# THE DEVIL WENT DOWN TO LAUGHLIN

## VEGAS SLAYERS - BOOK 3

## CHRISTINE POPE

DARK VALENTINE
PRESS

THE DEVIL WENT DOWN TO LAUGHLIN

Copyright © 2025 by Christine Pope

ISBN: 978-1-946435-87-3

Published by Dark Valentine Press

Cover design by Indie Author Services

Book formatting by Indie Author Services

# Chapter One

—·((·◌·))·—

CALEB LOCKWOOD DIDN'T LIKE TO THINK of himself as a hoverer, but he still found himself going back and forth from the kitchen more times than he would have liked—trying to decide whether it was time to get the bottle of Cristal out of the fridge or whether he should wait until Delia got here, starting to pour some cashews into a bowl and then wondering if nuts would be too much in addition to the strawberries and artisanal crackers and cheese he'd picked up at a gourmet shop just the day before.

Oh, the hell with it. Delia already knew he wasn't the most understated guy in the world. In fact, she probably expected him to go kind of over the top to celebrate the sale of his former house.

He got out the bowl of nuts and set it on the coffee table in the living room. The weather was far too warm to even think about having a fire in the floor-to-ceiling fireplace that dominated the space—now that it was the beginning of May, temperatures in Las Vegas had parked themselves in the mid- and upper eighties—but he still preferred to hang out in here unless he was watching TV. That activity had been relegated to his man cave on the lower level next to the garage, where his hundred-inch television held court.

Good thing he'd gotten over his dithering about the cashews, because the doorbell rang just a few seconds later. Caleb still hadn't given up hoping that one day they'd get past the point where Delia felt the need to use the doorbell, that maybe they'd be close enough that she'd have a key to the house, but they weren't there yet.

No, despite everything they'd gone through together—haunted houses and demon attacks and supernaturally charged poker tournaments—he was still firmly stuck in the friend zone.

But he smiled anyway when he opened the door, glad that she'd been able to carve out some time from her busy schedule at the real estate business she co-owned with her mother so she could come to the house and celebrate the closing of escrow on his previous home, the place where he'd first landed when he came to Las Vegas. However, he'd quickly realized that he far preferred this property, the one he'd ostensibly bought to flip.

This was his home now, and he knew he wasn't going anywhere.

"Congratulations!" Delia told him. She was holding an elegant white orchid in a black pot, something he knew she'd chosen because it would go perfectly with the black-and-white color scheme of the house.

And it seemed she'd decided to carry that theme into her outfit, since she was wearing a sleeveless white blouse with some black embroidery around the neckline and black skinny jeans. Against her copper-red hair, the stark tones of the ensemble were particularly striking.

Maybe one day he'd stop getting blown away by her beauty all over again any time he saw her after a gap of more than a few days.

Probably not, though.

"Thanks," he said, stepping aside so she could enter the foyer. Not even a glance around, which didn't surprise him too much. After all, she was the one who'd helped him pick out the flooring and the light fixtures and the white-veined black soapstone that covered the fireplace and stretched up to the vaulted ceiling. "I'm glad you didn't think I was going over the top with this."

"Of course not," she assured him as they headed into the living room. "Closing escrow is a big deal."

"Even though we already went out to dinner to celebrate when I accepted the buyer's offer?"

"Even then," she replied at once, a slight twinkle in her blue-gray eyes. "I mean, it's great to get an offer and accept it, but until escrow closes, a deal doesn't feel finished."

No, it hadn't felt anything like a *fait accompli,* especially since the buyer's offer was contingent on their own house selling. Their home had already been in escrow, but if that deal had fallen through, the whole transaction could have collapsed like a house of cards.

And while there had been other people interested in the property, he liked the couple who wanted to buy the house. They were in their mid-thirties with two kids, and he knew they'd appreciate the mid-century Brady Bunch vibe of the place. Having to start all over again with another set of buyers hadn't seemed very appealing.

Especially since Delia's prophecy about the collapse of Aegis Holdings had come partially true. The company—which appeared to have been run by demons or at least people possessed by them—had fallen apart after the poker tournament at the Desert Paradise casino just a month earlier. That tournament had been specifically set up to channel diabolical energy through Las Vegas and utilize it for some purpose neither he nor Delia had yet been able to discover, but after Caleb had foiled their plans...using his own quarter-demon powers in a way he still hadn't quite been able to figure out...Aegis Holdings and most of the people who worked there had pretty much disappeared off the map. The homes they'd owned had been put up for auction, and the glut of properties had caused housing prices in Las Vegas to cool a bit.

Luckily, his former house was already under contract before the shit really began to hit the fan, and, thank God, the couple who were buying the place hadn't tried to pull out or renegotiate. Maybe they'd decided it was better to go with a bird in the hand, or maybe they figured the market would bounce back soon enough and it was better to ride out the momentary turbulence.

"But it feels finished now," he said, and Delia smiled.

"Yes," she said, her tone cheerful. "I should have a cashier's check for you tomorrow afternoon at the latest."

Since today was Sunday, that meant the escrow company was going to be on it first thing Monday morning. While Caleb didn't exactly need the cash —he had several million bucks stashed in a bunch of banks and credit unions around town, and around the same amount in various investment accounts that his broker handled—he wanted the sense of completion that getting the roughly three-quarters of a million the house had fetched would give him.

Even if it meant he'd have to open a few more accounts so none of them would go over the $250K FDIC-protected limit.

Or maybe it was time to start thinking about offshoring his money, even though he'd avoided that step so far because he wasn't sure whether his fake credentials would hold up under the extra scrutiny. When he'd escaped from Hell and come to Las Vegas, a few inquiries...and a few thousand bucks slipped into the right palms...had gotten him a birth certificate and a credit report under his adopted name of Caleb Lowe. He'd used the birth certificate to get a Nevada driver's license, but he hadn't tried for a passport yet.

Everything was going pretty smoothly, and he hadn't wanted to rock the boat.

Delia had moved toward the coffee table and was looking down at the bottle of champagne in its silvery cooling sleeve with some amusement. "Cristal, huh? You don't mess around, do you?"

He grinned and took a few steps toward her. "You know I don't do things by halves."

For a second, their eyes met. Caleb thought he could easily drown in those cool, watercolor depths.

Especially since right now he thought he

detected a certain warmth there...unless he was just fooling himself, which was distinctly possible.

Before the moment could get too tense, though, he thought he'd better speak again.

"Ever had Cristal?" he asked, his tone deliberately casual.

Now Delia grinned back at him, her entire face lighting up. She was beautiful all the time, but when she smiled like that, she was positively incandescent.

"As a matter of fact, I have," she responded, still looking amused. "One of my friends from college got married to the son of a local developer, and they had a crazy, extravagant wedding. Swans wandering around on the lawn at the country club and a five-course meal and Cristal all 'round—and an open bar for those who weren't into champagne. The whole thing must have set them back around a million bucks."

That was a lot of money to blow on an event that only lasted for one day. Caleb came from wealth himself—he was the third generation of demons and part demons from Greencastle, Indiana, and his father had been president of a local bank—but even he was sometimes surprised by the way people threw their cash around.

Then again, he'd happily spend that much or more to make sure Delia had a perfect day.

Which was kind of nuts, he knew. They

weren't dating...they hadn't shared even a single kiss...but he still knew she was the only woman in the world for him.

And not just because she knew the truth of who and what he was and didn't seem to care a single bit. Sure, she'd been shocked at first, but now she was someone he had never expected when he moved here, a close friend and a true ally when the supernatural shit hit the fan, which had happened a lot more than he'd planned for.

"The heart wants what it wants," he remarked, and Delia's grin only broadened.

"I suppose so," she said. "Still, I don't think it was a very good investment, considering they got divorced just three years later. No pre-nup, so I think they're still arguing about who gets the condo in Cabo."

"Well, luckily, my real estate deal turned out a bit better than that," Caleb said. He didn't want to dwell on her friend's divorce and would much rather focus on the happy news that had brought Delia here in the first place. "So, I think it's time for champagne."

She nodded, although a certain sly glint in her eyes told him she understood exactly why he'd changed the subject. "And with these high ceilings, you don't have to worry about blowing a hole in all that new drywall."

As if he'd be that clumsy when opening a

bottle of champagne. Okay, he didn't have a huge amount of experience, but all it needed was a little dip into his demonic powers to make sure the cork slid out easily, and soon enough, champagne was flowing into their waiting flutes.

"Very smooth," Delia observed, her mouth quirking ever so slightly. "Have you been practicing?"

"I don't need to practice," he replied.

Her expression sobered a bit, and she gave him a considering look. "No, I don't suppose you do."

Rather than respond directly, he lifted his glass. "Let's toast to the Baumanns and their drama-free escrow."

Delia raised her glass as well. "Good idea."

They clinked their flutes together gently, and then each of them took a sip of Cristal. Caleb wouldn't pretend to know too much about champagne—although he'd been studying wine lately, wanting to make sure he wouldn't embarrass himself when he took Delia out to dinner—but he thought this was still probably the best bubbly he'd ever had.

"Go ahead, take a seat," he urged her, and she settled herself on the sofa, an appreciative glow in her eyes.

"That's some good stuff," she commented, then looked over the food he provided, spread across the glass and black iron coffee table. "And so is all this."

"It's not every day you sell a house," he said as he sat down as well. On the sofa, too, but far enough away that she couldn't possibly view his presence as invading her personal space.

"Unless you're a real estate agent," she said with a smile before sipping some more champagne.

"True," he agreed. "Speaking of offers, have you heard back about the house in Wyeth Ranch?"

Because although the collapse of Aegis Holdings had rocked the Las Vegas real estate market, that didn't mean he didn't plan to take advantage of it. The property in Wyeth Ranch would be one of their most recent acquisitions if they managed to snag it, and it hadn't yet been updated and therefore was going for a lot less than most of the other houses that were being liquidated.

"The auction is on Wednesday," she replied. A flicker of worry came and went in her expression, and Caleb could tell she wasn't completely thrilled about getting involved with Aegis again, if only in a peripheral way.

While he understood her trepidation, he thought she was being a bit too cautious. They'd walked the property with a bunch of other investors who'd been on the same tour set up by the auction company, and he hadn't detected a single hint of demonic activity in the place. It might have once been owned by a positively diabolical outfit, but the house itself was just an ordinary three-two built in the late eighties and in dire need of some updating.

Also, Delia hadn't sensed anything off about the house, either. Although she still steadfastly refused to call herself a psychic, they both knew her powers—which had started as the simple ability to speak to ghosts and help them move on to the next world—had begun to shift and expand after the incident at the Desert Sands casino.

Well, also after they'd met Ty Carter, a local tennis pro who might or might not be an angel, or at least part one, just as Caleb was part demon. Ty had all but admitted that Delia's strengthening powers had something to do with him, even though he'd also said they would have expanded without his intervention, if not as quickly.

Anyway, Delia hadn't felt anything wrong about the house Caleb wanted to pick up as a cheap flip, which meant he was willing to bid up to a fairly decent price to get his hands on the place. He'd had so much fun working on this house with her that he wanted to do whatever he could to repeat the experience...and making a little extra money on the side wouldn't hurt, either.

Also, with the escrow company sending him the payment for the Piñon Drive house sometime tomorrow, that meant he'd have plenty of liquid funds to step in and pay cash if he did manage to have the winning bid.

"Will you help me with the bidding?" he asked. The auction was being held online, but this would be the first time he'd done anything like this, and he thought it would be good to have her there for moral support.

Delia's head tilted to one side, and he thought her expression was one of genuine regret. "I can't— I already had a couple of showings scheduled with a new client when I found out about the auction. But you'll do fine on your own. Just make sure you don't go over $375. That place is going to need at least another sixty or seventy thousand in renovation costs, and you'll price yourself out of that neighborhood if you go too crazy."

Just another thing he loved about her. She was an awesome fellow demon slayer—and she had a brain for real estate unlike few other people he'd met.

"Got it," he said. Honestly, it shouldn't be that big a deal. This particular auction was the kind where you put in your best bid and hoped it would be enough, not the sort where you had to hover over your computer and keep bidding up in increments at the last minute. "Some cheese?"

They both created little plates of nibbles for themselves, and for a moment or two, they ate quietly and drank champagne, both of them content to enjoy the moment. But then he glimpsed a twinkle in her sea-colored eyes again.

"You would have had more money to put into the project if you hadn't given all your tournament winnings away."

Because of that glint he'd caught in her eyes, he knew she was teasing him just a little. After all, it didn't really matter where the money came from for a reno project; you still needed to stick to the budget no matter what.

"I didn't want to keep it," he said. "Sure, I know the casino was just a pawn in Aegis Holdings'—and Hank Bowers'—plans, but that money felt tainted to me. Much better to give it away."

The whole fifty grand had gone straight to Desert Paws Animal Rescue, a local charity that made sure stray dogs went to loving homes and which also sponsored free and low-cost spay and neuter clinics. Caleb didn't feel entirely settled enough yet to get a dog...even as he still couldn't help missing Riley, the German shepherd who'd been his constant companion when he was growing up...but he thought giving a large donation to an organization that worked hard to make pets' lives better was a good way to show his love for animals.

Maybe a little strange for a part demon, but...as he'd pointed out to Delia on more than one occasion...he was far more human than he was demon.

He'd made sure the donation was anonymous,

of course. This wasn't about getting adulation for his good works, or whatever. She was the only person he'd told, mostly because she'd asked him point-blank what he planned to do with the prize money and he'd immediately responded that it was going to charity.

"Well, it went to a good cause," she agreed. "And I can see why you might have felt hinky about keeping the money. Have you heard anything about Hank or the other people who were involved in the scheme?"

Because while some had appeared to be true demons and had promptly disappeared straight back to Hell, others, like Hank Bowers, had reverted to their human forms once the demons that had possessed them had been vanquished.

"Hank's still in the hospital," Caleb said. "Ty made up a story about him having a heart attack to explain why he collapsed in the middle of the casino like that, but it turns out his real story wasn't too far from the truth. I think Hank's human body couldn't handle the stresses the possession put on it, let alone all those crazy energy fluxes during the final round of the tournament. He had a stroke, and from what I've heard, he's probably going to get moved to a convalescent facility soon. It doesn't sound as if there's much hope for any real improvement."

And he wasn't sure what to feel about that.

Caleb didn't know how Hank had gotten involved with Aegis Holdings—had he agreed to the possession in exchange for power and wealth, or had he been yet another innocent victim of demonic machinations?—but whatever the truth of the matter, no one deserved to end up in such horrible circumstances.

"That's awful," Delia said, sympathy clear in every plane and angle of her lovely face. "I had no idea."

No, because she'd been crazy busy this past month. Her parents had come back from their anniversary trip to Hawaii about five days after all the insanity at the Desert Paradise poker tournament, but even though Delia no longer had to carry the whole load of Dunne & Dunne Realty on her shoulders, it sounded as though business had picked up, with a lot of people trying to find properties and close on them before the real heat of the summer descended.

"It's not good," Caleb agreed. Although it felt a little strange to be sipping champagne while discussing such a grim topic, he wasn't about to let the Cristal go flat.

So he drank some more and popped a few cashews in his mouth...and hoped she wouldn't ask about the person he really didn't want to discuss.

Aaron Sanchez.

Sure, there hadn't been anything going on

between him and Delia, not really, but Caleb kind of hated that she'd gone out with the guy for drinks. He didn't have a single claim on her other than friendship, but....

However, revealing how that one not-quite date still rankled would only make him sound like some kind of possessive jerk, so he knew he'd have to be as neutral as possible when discussing the man.

"And Aaron?" Delia prompted, just as he'd feared she would. "I know Ty said he collapsed, but I haven't heard anything from Aaron at all. Do you think he's in the hospital, too?"

Well, at least he could relieve some of her fears on that topic. "Not that I know of," Caleb replied. "He wasn't possessed nearly as long as Hank Bowers—and is several decades younger—so from what I was able to gather, the paramedics checked him on the scene and let him go. I don't know what happened to him after that."

"Oh."

Expression thoughtful, she put a slice of Humboldt Fog cheese on a rosemary cracker, bit into it, and then washed down the morsel with a swallow of champagne.

"You haven't heard from him?" Caleb asked next. Maybe that question might have sounded a little too desperate, but he needed to know...

although he guessed Delia would have probably mentioned it if Aaron had reached out to her.

She shook her head as she set down her champagne flute. "No. I suppose I could have contacted the agency where he works to find out if he was okay, but I've just been so busy and...."

The words trailed off, both her tone and her expression somewhat uncertain, as if she honestly didn't know for sure whether she could unearth a concrete justification as to why she hadn't followed up to determine whether Aaron Sanchez was all right.

"Don't worry about it," Caleb told her, hoping he sounded reassuring and not at all relieved that she hadn't allowed Mr. Sanchez to occupy too much space in her brain. "Like I said, it sounds like he walked out of the casino under his own power. Maybe he left Las Vegas to regroup. Sometimes it takes a while to recover from a demonic possession."

"Sort of like the flu," Delia said, and gave a shaky laugh.

"Something like that," Caleb replied. It was obvious she was still worried, but at least she seemed willing to accept his explanations about what might have happened. "People react differently to that kind of thing."

"Do they....?" Once again, the words faded away, although this time, he got more the sense that she was grappling with the best way to phrase the question. "Do people remember what happened to them when they've been possessed?"

"It depends," he said. Then he wanted to shake his head at himself. Here he was acting like he was some expert on demonic possessions, when the truth was that his father had told him very little about the demon side of his nature, much preferring to focus on the human lives they'd all been leading in their quiet Indiana town. Caleb had learned to use some of the powers Daniel Lockwood had passed down to him, but otherwise, it wasn't as if he'd attended some school for demons and learned all sorts of arcane lore about them.

In fact, most of what he knew, he'd learned from books and movies and websites, all of which could have been a load of utter bullshit.

Delia was still watching him, the elegant arches of her brows lifted ever so slightly. "Depends on what?"

He shrugged. "A whole lot of things. But everything I've read seems to say that the longer you've been possessed, the harder it is to snap back once the demon is gone. That's why Hank Bowers is headed for a convalescent home. Aaron, on the other hand, seemed to have only been possessed for a couple of days. That probably wasn't long enough to totally mess him up."

And, to be fair, it wasn't as if Caleb wanted the

guy to drop dead or something. On the other hand, if Aaron had been so rattled by his experiences in Las Vegas that he decided to walk away from everything and head home to Laughlin...Delia had mentioned that was where the guy had grown up... then Caleb wasn't going to be too sad about the situation.

Looking thoughtful, she sipped some more champagne. In fact, her flute was now nearly empty, so he reached for the bottle of Cristal and carefully poured some more for her, then refilled his own glass as well.

"I'm glad to hear it," she said at length. "I mean, there was never going to be anything between the two of us, but it was totally terrifying to see what happened to him after that demon took over. That's the sort of thing you expect to see in a horror movie, not real life."

Unless in real life you were hanging out with a quarter demon, in which case you might have a higher-than-average chance of running into something diabolical.

Maybe he should feel guilty about that. After all, he was the one who'd sought Delia out after seeing her walk through one of the casinos where he'd been gambling back in January. At once, he'd been able to sense there was something unusual about her, a kind of power that most mortals didn't possess, something that went far beyond her natural beauty and the self-assured way she carried herself.

Back then, he hadn't known exactly what that power even was. He'd only known that he wanted to find out as much as possible about her.

Now he knew that she'd been a singer in a punk band in high school and college, but had ditched her Doc Martens and the hair dye that made her naturally copper tresses something closer to what Woody Woodpecker might have sported for a much more professional look once she got her real estate license and started working with her mother at Dunne & Dunne. She was an only child and had a tank full of fish at home—freshwater, not salt, because she'd told him a saltwater setup was too much work—and although she tried to stick to salad and chicken most of the time, she wasn't above indulging in a burger or pizza when the occasion warranted it. Her favorite color was blue, but more teal or turquoise than cobalt or navy, and she had a hidden weakness for rom-coms and Hallmark holiday movies...although she'd vehemently deny it if you inquired about her viewing preferences to her face.

And she was also the bravest, toughest, most incredible woman he'd ever met.

"Sometimes real life can be a horror movie," he said, recalling some of the choicer battles he'd had with his father, mostly over where he planned to go to college...and what he'd wanted to do with his life.

Once upon a time, he would have wanted to be the person directing those horror movies. If nothing else, he would have had a unique perspective.

That wasn't going to happen, though, so he'd tucked his dream of working in the film industry away, along with a whole bunch of other half-formed hopes and plans.

Funny how being a quarter demon could really limit your options.

Delia shifted on the couch, and for a wild moment, Caleb thought she was going to reach over and take his hand, maybe wrap her fingers around his so she could offer him some much-needed comfort.

That didn't happen, of course. They might have touched here and there while in the middle of battling a demon or during other similarly fraught situations, but overall, they'd both studiously avoided any kind of physical contact.

Maybe she was worried about what even a simple hug might lead to.

"Considering everything that's happened over the past few months, I can't really argue with you," Delia remarked. She set down her flute of champagne and reached for a strawberry.

He really didn't want to watch her eat it and

see the way those luscious lips of hers wrapped around the red, juicy fruit, so he looked down at the cheese board and pretended to be engrossed in deciding which kind he should consume next. Just as he was reaching for a slice of Manchego, however, the doorbell rang.

Delia sent a puzzled glance in the direction of the foyer. "Were you expecting someone?"

"No," Caleb said shortly.

He never had visitors, unless you counted someone dropping off DoorDash when he was too lazy to go out and bring something back himself. Twice a month, he had a cleaning crew come in, but they'd just been here on Thursday and weren't supposed to be back for another week and a half.

Especially since Sunday wasn't even their regular cleaning day.

"Probably Seventh-Day Adventists or something," he said, then brushed his hands on the knees of his jeans and stood.

"Would they be coming around on a Sunday, though?" Delia responded doubtfully.

Probably not. Caleb had to admit that he had no idea what proselytizers' schedules look like, mostly because they'd given his childhood home in Greencastle a wide berth. For all he knew, they'd been able to sniff out something wrong about the house, even though to everyone else in town, the

Lockwoods had looked like a perfectly normal—if especially prosperous—family.

"I'll see who it is," he said.

Probably schoolkids trying to raise money for football uniforms or something, he told himself as he walked over to the foyer. Or maybe Girl Scouts, although again, he had no idea whether this was even the time of year when they'd be going around and hawking cookies.

When he opened the door, however, he saw the last person he would have ever expected.

Aaron Sanchez, looking like about fifty miles of bad road.

"I need to talk to you," he said.

# Chapter Two

—·《《·☾·》》·—

DELIA DIDN'T QUITE LET OUT A GASP WHEN a grim-faced Caleb led Aaron Sanchez, of all people, into the living room, but she was shocked nonetheless. A little over five weeks had passed since the calamitous poker tournament at the Desert Paradise casino, but Aaron looked as if he'd aged five years. His dark eyes were hollow and haunted, and she guessed that he must have lost at least fifteen pounds or maybe more, his once-athletic build now downright gaunt.

It sure appeared as if he hadn't survived his demon possession quite as well as Caleb had claimed.

Aaron's gaze caught the half-drunk bottle of champagne in its silver cooling sleeve, the big live-edge black walnut charcuterie board with its complement of fancy cheese and crackers and fruit. "I've interrupted something," he said.

Rather than offer a demurral, Caleb only replied, "Sort of, but it's okay. Why don't you sit down?"

Looking relieved that he wouldn't have to remain standing any longer, Aaron slumped into one of the club chairs that faced the couch.

"Do you want some champagne?" Delia asked, then wondered if maybe that had been a mistake. For one thing, she wasn't sure if anyone who looked like the man in front of her should be drinking, and second of all, the Cristal wasn't really hers to offer. Maybe Caleb would just shrug off the expense, but still, that bottle had to have cost him at least three or four hundred bucks, depending on where he'd bought it, and he might not have liked her offering it as if the champagne was a cheapie he'd bought at the local grocery store.

But Aaron immediately shuddered and said, "No...no alcohol. Some water, maybe?"

Caleb had remained standing, so he said, "I'll go get it. Just take it easy."

He hurried into the kitchen, leaving Delia to sit there and try not to look too awkward. "But maybe some food?" she ventured. What in the world had happened to the guy? Knowing she sounded just like her mother, she added, "You look like you could use something to eat."

Aaron's gaze moved to the assortment of cheese and crackers and fruit on the coffee table. "Maybe."

Despite how noncommittal he'd sounded, he did actually sit up straighter, get a napkin, and then put some Irish white cheddar on a cracker. Just as he popped the morsel in his mouth, Caleb reappeared with a glass of water.

"Here you go."

Because Aaron's mouth was full, he couldn't do much more than nod. However, he reached for the glass as soon as he was done chewing and washed everything down with a big swallow.

"Thanks," he said. "That helps."

Caleb sat back down on the couch but leaned forward, his gaze frankly curious. "No offense, man," he said, "but you're not looking so great. Everything okay?"

Aaron made a hoarse sound that Delia guessed was supposed to be a laugh. He seemed to realize how bad it had sounded, because he quickly gulped down some more water.

"No," he said after he set his glass of water on the table in front of him—not bothering with a coaster, Delia noticed, but she figured they could ignore that oversight, considering how out of it he seemed.

Besides, the coffee table had a glass top, so the worst damage a drink could do would be to leave a ring behind.

"Things have basically gone to shit," Aaron went on. For a second, his gaze slid to the partially drunk flute of champagne in front of Delia, and she wondered if he was regretting the way he'd refused a glass a few moments earlier.

"I'm sorry," she said, and she knew she genuinely was. Just because she hadn't shared a single speck of chemistry with the guy didn't mean she wanted him to suffer. "What happened?"

He pushed a hand through his hair, which was in desperate need of cutting. And since he'd always been so put together, obviously wanting to present a professional appearance when he met with clients or hosted an open house, the contrast with the way he looked now was even more jarring.

"Everything's wrong," he replied, then looked over at Caleb. "I sort of remember being at the semifinals of that poker tournament where you were playing, but everything after that...well, until about four days later...is a total blank."

One of Caleb's eyebrows lifted ever so slightly, which seemed to signal that this information, while interesting, hadn't surprised him very much. Was that a byproduct of being possessed by a demon? That your memory would be completely erased?

In a way, Delia believed that might be a blessing. She didn't think she'd want to recall anything of a time when her body wasn't her own, when some horrible supernatural being was basically making her its puppet.

"What happened after those four days?" Caleb asked.

"I woke up in my condo," Aaron replied. "I was lying on the couch, fully dressed. I think they might have been the clothes I wore to the tournament finals, but since I don't remember anything about that day, I can't say for sure. All I do know is that I felt like I had the mother of all hangovers."

Not too surprising, if he'd been blacked out for days. Maybe this wasn't about demons at all. Maybe he'd just gone on a massive bender. After all, she had no idea about his relationship with alcohol. Yes, he'd had two beers when they met for drinks at the bar at the Hard Rock, and that wasn't exactly what you could call excessive drinking, but he could have been putting on a public face for her when, in actuality, he hit the hard stuff on a regular basis.

Then again, he'd just looked as if the mere thought of drinking champagne was enough to make him sick, which wasn't the kind of behavior you'd usually see in someone desperate for some hair of the dog.

"It might be good that you don't really remember," Caleb remarked, although it seemed clear he wasn't going to elaborate, not when it appeared that Aaron didn't recall anything about his possession or the demons who'd done their best to hijack the Desert Paradise poker tournament for their own purposes. "What happened after that?"

"I slept for a couple more days." He paused there, looking shamefaced. "And then I woke up to a message that I'd missed a bunch of appointments and Keller Williams was letting me go. That's the real estate agency where I worked," he added, obviously for Caleb's benefit, since Delia knew very well which agency Aaron worked for.

"I'm sorry," she murmured, and his shoulders hunched.

"Whatever. I deserved it. I mean, I was out of it, but I should have been able to muster enough energy to call in sick."

Delia wasn't so sure about that. Although she'd be the first to admit that she was far from an expert on such things, it sure sounded to her as if Aaron Sanchez had suffered some major psychic blowback from his possession, and that his mind had shut down for a bit to help him recover.

Also, right then she heard the briefest whisper of his thoughts in her mind, just enough to catch a few words.

*I fucked up. I really fucked up.*

Everything about those two brief sentences resonated with contrition and despair. She might have been very new to this latest facet of her talent, the one she originally had thought helped her communicate with ghosts and nothing else, but she refused to believe what she'd heard was anything but genuine.

"They still should have given you a second chance," she said gently. "You were ill. But you're a good agent. I'm sure you'll find another agency that will take you."

Aaron only shook his head. "I'm done with Las Vegas."

His tone was flat, and Delia sent a quick, sideways look at Caleb, who only shrugged ever so slightly.

"I don't know—" she began, but Aaron immediately interrupted her.

"Well, *I* know. Losing my job was bad enough, but then I had my condo pulled out from under me, too."

Once again, Delia darted a glance at Caleb. The situation with Aaron's condo had been sketchy from the start, since they both knew Aegis Holdings owned the property. They'd thought maybe the condo had been a bribe to get Aaron to cooperate with the demons running the company, although she still hadn't caught the smallest hint that he'd had any idea what they were really up to.

"What happened with your condo?" Caleb asked.

Aaron picked up his glass of water and gulped some of it down. Not looking directly at either one of them, he said, "It was a rental. I guess the owners were in default and I didn't even know about it... not until I woke up to an eviction notice yesterday."

Ouch. It was a sad story that happened all too often, although most of the time, the bank took back its properties because the owners had stopped making their mortgage payments due to insolvency or simple negligence, rather than having their entire organization collapse and its employees either depossessed or sent back to Hell. Still, she was a little surprised that Aegis hadn't paid cash for the place and instead obviously had some sort of mortgage on the condo.

Had they really been that leveraged?

"I'm so sorry," Delia said, even as she wondered what Aaron really needed from her and Caleb. He might have gotten fired, but he was still a real estate agent and could have gathered his resources to find himself another place.

She also hadn't missed how he'd carefully avoided any mention of his connection to Aegis Holdings, although she wasn't sure whether that was because he actually was trying to hide something or because he'd blacked out so severely following the incident at the Desert Paradise casino that he didn't even remember the way Aegis had been bankrolling him.

*Allegedly*, she reminded herself. All she and

Caleb had had to go on was a bunch of suspicions and some somewhat sketchy information that her private detective friend Prudence had dug up. There still might have been an entirely logical reason for the way Aaron had suddenly paid off his student loans and bought a brand-new BMW.

However, since Caleb's expression managed to be both skeptical and sympathetic at the same time, she guessed he was also having a hard time trying to decide how much of any of this he was supposed to believe.

"But I found an Airbnb where I can crash for now," Aaron went on quickly, as if to reassure her and Caleb that he wasn't asking to sleep on their couch or something. "And I'll figure something out. What I really want your help with is my grandmother's house."

Delia had a feeling she looked genuinely confused by that *non sequitur,* and Caleb seemed puzzled as well, brows knitting together as he appeared to process the other man's comment.

"Your grandmother's house?" she repeated.

Aaron swallowed some more water and then put his glass back down on the coffee table—this time using a coaster, as if he'd just realized he'd made sort of a *faux pas* by not utilizing it earlier.

"Yes," he said. "She died last fall, around the middle of November. There was a lot of debate about whether we should even sell the place at all,

33

since it's been in the family for a long time, but it needs a bunch of work, and my parents didn't want to tackle the project. So they asked me to handle the sale."

"I'm assuming it's more of a problem than you expected," Caleb commented dryly.

A grimace, and Aaron said, "That's putting it mildly. I mean, I didn't hear or see anything when I was taking pictures of the house, but the first buyers backed out of the contract after they went in to measure everything for their furniture, and they heard strange noises coming from the basement."

"Possums, or maybe rats?" Caleb asked, seizing on the most logical explanation for those sorts of sounds...even though he doubted a simple rodent invasion would have been enough to send the man over here, looking for help.

"No," Aaron replied, his tone flat. "I had an exterminator come in and look everything over. He said there weren't any signs of a rodent infestation, and I had a plumber check out the whole house, too, just in case there was something wrong with the pipes. So I put the house back on the market, but every time people would go to view the place, they'd hear more weird noises. One time, a door handle came loose and went flying across the room. It almost hit the agent who was showing the house right in the head."

Delia couldn't help wincing—not just because she guessed that an antique brass or crystal doorknob could have done some serious damage if it had actually connected, but also because it sure sounded as if Aaron's grandmother's house was haunted.

And that explained why he'd come to her for help...although Delia wasn't sure how he'd managed to track her down at Caleb's house.

"You want me to talk to the ghost," she said, and at once, Aaron's expression brightened, although the brightest smile in the world couldn't erase the shadows under his eyes.

"Would you? I mean, everyone in town knows about your sideline, and it sounds as if you have a pretty good success rate."

That she did. Once or twice, she'd come across a spirit so recalcitrant that no matter what she said or did, it wouldn't budge, but those instances were few and far between.

Before she could respond, though, Caleb sat up a little straighter and fastened Aaron with a direct look, his eyes somehow appearing darker than their usual friendly brown. Most of the time, her quarter-demon friend appeared laid-back in the extreme, but when he stared at you like that, it was better if you didn't try any shenanigans.

"How did you know to find Delia here?" he demanded.

Aaron gave a very weary shrug, as if he almost didn't have the energy to even lift his shoulders a fraction of an inch. "I went to her house first," he said. "But her neighbor said she'd gone over to her friend Caleb's place."

Mrs. Gallina, flapping her jaw again. The woman meant well, but because her children were all grown and had relocated to various towns up and down the West Coast, she had decided to transfer all her protective instincts to Delia, who, as a woman living on her own, apparently needed a mother figure looking out for her.

Never mind that Delia's own mother lived only fifteen minutes away and certainly could have been there quickly enough to help out if an emergency arose.

Anyway, Mrs. Gallina had seen Delia hurrying out to her car with the potted orchid in her arms—she'd been running late and had backed out of the garage before she realized the plant was still sitting on the kitchen island, and had gone into the house through the front door rather than wasting time opening the garage door—and the woman had asked if the orchid was a gift. Even though she knew all this had been making her even later, Delia had told her neighbor that the plant was a present for her friend Caleb, who'd just sold his house. After that, she'd murmured breathlessly that she was running late and needed to get going, but the encounter would have provided enough information about where she was headed that Mrs. Gallina could have passed it along to Aaron Sanchez.

Except....

"Did this neighbor give you my address or something?" Caleb inquired, one brow lifting at an angle that told Delia he wasn't too thrilled by any of this.

Aaron had the grace to look sheepish. "Well, I'd sort of heard through the grapevine that you two were spending a lot of time together, so I kind of looked you up online a while back when I was thinking of asking Delia out."

This piece of explanation only made Caleb set his jaw, and Delia knew Aaron was just digging his hole that much deeper.

To be fair, property records weren't a state secret. She didn't know why Caleb hadn't set up a trust to buy his current house, because doing so would have helped a little to obfuscate the identity of the owner, but she supposed everything had moved so fast that he really hadn't had the time to put the necessary paperwork together.

But at least the house was listed on the county recorder's website as belonging to Caleb Lowe. As far as Delia had been able to tell, she was the only person in town who knew he was really Caleb Lockwood...and she intended to keep it that way.

However, she couldn't help thinking it had

been just a little stalker-y for Aaron to investigate Caleb as a possible rival.

"Well, that explains it," she said as brightly as she could, even while shooting Caleb another of those sideways looks that she hoped would tell him he needed to drop the whole thing about Aaron hunting down his address. "And of course I'll come to your grandmother's house to see if I can find anything that feels strange."

Caleb's fingers tightened on his knees, and she could tell he was practically stomping on his tongue not to interject.

Good. They were friends, of course, and she was always willing to listen to his advice and insights, but in the end, she was a grown woman who could make her own decisions.

And so far, she'd never turned down someone who was asking for help with their haunted house.

Even if Aaron had recently been possessed by a demon and still looked positively hag-ridden.

Because she'd been able to dip into his thoughts a few minutes earlier, Delia thought it couldn't hurt to try again. Just by reading his expression and his body language, she couldn't pick up on anything that indicated he was lying or misrepresenting the situation, but....

*Gotta sell that damn house. My parents want it gone, and the thirty percent they promised me would go a long way toward digging me out of this hole.*

After that, what she saw in her mind was more a set of impressions than actual words...money mysteriously being sucked out of his bank account...the dealership where he'd bought his BMW threatening to repo the thing unless he came up with a couple grand in the next ten days...but it was enough to show her that Aaron Sanchez's financial situation was pretty dire.

Even if the family was willing to get rid of his grandmother's house at a fire sale price, thirty percent would probably net him six figures. That would certainly be enough to stop the bleeding, even if he'd still need to establish himself at another agency soon if he wanted to get his money flowing in the right direction.

However, what she'd heard with her mind was certainly enough to prove that everything he'd told her was on the up and up. Caleb could look as disapproving as he wanted, but he didn't have the final say on any of this.

This was her business...and her decision.

"I'm really booked up tomorrow," she said, and gave Aaron a sympathetic smile. "But Tuesday looks pretty open. How about we set up a meeting for me to walk the house on Tuesday afternoon sometime?"

The relief on Aaron's face was so obvious that you probably could have used it as an illustration next to the word's entry in a dictionary. "Tuesday afternoon would be great. Does three o'clock work?"

It would; she had one appointment to show a house at ten-thirty, but nothing after that. Even if she didn't head down to Laughlin until after lunch, she could easily make it by three.

Well, barring accidents, construction, and all the other complications that could turn a simple hour-and-a-half drive into something much more arduous, but she'd been to Laughlin plenty of times and had never run into any trouble before, so she thought it should be totally doable.

"Sure," she replied. "Just text me the address, and I'll meet you there."

Aaron nodded, looking grateful. "Absolutely."

He got out his phone and entered a quick message, and a moment later, her phone pinged from somewhere within her purse. Caleb looked even less thrilled by this exchange, probably because it reminded him that she'd gone out with Aaron once, and he still had her in his contacts.

Well, Caleb could think what he wanted. It wasn't as if she was going out with him, so he didn't have any say in her personal life. Besides, it had been one and done with Aaron, and she knew she had absolutely no interest in pursuing anything else with him except—she hoped—finding out what was going on with his grandmother's suppos-edly haunted house.

All the same, Caleb's not-so-hidden jealousy might have been amusing to watch if it hadn't made her brain go in directions she wasn't sure she wanted to explore right now.

She got out her phone, looked down at the address Aaron had just sent her, and smiled. "Got it. Then I guess I'll see you Tuesday afternoon."

At least he got the hint, because he stood at once, saying, "See you then. Just call or text if you're running late or something." He paused for a beat or two before he added, the words now directed toward Caleb, "Sorry for interrupting your celebration."

"No biggie," Caleb replied, even though Delia thought it was probably a bigger deal than he wanted to let on. "Good luck with your grandmother's house."

There wasn't much left to say after that, so Aaron mumbled a quick goodbye and then let himself out. Quiet descended...although it didn't last for long.

"I don't like it," Caleb said, and Delia crossed her arms. She'd already been pretty sure he wasn't about to drop this and move on to more neutral topics, but she didn't much like being proven right so quickly.

"Why not?" she returned. "I mean, cleansing homes of spiritual presences is part of what I do."

"I know that," Caleb said, both his tone and

his expression now openly irritated. "But are you forgetting that he was being controlled by those bastards at Aegis only a month ago?"

More like five weeks, but Delia decided it was better to let it go. "I haven't forgotten," she said calmly. "As far as we can tell, though, Aegis has totally fallen apart, so it doesn't seem as if they're much to worry about anymore. Besides, I saw Aaron's thoughts. He's not lying...and he's in a lot of financial trouble. If I can get the house cleansed, it'll help him out a lot."

Caleb's brows drew together even further, creating an obvious line between them. "You were able to read his mind, just like that?"

"Well, I wouldn't say it was 'just like that,'" she responded. Her tone was gentler than maybe it should have been, but she didn't want to get into an argument. "More like I caught one of his thoughts early on, and that somehow made it easier to try to take a second look a little bit later. It's still not anything I can control with any degree of certainty."

For a moment, Caleb didn't say anything. In fact, he reached over and picked up his glass of champagne. The Cristal still fizzed gently inside, but it wasn't nearly as exuberant as it had been some twenty minutes earlier.

Then, "Have you tried to read my mind?"

"No," she said at once. Part of her wanted to be

offended that he would even ask such a question, although she understood why her off-and-on ability to read minds might have been preying on his thoughts. "At least," she added, since he didn't look completely convinced, "I haven't tried on purpose, and I honestly haven't seen anything of what's going on in your head. For some reason, it's easier with Aaron. I have no idea why."

Caleb tapped a finger against the side of his champagne flute. "Maybe because his were the first thoughts you were able to hear when your powers started to expand?"

That seemed like as good a theory as any other. It was true that she'd caught just a snippet—a not-very-flattering one—from Aaron's mind right after she'd told him she didn't kiss on the first date. At the time, she'd been more shocked than anything else by that glimpse into his mind, but now she thought she could see why it might have been easier today to catch at least a hint of what he was think-ing, simply because she'd already done it before.

"It's possible," she said. "And for all I know, your thoughts are more shielded because of your demon blood. It's really hard to say, since I'm kind of flying blind with all this."

That was for sure. She'd had years to get used to her ghost-whispering talent, since it had appeared when she was only seventeen, and she'd now had more than ten years of living with it. This mind-reading thing? It had come on the scene only five weeks ago, and because she hadn't even tried to work with this strange new gift—mostly, she'd just hoped it wouldn't pop up during an inopportune time, like a client meeting or something—she didn't have much idea of what it could or couldn't do.

If Ty Carter had stuck around and tried to work with her on the newly expanded talent, then maybe she'd have a better grasp on her ESP, or whatever you wanted to call it. But he hadn't made the slightest attempt to get in contact, although Pru had reported that he appeared to still be teaching tennis at the DragonRidge country club, just as he had been for the past five years. Maybe he'd decided there was no reason to stay in touch, since the immediate danger appeared to have passed. Delia thought that was a little crappy, considering he'd admitted that he was the one who'd prodded along her psychic talents and gotten them to expand, but maybe he thought she was a big girl and could handle all this on her own.

The angry set to Caleb's jaw had relaxed somewhat, telling her that he understood she was at a loss here and was just trying to muddle through everything as best she could. "It must be rough," he said. "Sorry I jumped down your throat."

She summoned a smile. "I don't think you did exactly that," she replied. "I mean, I understand why you would be worried about all this. But it sure feels to me as if Aaron isn't being influenced by any outside forces. He's just trying to figure out a way to survive—and the best way for him to manage that is to get his grandmother's house sold."

"And the best way for that to happen is for you to get rid of whatever spook has taken up residence there," Caleb said. He let out a breath and sipped some more champagne. "I get it. I still don't like it...but I get it."

"I'm sure it'll just be your standard de-haunting," Delia said, glad she wouldn't have to keep persuading him there was absolutely nothing to worry about. "In fact, since Aaron didn't mention that the house had been haunted before this, I have a feeling it's his grandmother's spirit not wanting to let go of the place where she lived for so many years."

The beginnings of a frown touched Caleb's brow. "Won't that make it harder to get rid of her?"

At least Delia felt pretty secure on that front. After all, she'd done this sort of thing many times before. "Not necessarily. If she only died about seven months ago, then she hasn't been haunting the house for very long. A lot of the time, the longer a ghost has taken up residence, the more difficult it is to convince them to let go."

He appeared to mull over those words for a

second or two before giving a reluctant nod. "If you say so."

"I do."

In fact, the more she thought about it, the more she guessed that this would be a relatively easy cleansing. She could probably be in and out in less than an hour.

Piece of cake.

# Chapter Three

—·《《·☾·》》·—

THE MORE SHE RESEARCHED ALBA Sanchez, though, the more Delia wondered if she might be dealing with something much more than a simple haunting.

Oh, the woman had definitely passed away last fall...in November, just as Aaron had said...but Delia still found a few mentions online about her that sent up more than one red flag.

The supernatural kind of flag, anyway.

It sounded as if Alba had been something of a *curandera,* or herbalist, who used folk remedies from her native Mexico to help others in the family, as well as many others in the Laughlin area who weren't satisfied with the options offered by the more traditional medical community. She delivered babies and sat with people at their sickbeds, and more than one person claimed they'd been miraculously cured of cancer or MS or some other autoimmune disease thanks to the medicine she'd provided.

Not so long ago, Delia might have thought this was all a load of crap, just the placebo effect working in overdrive. Now, though, after realizing that demons...and angels...and all sorts of other supernatural entities and powers were very real, she knew her mind was much more open to the possibility that there was a lot more in heaven and earth than she'd ever imagined.

Which meant she had to allow the idea that Aaron's grandmother had possessed some sort of magical healing gifts.

However, some other items Delia had found—such as mentions of Alba organizing potlucks and fundraisers at her local church, St. John the Baptist—made it sound as if she'd also been very devout.

Had Alba ever experienced some dissonance in trying to reconcile her strict Catholic beliefs with the powers she'd apparently possessed?

Hard to say. Then again, Delia would have thought that someone so obviously religious wouldn't have any trouble moving on. After all, Alba must surely have believed in Heaven, and if she'd spent a good part of her life helping people, then she should have had an express ticket to the pearly gates.

Delia had been doing most of her research on her computer at the office, since she had just enough appointments booked that Monday that she wouldn't be allowed the luxury of working from home. In fact, she hadn't gotten as far as she would have liked with her investigation into Alba Sanchez, since between writing up an offer for a home she'd shown the previous Friday and fielding phone calls, her free time had been fairly limited.

In fact, Delia had to turn away from the computer once again to answer the phone, only this time, it was welcome news.

The loan on Caleb's house had been fully funded, and that meant the title company would be sending the cashier's check by courier later this afternoon.

That was pretty much what she'd told him was going to happen, but still, until the money was physically in his hands, she knew she'd still find herself worrying whether something catastrophic was going to happen at the last minute to prevent him from getting his payout.

She was just about to call him and give him the good news—and tell him he should be able to swing by after three to pick up the check—when her phone rang.

Not a client, though.

Her friend Prudence.

Delia had asked Pru to look into Alba Sanchez

as well, just because she knew that Pru's private detective license made her a lot more efficient when it came to digging up information about people. However, she was still a little surprised to hear from her friend, just because Pru generally preferred to text rather than call.

"What's up?" Delia asked after she lifted the phone to her ear.

"Found some stuff," Pru replied, sounding cheerful.

Then again, she was usually in her happy place when she got a chance to do some investigating that didn't involve cheating spouses or insurance fraud, so her upbeat tone wasn't too surprising.

"Like what?" Delia didn't think Prudence could have found anything too incriminating... Alba Sanchez didn't seem like the sort of person who would have too many buried bodies in her past...but you never knew.

"The house you think is haunted?"

"Yes?" Delia replied cautiously. She hoped Pru hadn't discovered that the place was reputed to be a site for satanic rituals or something similarly messy. That would make it a lot harder to sell.

"Well, it's one of the older homes in town. Sounds like the Sanchez family came to Laughlin in the 1940s to get jobs while Davis Dam was being built, but unlike a lot of other people, they stuck around afterward instead of moving on to the next project."

Okay, so they'd been there for going on eighty years. That might not have sounded like much to people from the East Coast, where local history went back a lot further, but it was practically an epoch in Nevada time.

"I don't know if the ghost has been around that long, though," Delia replied, realizing how dubious she sounded. "No one ever mentioned any supernatural activity in the house until recently, so I really think the ghost is the woman who died there last fall."

"This doesn't have anything to do with the ghost," Pru said. "No, I just found it interesting that the Sanchezes have always owned the house. Since they've been in town so long, they've done pretty well for themselves—I guess Alba's husband Carlo was Don Laughlin's right-hand man in the 1980s and was involved in a lot of the casino development back then—but even though they bought a big house in Bullhead City across the river at around the same time, they always made sure someone in the family lived the original house that Carlo's parents built. It sounds like it was Carlo's older sister's home for a while. She was there for around ten years and left it to her kids in her will, but they never actually lived in it. And after Carlo passed away, Alba moved in."

On the surface, it didn't sound so strange that she might want to live in the home her late husband's family had built. If Alba and Carlo had shared a more spacious house on the other side of the river...Bullhead City, Arizona, was actually much bigger than Laughlin itself...maybe Alba had decided it would be better to downsize rather than rattle around in a McMansion all by herself. It wasn't as if Delia hadn't seen that same story repeat itself plenty of times over the years. Living in a large home by yourself could be challenging as you got older, especially if you had any serious health issues to deal with.

And as for keeping the house in the family, well, Delia had seen that scenario play out plenty of times as well. The older the generation, the more they wanted to cling to what might have been the house a father or grandfather had built. It wasn't until those properties got passed down to the kids or grandkids that they went on the market, mostly because the people who inherited them wanted the cash and didn't want to deal with the complications and expense of a lengthy reno on an old house.

The only really surprising thing here was that Carlo's nieces and nephews hadn't sold the property outright when their mother died, rather than hang on to it so their aunt could move back to her original home during her final years.

"Any record of Alba buying the house back from her nieces and nephews?" Delia asked.

"Not that I could see. The property records are kind of muddy, to be honest. Carlo was definitely on the deed, but it looks like giving it to Lorena— Carlo's older sister—was more of a handshake thing than anything else."

Again, probably because they knew they weren't going to sell the place or even rent it, so the legalities wouldn't have seemed like that big a deal.

"What about Carlo and Lorena's house in Bull-head City?" Delia asked next, and Pru replied right away.

"Oh, that one was much more cut and dried. Carlo left it to Aaron Sanchez's father, Joseph, and he sold it about six months later. Made a chunk on it, too, since it was right on the river and was paid off. It went for a little over a million."

That was a lot of money. The amount involved made Delia wonder why Aaron hadn't asked his parents for a short-term loan, since—well, unless they'd immediately gone out and gambled it all away—they must have been sitting on a decent chunk of cash.

But it was very possible that he hadn't wanted to let on how dire his financial circumstances actually were. Taking a percentage of the sale of the old homestead was one thing, since he'd be providing the necessary expertise to make sure it went for top dollar. Coming right out and having to admit that he'd lost his job with Keller Williams and that his supposed business partners...or whatever Aegis Holdings had been to him...had gone out of business might have been too big a blow to his pride.

No way of knowing why Aaron's parents had decided to sell the place after it seemed the Sanchezes had worked damn hard to keep the old house in the family. It didn't sound as if they needed the money.

Delia supposed she could have reached out to him and asked, but that sort of question felt awfully intrusive...and would also let Aaron know that she'd been doing some serious digging into the situation.

After all, she didn't need to know all the ins and outs of his family dynamics. It was enough to know that they wanted to get rid of the place, and that it seemed to be haunted now when it hadn't been before.

Oh, and also that Aaron's grandmother appeared by all accounts to have been something of a witch, although Delia had a feeling that the clearly devout Alba Sanchez would have given them holy hell—pardon the expression—if anyone had dared to say such a thing to her face.

"I can keep poking around if you want," Pru ventured, and Delia realized she'd waited just a little too long to respond to her friend's comment.

"No, no, that's fine," she said hastily. "I kind of doubt you're going to find anything else of much use, and I know you have better things to do."

Something that sounded like a snort came through the iPhone's speaker. "Oh, you mean like rooting around in some deadbeat's financials to prove he was off playing around in a climbing gym when he was supposed to be home flat on his back with a work-related spinal injury?"

Delia couldn't help smiling. "Yeah, something like that."

"Then sure, I suppose I have better things to do. But I'll message you if I find anything else that looks interesting."

"Sounds good. Thanks for getting back to me on this—I appreciate it."

"No prob."

They ended the call there, and Delia set her phone down on the desk in front of her. She'd only started to swivel back toward her monitor when her mother paused in the doorway to her office. Not quite thirty years older than her daughter, Linda Dunne had the same oval face and blue-gray eyes, although her hair was light brown, expertly tinted with just a few highlights here and there. They still weren't quite sure where Delia had gotten her red hair, although the main suspects appeared to be her great-grandfather on her father's side and Linda's grandmother, who'd apparently been more auburn than true red but who seemed to have passed those gingery genes along to her granddaughter.

"Busy today," Linda remarked, and Delia did her best to ignore the stab of guilt that had gone through her.

Yes, she'd been busy...but only about half of what she'd done at the office today had anything to do with her actual clients.

"A little," she allowed, then added, "I just heard from the title company that the funds for the Piñon Drive house cleared. They're going to send a cashier's check over this afternoon, and Caleb Lowe will be here around three to pick it up."

Her mother's expression grew thoughtful. "You've been spending a lot of time with him."

It wasn't a question. Normally, Linda Dunne would never interfere with her daughter's business, but it must have caught her notice that Caleb Lowe wasn't what you could call an ordinary client.

"I suppose so," Delia said lightly. Why did it feel as if her mother was inquiring about the latest guy she'd been dating, even though there was absolutely nothing of that nature going on with Caleb?

*Maybe because you kind of wish there were,* passed through her mind.

She ignored the thought as best she could.

"He needed help with his house," she went on. "And it sounds as if he wants to do some more flips. I kind of missed doing that, so it's fun that I've met someone willing to bankroll the projects, and all I have to do is provide some creative input."

"Not to mention getting the commissions when you find properties for him," her mother responded. Nothing in her tone or expression showed that she had a problem with the arrangement, and yet Delia still felt as if she needed to justify herself.

"Well, that, too," she said, even though she knew that Caleb had earned a real estate license a while back and could have handled those transactions himself. However, she also got the feeling that he would probably continue to have her manage any acquisitions for him, partly because she was much more experienced in that kind of thing...and also because he knew she needed the money and he didn't. She made a decent living and certainly didn't have to worry about keeping a roof over her head or even allowing herself certain luxuries like a spa day every once in a while or almost exclusively buying Cole Haan shoes because they were the only heels her feet could tolerate for more than a few hours at a time, but she certainly didn't have millions stashed away like he did.

A beat or two passed while her mother seemed to study her for a moment. "It isn't anything more serious than realtor and client, is it?"

That was a loaded question if Delia had ever

heard one. There might not have been anything romantic going on between her and Caleb, but on the other hand, they'd passed "simple business relationship" status months ago.

"We're friends," she said simply. "We like working together. But we're not dating or anything."

Once again, Linda was quiet. This time, her expression seemed to border on skeptical, although Delia hoped her mother would be able to infer from her daughter's tone that she really didn't want to discuss the subject any further.

Then she said, "That's too bad. He seems like a nice young man from what I've seen of him."

Considering she'd only been briefly introduced to Caleb and otherwise had just caught glimpses of him as he came and went from the office, Delia had a feeling her mother was mostly impressed by him because it was clear enough he had money and she wouldn't have to worry about her daughter dating a deadbeat or something.

And she also had to wonder if her mother would think Caleb was quite so "nice" if she ever found out some part of him wasn't even human.

Of course, Delia would never share Caleb's secret with anyone. He'd been surprisingly frank with her, but she'd also noticed that he didn't seem eager to tell anyone else about his otherworldly origins.

Well, of course not. She wouldn't pretend to know everything about his personal life, and yet she could tell he hadn't made any other real friends during the months he'd lived here in Las Vegas. He seemed on friendly terms with his new neighbors—who were probably just happy that the renovation was now finished and the improvements he'd done on the house had removed the upscale neighborhood's one remaining eyesore—but she guessed that friendliness didn't amount to much more than waving when they drove past or maybe having a chat about the weather or some other harmless topic when they happened to be in their respective backyards at the same time.

"He is nice," Delia said. "And easy to work with. But we're keeping things professional."

"Your choice...or his?" her mother pressed.

"Both," Delia replied calmly. "Sometimes it's not so hard to tell that it's better to just be friendly and nothing more."

That comment sounded reasonable enough. For all she knew, it was only the truth, and those stray glances she caught from him from time to time didn't mean anything at all.

She wasn't sure how she wanted to feel about that. From the beginning, she'd been forced to acknowledge that Caleb Lockwood was very attractive, and she knew she got along better with him than any other man she'd ever met...but she'd also made herself believe the last thing she wanted was to get involved with a man who happened to be a quarter demon.

Now, though, she didn't know what to think. If he reached out and told her he wanted something more, would she be brave enough to accept the truth that had been hiding in her heart for quite some time now?

She honestly didn't know. Somehow it seemed easier to face down an army of demons when armed with nothing more than a few vials of holy water than it was to admit that she maybe...just maybe...wanted something a little more than merely friendship with Caleb Lockwood.

Linda had far too much control of herself to sigh, but Delia could still tell her mother was disappointed by that response. It had been a very long dry spell...Delia's breakup with her ex-fiancé had been almost two years ago now, and she sure wasn't going to count that one date with Aaron Sanchez as anything more than a mistake...and she knew her mom had been hoping her daughter would get back out there at some point.

Thank God she was still about eighteen months away from her thirtieth birthday. Delia had little doubt that when that momentous occasion rolled around, her mother would really up the pressure about getting married and settling down. While she wasn't as strident as some of

Delia's friends' parents, Linda had also made it crystal clear that she'd be less than thrilled with her daughter if she didn't get at least one grandchild.

"Well, you know best," she said, although her tone seemed to indicate she wasn't entirely sure whether her daughter actually did know best.

Mercifully, Delia's phone rang right then, so she was able to reach for it while giving her mother an apologetic glance, and Linda took the signal for what it was and melted away.

Sometimes, working with family could be a real pain in the ass.

---

Caleb made sure to be right on time for his appointment with Delia. While he was glad to finally be getting the money from the sale of the Piñon Drive house—okay, the transaction had gone smoothly enough, but he was still sort of astonished by how long it took even the simplest mortgage to process—he was looking forward to seeing her for an entirely different reason. The day before, she'd been dead set on helping out Aaron Sanchez and his family, and yet Caleb still hoped he'd be able to convince her that this whole thing was a very bad idea.

She smiled as he entered her office, but at the

same time, she also looked tired, as if she had way too much going on.

Maybe she did. While she discussed her work sometimes if she thought something particularly interesting or amusing had happened, a lot of it was still opaque to him.

But if she was overloaded at the office, then taking off to Laughlin for the day didn't seem like a very good idea.

"Here you go," she said after she'd greeted him and he'd sat down in the chair facing her desk. By this point, her office with its white oak furniture and plants everywhere felt almost as familiar to him as one of the rooms in his own house. She slid an envelope across the desktop toward him. "Seven hundred and fifty-eight thousand dollars."

"A good day's work," he replied with a grin, although he didn't reach for the envelope. It was far too warm now for a jacket, so he didn't have a convenient pocket he could slide it into.

"Well, it took a bit more than a day," she returned, and her mouth lifted a little at the corners. Not a complete smile, but the shift in expression made her appear a little less tired.

"True. But it's done now, so we can look forward to the next thing." He leaned forward slightly as he added, "I really wish you'd think again about going down to Laughlin. The whole thing is giving me a hinky feeling."

Her posture grew a little more tense, but her expression remained pleasant enough. "So, you're getting psychic abilities now, too?"

"No," he replied at once, refusing to take the bait. "This is more of a gut feeling."

"I don't go back on my promises," she said, her tone flat.

Good to know, although Caleb was forced to admit that he didn't like the idea of her making promises to Aaron Sanchez. Maybe she was right and he was completely innocent, his memory of his dealings with Aegis Holdings wiped right out of his memory banks, but he still didn't trust the guy.

"Then let me come with you," Caleb said, surprising himself. He'd thought of several ways he might dissuade Delia from going to Laughlin, but none of those scenarios had included him tagging along.

She chuckled. "It's just a plain old haunted house, Caleb. No demons. There's no reason for you to be there."

"That you know of."

Her shoulders lifted slightly, and she reached for the mug that sat on the desktop near her. It was the white one that he knew she used for water and nothing else, since it was late in the day to be drinking coffee.

"Nothing Aaron described sounded like anything more than evidence of your regular, garden-variety haunting. It's probably going to take me longer to drive down there and back than it will for me to convince his grandmother's ghost to move on."

"It could be a demon masquerading as a ghost," Caleb suggested, even as he realized he was starting to sound a little desperate with all these excuses. Maybe he should have backed off, but some niggling sixth sense kept telling him the house in Laughlin was *no bueno.* "That sort of thing has happened before, you know."

"I didn't know," she said, her tone a little too even. "I've never run across anything like that in all the hauntings I've worked on. Then again, I didn't know demons were real, either, until a few months ago."

"Then trust me on this one," he said. "Besides, wouldn't it be more fun if I tagged along? We could pick up a bunch of junk food, make it into a real road trip."

A reluctant smile tugged at her mouth. "Maybe it would be more fun. But that's not why I'm going. I'm trying to help someone out."

Yes, he knew that, and maybe he was being an utter jerk for trying to insert himself into a situation where he really had no business being there. As she'd said, this sounded like an ordinary enough haunting. At best, he'd provide some company she probably didn't need.

At worst, he might prove to be more of a distraction than anything else.

"Besides," she went on, "I noticed that some more of the Aegie properties went up on the auction sites this afternoon. You'd be much better served to go take a look at them while I'm out of town in case the bidding gets too hot on the one we're interested in. Then, when I get back, we can walk the most promising ones together and decide which ones we want to bid on, since the next auction won't be happening until Thursday afternoon."

Under normal circumstances, this would have sounded like a good plan. However, Caleb couldn't prevent himself from believing that it would be much better for him to stay by Delia's side and offer whatever support he could.

"I suppose so," he said, as noncommittally as he could. "But if the next auction isn't until Thursday, then there's no reason why we couldn't view the properties together sometime on Wednesday afternoon after you get back to Las Vegas. By then, we'll know whether we got the first one or whether we have to keep looking."

Her full lips compressed slightly, and he got the distinct impression that she was getting a little tired of his bullheadedness. She took a sip of water from her mug and then set it back down on the desk before giving him a very direct look.

"I understand that you're worried," she said. "But I've got this. Or have you forgotten that I've been cleansing houses for almost ten years and did just fine before you came along?"

If it had been anyone else, he might have let his temper flare at her stubbornness. Something about Delia made him want to be better than he used to be, so he did what he could to tamp down the flare of irritation that raised its ugly head.

"No, I haven't forgotten," he said evenly. "On the other hand, you have to admit that the landscape has changed a little since you first got in the ghost-whispering business."

There was no way for her to contradict him on that front, not when she'd seen Robert Hendricks transform into the demon Calach back in January...not when she'd watched the demonic goons from Aegis Holdings nearly raise enough black energy during the poker tournament at the Desert Paradise casino to level a city block.

"It has," she said, her tone almost too calm. "And I've changed, too." Incongruously, she smiled. "Also, you know I don't go anywhere without holy water in my purse. It'll be fine."

He'd seen her wield the stuff, too, fearlessly splashing the blessed liquid right in Calach's face without blinking an eye.

No, Delia Dunne could definitely take care of herself.

Most of the time.

"I don't want anything to happen to you," he said.

Her smile faded, and those clear, blue-gray eyes met his without fear.

"It won't," she replied.

# Chapter Four

—·《《·✿·》》»·—

AT LEAST CALEB HAD FINALLY RELENTED. Or rather, she'd agreed to check in with him regularly while she was out of town, and even though Delia could tell he would much rather have accompanied her to Laughlin, he'd backed off enough to say that should work...but if more than an hour passed and he didn't hear from her, then he'd jump in his car and blaze a trail down there to find out what had happened.

She supposed she had to be content with that.

Before he'd left her office, she handed over printouts of some additional auction properties she thought might work well as flips, homes that weren't priced too crazy and also didn't need such extensive renovations that he couldn't still make a decent profit on each of them.

He hadn't looked too thrilled, but he hadn't argued, either, and had told her he'd check them out. For all she knew, he'd do that before she even got on the road, since she had that one client at ten-thirty to handle and wasn't sure whether she'd be able to leave the office before noon.

As it turned out, though, the house showings on Tuesday morning didn't take as long as she'd expected, since her client fell in love with the first property and didn't want to look at any others. Because she'd been unexpectedly gifted some extra time, she texted Aaron to see if he could meet with her at one instead of three.

He replied that meeting earlier would be great —she had a feeling he wanted to get all this over with as quickly as possible—so she stopped at In-N-Out on her way out of town and grabbed an early lunch before heading down to Laughlin.

As she took a bite of her burger, though, she couldn't quite help experiencing just the slightest twinge of guilt. If she'd taken Caleb up on his offer to accompany her, they could have gotten these burgers together, and maybe added some candy or a couple of Little Debbies or something equally calorie-laden and unhealthy for the return trip to Las Vegas.

No, better for her to be doing this alone. She hadn't heard from him this morning, so she didn't know whether he'd gone to look at the auction properties already or whether he'd put the errand off until later in the day, figuring she wouldn't get back from her ghost-whispering mission until sometime after five or six at the very earliest.

If he was going to look at the houses after lunch, then at least she knew he'd be safely occupied for a while.

It was possible she shouldn't even be looking at the situation that way—she'd known he was only trying to help when he offered to come along, and was doing his best to keep her safe—but she still didn't like the hidden assumption that she couldn't handle whatever was thrown at her.

As she'd told him yesterday, she'd been doing this kind of thing for a long time.

The drive wasn't anything to write home about, just long stretches of dry desert and asphalt that shimmered from the heat and created multiple mirages on the highway ahead of her. Since she'd gone this way plenty of times before, she'd known what to expect, and had her old school punk playlist queued up on her iPhone, X and the Circle Jerks and Black Flag and the Dead Kennedys and a bunch of others whose raucous tunes would effectively kill the silence inside her little Hyundai Kona.

That music had been the soundtrack for most of her high school and college years, and although she didn't listen to it as much as she used to, she still liked to break it out when she knew she'd need something to fill up the monotony of a long drive —or to give her the energy for a task she disliked, such as cleaning out the fish tank at home. She had a housekeeper who came by twice a month, but she would never expect Lupe to deal with that tank.

And as "Johnny Hit and Run Pauline" started to blare through the speakers, Delia couldn't help smiling at herself. She wondered what the eighteen-year-old version of herself, lead singer for Final Girl, the chick who wouldn't take off her Doc Martens even in hundred-degree weather, would think of real estate agent Delia with her cleaning lady and her mortgage and her carefully renovated suburban home.

She'd probably think she was a total sellout.

Oh, well.

Off in the distance, the tall shapes of the casinos that clustered along the riverfront began to rise against the desert's yellow expanse, and when she passed the turnoff for the Davis Dam, she knew she was getting close. Onto Casino Drive, and then another turn onto L Street, moving past what felt like acres of trailer and RV parks. So far, she hadn't seen a single real house, and she wondered if her nav was pointing her in the wrong direction somehow.

But then she noted a cluster of cottonwoods and willows and a single driveway with a gate, and she realized that was where she was supposed to turn off. At first, she couldn't see anything of the house at all, but once she was past the trees that surrounded the property, she spied a white-painted two-story home with light blue shutters, kind of your standard American farmhouse in appearance and definitely incongruous amidst all the RVs and casinos that otherwise dominated the Laughlin landscape.

A black BMW was parked in front of a detached structure that Delia guessed was the garage. The car had to be Aaron's, so it didn't look as if the finance company had repo'd it yet.

Or maybe he'd borrowed some money from family to get his payments up to date. Either way, it wasn't her business...and she wouldn't ask.

She came to a stop next to the BMW and turned off her Hyundai's engine, then got out. Almost at once, a hot, dry wind tugged at her hair, even though she'd pulled it back into a ponytail. Before she'd left work, she'd gone into the bathroom and changed out of her skirt, heels, and blouse into jeans and a sleeveless top and some sandals, an outfit she'd brought with her after she realized the day before that it would be better to be dressed practically for this mission.

Just in case.

Almost as soon as she'd gotten out of her little SUV, Aaron emerged onto the front porch of the house. He looked much better than he had yesterday, since it seemed as if he'd gotten a haircut and a decent night's sleep in the interim.

"Hey, there," he called. "Did you have any trouble finding the place?"

"No," she said, then made her way along the little gravel path that wound its way to the door. The grass surrounding the path was yellowed and in definite need of a watering, and again, she could tell that Aaron's great-grandparents obviously hadn't worried about fitting in with the desert landscape, not with that lawn and all the trees that surrounded the property. "Although I'm starting to wonder if this is the only real house in Laughlin."

He grinned at her as she came up the porch steps. "No, there are real houses, but most of them are to the south of here, near the Colorado River bend. My family hung onto this place even though developers kept trying to buy them out."

Delia could see why anyone who'd built the RV parks or the casinos would have wanted this plot of land, since it did sort of sit right in the middle of what was otherwise mostly commercial real estate. Pru hadn't mentioned anything about that, although Delia guessed all those offers—if they'd even happened—had been informal, verbal affairs and nothing that would have been put in the public record.

"I'm glad they did," she said. "It's always fun to

come across these holdouts in the middle of boring suburbia or retail areas." She paused there and glanced around. The paint on the siding was fading, and she could see evidence of some wood rot on the porch columns, but those were easy fixes. "If developers are so interested in this place, why not sell it to one of them rather than a private party? Then you wouldn't even have to worry about whether it was haunted or not, since the developers would just bulldoze the house anyway."

Aaron didn't quite wince, but she could tell he wasn't too thrilled with her assessment of the situation. "Not possible," he said shortly. "I finally convinced my parents to sell the house—a lot of the family isn't even in the area anymore, and there wouldn't have been a lot of takers in the first place —but my father flat-out told me that selling to a developer was off the table. It has to go to someone who'll preserve the property."

If that was the case, then even leaving aside the haunted-or-not aspect of the situation, they were going to have a much harder time unloading the place. People wanted to live in real neighborhoods, not in a carve-out of a couple of acres in the middle of unending RV parks.

But Aaron probably knew that as well as she did, so Delia didn't see any reason to bring it up.

"Okay," she said. "Then I suppose we might as well go inside and check it out."

He nodded, then turned around and opened the door to let her in.

Like a lot of houses of a similar vintage, it had a small foyer that had a staircase immediately facing the front door, with a formal dining room on one side and a sitting room on the other. A blast of cool, damp air hit Delia's face, telling her that the place only had a swamp cooler, not real A/C.

Another strike against the house.

But again, Aaron must have known that, too. Anyway, she wasn't here to evaluate the home's shortcomings and give an honest assessment of its current market value.

No, she was here to see if she could sense the ghost who apparently lingered in the house and figure out the best way to convince it that it needed to move on.

There was something off about this place, though, an intangible quality she couldn't begin to describe. It didn't feel exactly like the sometimes oppressive sensation she sensed when she was in the presence of a particularly troubled or stubborn entity, but it still seemed to press on her, making each breath a little more difficult to pull in than it should have.

Aaron must have noticed something was wrong, because he asked, "Is everything okay?"

"I'm fine," she managed.

And oddly, as soon as the words left her

mouth, she did feel fine. Or rather, while she didn't like the sensation of the slightly damp air lying on her bare arms or the faint scent of mothballs that seemed to pervade the place, at least she could breathe properly.

As far as she could tell, no one seemed to have touched much of anything after Alba Sanchez died. A fussy-looking table and matching chairs still occupied the dining room, while the sitting room was crowded with a sofa and two matching chairs, all upholstered in the same powder-blue velvet. Matching velvet curtains hung at the windows.

"Are these all your grandmother's things?" Delia asked.

Looking somber, Aaron replied, "Yes. Because we weren't sure what to do with the house, we left all the furniture in place. Her personal items were given to people in the family according to her will, but everything else is still here."

"So...she left the house to your parents?"

For a second, his gaze slipped away from hers, and she thought again of how the house seemed to have been passed among members of the family without much ceremony. "Basically," he said. "My father was next in line to inherit. But then we decided to sell the place instead."

Aaron sounded casual enough, but Delia guessed that his almost offhand tone was his way of trying to minimize what had probably been some heated debate among the family.

"Well, then," she said, "I'll do my best to help you with that. Is it okay if I walk through the place on my own? Having someone else around can sometimes disrupt the energy of a space."

While this was true, she'd also conducted plenty of these walk-throughs with concerned clients nearby. But because she didn't know what she was dealing with here—and because the place had felt so odd to her when she first walked in, even though the strange, breathless sensation appeared to have subsided—she figured it was probably better to do this on her own.

Luckily, Aaron didn't seem to have a problem with that, because he replied, "Oh, sure. Is it okay if I wait on the porch?"

"Absolutely."

He flashed her a smile and went out the front door, then closed it gently behind him. For a second or two, she felt a little guilty about banishing him from the house, just because it was pretty hot outside, and even the damp relief provided by the whole-house swamp cooler was better than nothing.

But he'd be in the shade at least, and because it was plenty breezy outside, she thought the conditions wouldn't be too bad. Anyway, he shouldn't be out there for very long.

She hoped.

The question was, where to go first? Into the living room, with its overstuffed blue velvet furniture, or the dining room, which felt equally cramped thanks to the large buffet crammed with china that had been wedged up against a wall she guessed was shared with the kitchen?

She didn't know for sure, but if Alba Sanchez had been anything like Delia's high school friend Carmela's grandmother, then she'd probably spent much more time feeding people than she had lounging in the living room.

A moment to pause in the dining room and sense its vibrations, but Delia couldn't pick up on much of anything. The realtor and designer in her immediately wanted to imagine what the house would feel like with some of the walls knocked down, thereby creating a sense of space and airiness, although she knew that wasn't why she was here. Aaron and his family weren't remodeling the property to get top dollar, but only doing what they could to sell the place fast so they could get on with their lives.

All right, then.

Delia moved into the kitchen, which was actually larger than she'd expected. It occupied a sort of "L" at the back of the house, with the shorter leg given over to a breakfast nook with a big window that overlooked the backyard. From what she could see, the yard was mostly yellowed grass, just like the front, although it looked as if a vegetable garden of some sort had once occupied the long raised bed near one of the walls.

Whoever moved in here, they'd have a lot of work ahead of them. Trying to keep up that much grass out here in the middle of the desert didn't make much sense, so they'd have to either tear up the lawn and cover the dirt with gravel and drought-tolerant plants, or they'd need to invest in artificial turf.

Well, it wasn't her problem.

Belatedly, she realized she was supposed to have checked in with Caleb. She'd already let him know she wouldn't call while she was driving, but now that she was here in Laughlin, she needed to get in touch and at least assure him she'd arrived safely.

A text should be fine, though.

*I'm in Laughlin. Aaron just let me into the house and is waiting outside while I check out the place. I'll let you know if I find anything.*

A second or two went by, and then Caleb messaged her back.

*Thanks for the update. Just walked the first house. It's a little smaller than I was looking for, but all the fixes are cosmetic & I think it's a good candidate as long as no one bids it up too far.*

That was good news. If nothing else, having

him preoccupied with another flip sounded like a good way to keep him out of trouble.

*Great! I'm interested to see what you think of the other houses.*

*I'll let you know.*

*Okay. Gotta get back to work.*

*Good luck with the ghost.*

She sent a tongue-out emoji in response to that comment, then slipped her phone back into her purse. While she was texting with Caleb, she'd kept one ear open, thinking that maybe the ghost would want to sidle up when she was otherwise occupied. For now, though, the space still felt entirely too neutral.

Maybe that was the point. It was always hard to say what a spirit knew or didn't know about what was going on in the physical world, but Delia wondered if maybe Alba Sanchez had somehow sniffed out that she was there for more than just a simple walk-through of the property.

"Alba?" she ventured, then immediately felt like an idiot. After all, she had just assumed that Aaron's grandmother was the person haunting the place, but she didn't know that for sure.

Dead silence—well, except the omnipresent background rumble of the swamp cooler—and yet Delia couldn't help feeling that something was still there, watching and listening.

Not exactly the most reassuring sensation in the world.

But she'd been in creepy spaces before, and she certainly wasn't going to turn around and walk out because she had the heebie-jeebies. Besides, she knew that ghosts...with a few notable exceptions... couldn't cause any real harm to the living.

She set her purse down on the counter and surveyed the space. If the golden oak cabinets and laminate countertops were any indication, the kitchen had probably been updated in the early 1990s but hadn't been touched since. Now the room was ripe for another remodel, although she knew she shouldn't be worrying about that.

At least no one had touched the original wood floors, which looked to be in surprisingly good shape. She hoped whoever bought the house would keep them, even if the new owners ended up making a lot of other changes.

Even though she had no real idea that Alba was listening, she knew she had to keep going.

"I just want to take a look around," Delia continued. "But if you want to reach out and communicate in any way, I'm listening."

Almost immediately, one of the cupboard doors swung open. She had been standing at least ten feet away, so she knew she couldn't have had anything to do with the sudden activity on the other side of the room.

Was Alba trying to send a signal of some sort?

It wasn't the first time Delia's had seen a spirit interact with the physical plane, so rather than running out of the house screaming, she walked as calmly as she could over to the cupboard in question to take a look. Unlike the buffet in the dining room, which was stuffed full of fancy china she guessed no one had wanted, the cupboard was empty, and she thought that Aaron's parents or possibly someone else in the family had come through and cleared everything out.

Or at least, almost everything.

She almost overlooked the mark. It was small, not much more than an inch high, and at first she thought it was simply a scratch, a careless blemish left behind when someone was putting something inside the cupboard.

But then she realized the mark she'd found had an intentional design of some sort, although she had no idea what it was supposed to be. While at first glance it looked something like a cross, all four arms were equal in length and had a sort of curved lozenge shape to them, and a small circle seemed to be superimposed where the arms connected in the middle.

Maybe it was some sort of Christian symbol. Delia hadn't been brought up in any particular religion, so she'd be the first to admit that she didn't know much about the different types of crosses that various denominations might use.

Then again, Pru had told her that Alba attended the local Catholic church. Delia didn't know what this symbol was supposed to be, but it sure didn't look like a crucifix to her.

Well, she'd take a photo and upload the image to Google search and see what it said.

She got out her phone once again and moved as close as she could without the cross-thingy turning too blurry. Then she took a series of shots and hoped that at least one of them would be serviceable.

Actually, several were, so she uploaded the most likely candidate and waited to see what Google had to say on the subject.

And waited...and waited....

The screen appeared to be frozen, even though Verizon claimed she had three bars of 5G. That should have been plenty to upload a simple image, especially since she'd only sent a medium-sized photo, not the high-resolution one.

Frowning, she closed the browser and reopened it, hoping that might have jiggered things loose. Once again, she attached the image to the Google search bar and waited.

And once again, nothing happened.

Okay, fine. She'd send the thing to Caleb and ask him to try looking it up. After all, just because

Verizon said she should have sufficient bars here, that didn't necessarily mean the company's assessment of the local situation was accurate. This wouldn't be the first time she thought she had a strong enough cell signal to do whatever she needed, only to have her service provider demonstrate otherwise.

She went back to their message thread and typed, *Can you check on this symbol and let me know what it is? My cell service is kind of shaky here.*

And then she attached the image and pressed the screen to send the text.

Again, nothing. Or rather, it looked as if the message had gone off into the ether the way it was supposed to, but there was no sign that it had been delivered. Since both she and Caleb had iPhones, she always got that confirmation when they were communicating this way.

Today, though?

Bupkiss.

For a moment, Delia wondered if she should go out onto the porch and ask Aaron if he usually had issues with sending attachments or surfing the internet on his phone when he was in this neighborhood. It could have been a dead spot, despite what the bars on her phone showed.

Something inside told her not to do that, though.

Instead, she kept her phone out and peered

inside the rest of the kitchen cabinets. No other strange symbols, unfortunately...at least, that she could find.

The space opened onto a service porch that held a Kenmore washer and dryer that looked almost as old as the cabinets and Formica counters in the kitchen. A pair of cupboards was mounted to the wall above the appliances, but when Delia peered inside—using her phone's flashlight to illuminate the interiors as best she could—she didn't see anything except one abandoned dryer sheet.

So much for that.

Trying to ignore the mounting frustration inside her, she went back through the kitchen and over to the other side of the house. Just past the sitting room was a small guest bath, something she guessed had been shoehorned in there around the same time the kitchen had been "updated," since in general, the front parlor or whatever you wanted to call it would have been somewhat bigger than its current footprint.

Beyond that was the room she guessed had been the home's main living space, since this was the only place where she'd seen a TV so far. It was mounted to the wall above the fireplace, which didn't look as if it had been used in years and in fact was filled with a large silk flower arrangement that needed a good dusting.

In here, Delia got the feeling more than ever

that someone was watching her. "Alba?" she ventured again.

One of the blue-striped curtains at the window moved ever so slightly. It could have just caught a current of air from the whole-house swamp cooler...or that faint flutter could have been caused by something else entirely.

Unease moved down her spine, even as Delia told herself she'd been in this particular situation plenty of times before. Not every ghost wanted to reveal itself, and sometimes it took a good deal of coaxing to get to a place where they could actually communicate.

That didn't mean she wouldn't keep trying, especially if it meant she wouldn't have to go upstairs. For some reason, that idea seemed extremely unappealing, even though it was a bright, sunny day and she knew she didn't have anything to worry about.

All right, more like hoped than actually knew, but still.

A soft footfall behind her nearly made her jump out of her skin, but then she realized it was only Aaron, holding his phone and looking apologetic as he stood just inside the entrance to the room.

"Sorry," he said. "I hate to bail on you like this, but I just got a call from an agency over in Bullhead City that I applied with, and they want me to come in now. I can't really blow them off, not when I need to get a new position as soon as possible. Are you okay with staying here by yourself?"

*Absolutely not,* her mind said at once, but Delia quashed that thought. She'd come here to cleanse the house, and she wasn't anywhere close to accomplishing that goal.

"Sure," she replied. "I think I've picked up on a few things, but I still don't know who's here or what they want."

Aaron's expression grew troubled. "I suppose I can try to reschedule—"

"No," she cut in. Considering the financial mess he was currently dealing with, the last thing she wanted was for her own cowardice to prevent him from getting a job he needed. "It's fine."

"You're sure?"

"I am."

He hesitated, but it seemed clear to her that he wasn't going to argue too much, not when he wasn't in a position to blow off a potential employer. "Okay." He reached into his pocket and pulled out a set of keys attached to a silvery fob set with what looked like inlaid turquoise and mother-of-pearl. "Here are the house keys. When you're done, you can text me and then leave them under the mat. I'll swing by and get them when I can."

Delia wanted to ask if that would be taking something of a risk, but she figured he knew the neighborhood better than she did and had a much clearer idea of what was safe and what wasn't.

Instead, she took the keys from him and put them in her jeans pocket. Since he was standing right there, she thought she might as well ask the question.

"Do you ever have problems with cell service here?"

He nodded, then said, "Oh, yeah. I guess I should have warned you about that. This property is kind of a digital sinkhole. It looks like you have service, but sometimes you still can't send a text or get the internet to work right. Calls usually go through, though, for whatever reason."

Well, that was something. Delia knew she'd been able to get at least one text out to Caleb, so it sounded as if the service was just unreliable rather than being completely nonexistent.

Obviously trying to be helpful, Aaron added, "If I need a clear signal, I usually drive up to Heritage Park. It's about five minutes from here—just go back out to Casino Drive and head north. The road ends there, so it's hard to miss."

"Thanks for the tip," Delia replied. Maybe it wasn't the most convenient thing in the world to leave the property altogether to get in touch with the outside world, but it was better than nothing.

"How long do you think you're going to be?"

he asked, and all she could do was give a noncommittal lift of her shoulders.

"It's really hard to say. I can sense someone in the house, but they don't seem very eager to make contact. I'll keep plugging away, though—it's still early enough that I can spend a couple of hours here and not have to worry about driving home in the dark."

Which she'd done once or twice when a client she'd worked with in Las Vegas had insisted on her handling a transaction in Laughlin. There really wasn't all that much to the drive, but all the same, she didn't like traveling over those long stretches of empty road, even if there were plenty of other cars sharing the highway with her.

"Okay," Aaron replied. "Then I'll swing by after I'm done with my meeting. If you're still here, great, but otherwise, I'll just pick up the keys and head home."

Wherever that was right now. He'd mentioned an Airbnb, but she didn't know whether it was located here in Laughlin or back in Vegas somewhere.

"Sounds good," she said.

"Good luck."

Why did that supposedly friendly admonition sound so ominous right now?

However, she only smiled and lifted a hand, and he did the same before he headed back outside.

She couldn't hear his car starting up, but that wasn't so strange—the windows in the house were mostly closed, although she'd noticed the one in the kitchen had been left open a crack so condensation from the swamp cooler wouldn't start to build up.

For a moment, she stood in the middle of the family room, not sure what she should do next.

Then she pulled in a breath and headed for the stairs.

# Chapter Five

WELL, AT LEAST HE KNEW DELIA WAS OKAY, although Caleb still didn't like the thought of her being down there in Laughlin all by herself. Most of the time, he would have said she could handle pretty much anything that was thrown her way, but the last few months had been just crazy enough that he would have felt a lot better if he could have been there for backup.

He wasn't, though. Rather than sit at home and brood, however, he'd looked up another of the Aegis Holdings houses that were going up for auction, not because he thought it was all that likely a prospect—the place was a townhouse, and the chances of making some serious cash on a home like that were a lot lower—but because he figured it was better than staying at his own house and doing nothing except fretting.

Also, he figured it couldn't hurt to see who else was looking at the place, just in case any of them seemed suspicious.

When he did the walkthrough, though, he could tell the other people inspecting the property —a husband and wife team he thought he recognized from the same house he was actually interested in, a few solo people who snapped pictures and took notes—were all nothing more than they seemed to be, just regular humans out to make a buck.

Or at least, he was about ninety percent sure they were nothing more than they seemed. He had to admit that his demon-detecting radar hadn't been as accurate as he might have liked lately. True, demons could be very good at hiding their natures, especially if they were several rungs up the ladder from the low-level demons Calach had sent after him in January, but still, Caleb thought he should have been able to catch at least a whiff of brimstone.

Nothing, though, and that meant he was driving home about an hour after he'd left, feeling vaguely unsatisfied and not sure what he should do with himself.

In more innocent times, he might have gone out and hit the casinos to pass the time and take the edge off his anxiety. After that clusterfuck at the Desert Paradise in March, however, he thought he might be happy if he never set foot in a casino again.

Besides, his investments were humming along, and with the prospect of flipping some properties in the near future, he knew he didn't have to go out and make money by using his demonic powers to influence a set of dice or ensure that he made black-jack whenever he liked.

Maybe he really should take up golf.

His phone pinged at him just as the garage door was closing, and he turned off his Range Rover's engine so he could slide the iPhone out of his pocket. A text from Delia.

*Can you look this up and let me know what it is?*

Obviously, there was supposed to have been an attachment, but he didn't see anything. Possibly she'd goofed or—more likely—she had enough cell service to get a text out, but her carrier had decided the picture she'd tried to send was too much for the system to handle.

At least she'd texted him, though, which meant she must be fine.

Of course she was fine. She'd driven to Laughlin, not a town in the middle of the Sinaloa cartel's territory or something.

He got out of the SUV and went into the kitchen. Cool air surrounded him, and he wondered if maybe he should have a beer to take the edge off. It was past three o'clock by that point, so he didn't think anyone could give him too much grief over having a drink.

Delia first, though.

*I got your message, but there wasn't an attachment. Do you want to try sending it again?*

While he waited for her to get back to him, he headed over to the fridge and pulled out a Voodoo Brewing brown ale, then cracked the tab and poured the beer into a pint glass. He swallowed some and looked down at his phone.

His text still showed as the last one in his and Delia's convo.

Well, maybe she'd set her phone down somewhere, or maybe she was now enough out of range that even a text couldn't get through.

That didn't feel right, though. She was in Laughlin, Nevada, not out in the middle of nowhere. He might not have visited the town yet, but even he knew it was a big tourist destination and therefore should have plenty of cell capacity.

Had her battery died?

He dismissed that thought almost as soon as it passed through his mind. The whole time he'd known Delia—going on five months now—he'd never once seen her phone run out of juice. It was her connection to her clients, and she was very careful about keeping it fully charged.

No, the cell connection down there must be screwed up somehow.

Another glance at the phone didn't reveal an answering text, which he'd already known. Still, he hated the thought of their one means of communication being completely unavailable.

An uneasy sensation inched its way down his spine.

What if it wasn't the cell towers at all?

What if she was really in trouble?

*Oh, shut up,* he told his brain, but it continued to manufacture worst-case scenarios.

After all, he'd seen an angry spirit attack her in this very house—okay, out in the backyard—so he knew that ghosts weren't always wispy blobs of vapor, entirely harmless. What if an equally vengeful specter was haunting Aaron's family's house in Laughlin? Would Delia even be equipped to handle that kind of assault?

She had holy water with her, but Caleb didn't know whether that would be enough.

Damn it.

He picked up the phone and entered her number, since by this time, he had it memorized and this was faster than going to his contacts list. Three rings, and then he heard her standard message.

*Hi, you've reached Delia Dunne. I'm sorry I missed your call—*

An annoyed breath passed his lips, and he touched his finger to his iPhone's screen to end the call. Maybe that was rude, and he should have just left a message anyway, but the whole point of him reaching out was to talk to her personally and make sure she was okay. If all he got was a recording, there didn't seem to be any reason to stay on the line.

And if she was all right, then at some point she'd probably notice that he'd called but hadn't left a message, in which case, she'd contact him anyway.

As much as he didn't like it, there didn't seem to be much he could do right now except sit and wait.

---

Even though it wasn't even two o'clock in the afternoon and Aaron had opened all the drapes and blinds to let as much light in as possible, Delia still flicked on the lights in the stairwell as she made her way up to the second story. True, the stairs were enclosed, so daylight didn't help much, but it wasn't as if she was going upstairs in the middle of the night or something.

All the same, the sconces on either side—unattractive things that she guessed had also been installed sometime in the 1980s—helped a little. Not all the way, because she could think of about a thousand places she would rather be, but it was still better than heading up there in the dark.

Okay, half-dark.

The stairs terminated in a landing with two doors facing her. One of them was a bedroom with nothing in it except a pair of empty white bookcases, and the other was a bathroom that looked fairly large, considering the age of the house.

Two more doors revealed two other bedrooms. The first looked to be about the same size as the one that faced the staircase, but the other was much bigger, obviously the master bedroom, even though it didn't have an *en suite* bath.

Again, a lot of houses of this vintage didn't have that amenity. Anyone who bought the place would have to deal with the setup as-is or figure out a way to steal some space from one of the other bedrooms to create a master bath and a decent-sized closet.

*Not your problem,* she told herself, but that was just how her brain worked. After being in real estate for so many years and flipping a dozen or so houses along the way, the second she set foot in a place, she started assessing its strengths and weaknesses, trying to determine what should be updated and what might be left alone to save a little money.

Besides, thinking about harmless stuff like how to reconfigure the upstairs to fit the needs of a twenty-first-century family kept her from wondering about the entity that appeared to have taken up residence in the house...and how she was going to get it out of there.

The secondary bedrooms were mostly empty except for the odd bit of furniture inside, like the bookcase in the room that faced the stairs. However, the main bedroom still had an entire suite of furniture—a four-poster bed, two night-stands, and a long dresser with a matching mirror that hung about it—as if no one had known exactly what to do with the outdated ensemble and had hoped maybe the new owners would want to keep it.

Fat chance of that.

All of the pieces had their share of scratches and dings, and besides, most people these days didn't want matchy-matchy bedroom sets like the ones their parents and grandparents had preferred.

Delia moved farther into the room and stood there for a minute, doing her best to sense its ener-gies. Again, she had that feeling of someone watching her, but nothing more than that. She certainly couldn't tell if the presence was male or female.

Or even if it was human.

A shiver inched its way down her spine, even though it was probably about four or five degrees warmer up here than it had been on the ground floor, the swamp cooler straining against the ninety-degree temperatures outside.

"I'm here if you want to talk to me," she said quietly, then waited.

Something went *thump* inside the closet.

Her heart made a valiant effort to leap into her throat, but she choked it down. She absolutely was not going to lose her shit in here, no matter how hard the ghost lurking in this house seemed to want to play with her.

Another swallow of air, and then she moved calmly over to the closet door—it was a sliding version, not a regular door with a walk-in space beyond—and pushed it aside.

The thing was empty except for a few forlorn wire hangers at one end.

So what had made that thump?

Nothing at all, it seemed.

Well, in a haunted house, you often didn't have a physical cause for the phenomena you might see... or hear.

Delia pulled her phone out of her purse and turned on the flashlight again, slanting the beam up toward the shelf that spanned the length of the closet. It was empty as well, but then something caught her eye.

The puffy cross shape that somehow reminded her of the petals of a flower, with the small circle superimposed at its center. This one appeared to have been written on the wall just above the shelf, right smack in the middle.

Just what the hell was that thing?

Her phone still said it had five bars, but she knew better than to trust it, not after what Aaron had told her about the reception here. No, she just took some snaps of the drawing—and this one did seem to be drawn on, rather than scratched into the paint—and then stepped away from the closet.

"Alba, what does that cross mean?"

Movement at the corner of her eye, although Delia realized it was only the curtains fluttering ever so slightly. More air currents from the swamp cooler...or something else?

Then the faintest of whispers.

*Not...a cross.*

It was impossible to say whether the person talking was male or female, and yet Delia still got the impression the speaker was a woman.

Alba?

"I'm here to help," Delia said clearly.

Something that might have been a ghostly chuckle.

*Can't help.*

"Yes, I can," she replied, hoping she sounded confident and not at all worried that she might be dealing with something here she hadn't been expecting. "I've helped many move on."

*Can't.*

That was all, and Delia frowned. Was the ghost trying to say she couldn't help, or attempting to tell her that it couldn't move on, for whatever reason?

"Why not?" she asked, willing herself not to get too frustrated. Communicating with ghosts wasn't like talking to another person—when they spoke at all, it was often in riddles or half-sentences, uttering statements that didn't seem to make much sense on the surface. She usually needed a good while to get to the heart of the matter and ascertain exactly what was keeping them on this plane.

And, as she'd pointed out to Aaron, it was still early in the afternoon. She had plenty of time to get this straightened out and still be on the road before nightfall.

*Danger.*

Cold once again trickled down her spine. Delia pulled in a breath and wished she'd brought her iced tea from In-N-Out inside the house with her—her mouth felt as dry as the desert that lay just a few hundred yards outside the oasis of the Sanchez homestead.

"Who's in danger?" she said clearly. "Or are you talking about the house?"

*House...stays.*

That made no sense at all.

Unless....

Was Alba trying to say that the house needed to

103

stay in the family, and that anyone else who tried to live there would be in some kind of danger?

Possibly. Delia didn't want to think that Aaron's grandmother might be the vengeful kind of spirit who played tricks on anyone who had the presumption to take up residence in her beloved home, but that sort of behavior was all too common among ghosts.

From what Pru had told her, though, it didn't even sound as if Alba Sanchez had spent most of her life here. She and her husband had lived in the house for a while, but they'd moved out in the eighties, and she'd only returned after she was widowed some five years ago.

"You don't want Aaron to sell the house?"

Dead silence.

For a second, anyway. From down the hall came a crash that made Delia jump...and then she realized that was probably the sound of the two bookcases getting knocked over.

Yes, it definitely seemed as if Alba wanted to keep the house in the family.

More than ever, Delia had to fight the urge to hurry down the stairs and get out of there, and let Aaron's family deal with the problem. But she'd told them she'd do what she could, and that didn't include running away at the first sign of trouble.

Also, while the spirit...who might or might not have been Alba...had expressed its displeasure in various ways, it hadn't done anything to threaten her personally. That made her think the ghost was more frustrated than anything else.

Well, that made two of them.

"Why can't he sell the house?" she pressed. "I know it's been in the family for eighty years, but is there some reason beyond that for wanting to make sure strangers don't buy it?"

*Guard....* came a whisper from the spirit.

Something about the atmosphere in the room felt almost thundery, although Delia told herself that could have simply been the damp air from the swamp cooler.

Or was it that she might be getting to the heart of the problem?

"Guard against what?" she asked.

*Guard.*

Well, that cleared everything up.

She tightened her grip on the strap of her purse, even as she reminded herself that she had plenty of holy water inside and there was nothing to be worried about.

Yeah, right.

And then....

Delia wasn't sure if she could have ever described what happened next, except that it felt as if someone had grabbed her by the arms and forced her eyes wider than they'd ever been, almost as if she'd been trapped in that awful scene from *A*

*Clockwork Orange* where Alex's eyes were kept open by those horrible metal gadgets.

In front of her was the symbol she'd seen scratched into the kitchen cabinet downstairs and written on the wall inside the closet, only instead of being an inch or so high, it appeared to be almost her same height, hanging in the air and surrounded by a golden glow that seemed to pulse like a heartbeat.

*Guard...protect.*

The symbol was some sort of sigil of protection?

But what had Alba been trying to protect against?

"Someone in the family needs to protect this place?" she asked.

The glowing symbol abruptly disappeared, and the curtains rustled again.

*Protect...or else.*

The thundery sensation in the room abruptly disappeared, and Delia pulled in a shocked breath. A glance around told her she was alone...and the heightened senses she still wasn't entirely used to only reinforced that impression.

Whoever or whatever had taken hold of her, it seemed to be gone now.

A symbol of protection. A sigil to ensure the safety of those inside this place.

But why? What was so important that Alba

had lingered after her death to make sure no one outside the Sanchez family ever lived in the house?

Delia had absolutely no idea, and with Aaron off at a job interview, she wasn't going to get the answers she needed any time soon. As much as she wanted to dash right back to Las Vegas, she knew that wasn't feasible, not until she got a chance to talk to him again.

However, that didn't mean she couldn't share what had just happened with Caleb and see if any of this made sense to him.

Not from here, though, not with the way the cell reception around the property was all kinds of screwed up.

She hitched her purse on her shoulder and resolutely made her way down the stairs, then went outside and locked the door behind her with the key Aaron had provided.

He'd said she could get a call out from Heritage Park...and that's exactly where she was headed.

# Chapter Six

Halfway through his beer, Caleb gave up and tried calling Delia again.

And texting.

And calling again.

Nothing seemed to get through.

What the hell was going on down there?

In desperation, he picked up the phone again and called Aaron. Delia had given him the guy's number just in case, but Caleb had never imagined he'd be calling the other man to check up on her like some kind of jealous boyfriend.

He wished he could play that role in her life... well, without the "jealous" part.

At least Aaron answered, and said in response to Caleb's question, "She was at the house, but I had to leave for an interview, so she stayed behind."

An interview? Was he serious?

"You left her alone there?" Caleb demanded.

Too bad his demonic powers weren't strong enough for him to reach through the phone and slap the jerk upside the head.

A pause. When Aaron replied, his tone sounded distinctly defensive. "Yeah, I did," he said. "She said it wasn't a problem, that she'd done this plenty of times."

As much as he hated to admit it to himself, Caleb knew that part was true enough. Delia had never given him an exact number, but he knew she'd been ghost whispering for around ten years. Even if she only had to cleanse six or seven houses in any given year—and he'd gotten the impression it was often much more—that still added up to a lot of ghosts.

But that had been before a bunch of demons had decided to start appearing in Las Vegas and causing all sorts of havoc. The supernatural world Delia inhabited now was very different from the one she'd lived in before he'd entered her life.

"Maybe so," Caleb said. "But I can't get hold of her, and she told me she'd check in regularly."

"It's probably not a big deal," Aaron replied at once. His tone was almost too smooth. Possibly, he was just trying to sound reassuring, but he came across as more condescending than anything else.

Of course, that could have simply been because Caleb still didn't like the guy and didn't trust him, no matter what sort of trauma he might or might not have suffered recently.

"The cell reception at the house isn't so great," Aaron continued. "I'm sure that's why you can't get through."

"I got a text from her earlier this afternoon," Caleb pointed out.

Although he couldn't see his face, he got the impression that Aaron had only shrugged. "Sometimes stuff gets through, and sometimes it doesn't. Tell you what—I just finished up here, and I was about to swing by the house and check on Delia anyway. As soon as I know something, I'll call you back."

"I thought you just said you don't have cell service at the property," Caleb returned, knowing a definite rasp had entered his voice.

However, Aaron still didn't sound too concerned. "I said it was iffy. But if it's acting up, I'll drive to a place I know that has good service, and I'll call you from there. Just give me about ten minutes."

Most of the time, that would have sounded like an adequate solution. Now even ten minutes felt far too long.

If Caleb had known where he was going, he could have simply teleported himself onto the property and searched for Delia himself. However, he'd never been there, and while there might have still been some photos of it online—even though Aaron had intimated that the house was currently off the market—it seemed simpler to wait and hear what he'd found.

If nothing else, Delia might get seriously annoyed with him if he appeared out of nowhere to check up on her. Caleb knew she didn't appreciate that kind of babysitting.

"All right," he said, not bothering to sound gracious. "I'll wait to hear back from you."

They ended the call there. For just a moment, he thought about opening up another beer but immediately shot down that notion. Although alcohol didn't affect him the same way it did people without a drop of demon blood in their veins, he still wanted to be as sharp as possible.

Just in case.

Instead, he poured himself a glass of water and took it and his phone with him into the living room, where he sat down on the couch to wait. Although he was generally very happy with the setup in his house, right then he thought it was sort of stupid that he'd put his big TV downstairs in the bonus room rather than here, where it would be more easily accessible.

But since he wasn't about to start rearranging the decor, he looked up a few stocks on his phone, read a couple of articles on Apple News, and checked his email.

To his surprise, he'd won the auction for the house in Wyeth Ranch. Since he'd already put down a deposit before he could bid, he now had forty-five days to come up with the rest of the money.

Well, that was something. Thank God for the time buffer, because right now, he had more important things on his mind than running over to the auction house's offices and handing over a cashier's check, the only form of payment they accepted.

About twelve minutes after he and Aaron had hung up, his phone rang.

"What did you find?" he asked.

Okay, sure, it could have been someone else, but Caleb didn't get a lot of phone calls, so he couldn't think who else would be contacting him. The auction house had already stated that all its communications would be via email, so he knew it wasn't them.

"Well, it looks like she left," Aaron replied, still in that just slightly too upbeat tone. "I gave her the keys, and everything was locked back up, and the keys were under the doormat, just like I asked her to do when she was done at the house. As far as I can tell, she did what she needed to do and got back on the road, because her car isn't here."

Delia was always careful with other people's property—how could she not be, when showing houses was part of her job?—so all this sounded pretty much exactly like the way she would have handled such a situation.

Except....

"If she managed to banish the ghost, why didn't she call you to let you know the house was cleared?"

"Well, she knew I was in a meeting. She probably didn't want to bug me."

Again, that didn't sound too off base for Delia, but the other man's blithe tone still grated. "Did you go inside? Was there a note?"

"I didn't see anything. But I don't know if she even would have had something to write with. There's not a whole lot left in the house."

Most people probably wouldn't have a pen and paper available. Delia, on the other hand, usually carried a small notebook and a pen with her for those times when she wanted to write something down but didn't want to use her phone's notepad function.

But maybe she didn't have her note-taking tools with her this time, for whatever reason. If that were the case, then she might have just gotten on the road and figured she'd call Aaron later to let him know what had happened with the ghost.

However, that didn't explain why she hadn't reached out to Caleb. She'd promised him she would check in, and it seemed as if she had...at first. The crappy cell reception could have been the real culprit here, but even so, there shouldn't have been anything stopping her from calling him once she was away from the house and out someplace where she got a decent signal.

The more he thought about it, the more suspicious the whole situation sounded.

Aaron spoke again. "Tell you what. I told her she should drive up to Heritage Park and make her calls from there, since that's my go-to place when I've been at my grandmother's house and needed to call or text someone and couldn't get a message out. The park is only a couple of minutes away. Let me go up there and see if I can spot her car. Delia might have already headed back to Vegas, but if she left the house only a few minutes ago, she could still be there."

That sounded like a long shot to Caleb, but he wasn't going to abandon any possibility, no matter how slim. "That could work. Thanks."

"Just give me a couple of minutes."

The call ended, and Caleb set his phone down on the coffee table to wait again. This time, though, it was a much shorter span before Aaron called back.

"I'm at the park. Her car is here."

Thank God. "What did she say about the house?"

A pause. Then Aaron replied, "Sorry, I think

you misunderstood. Her car is here...but there's no sign of Delia."

Shit. *Shit.*

By some miracle, Caleb's voice was nearly even as he asked, "Any sign of a struggle?"

"No. The car's locked, and nothing seems to have been disturbed. She just...isn't here."

Goddamn it. All his instincts had been screaming at him that Delia should never have gone down to Laughlin unaccompanied, but she'd insisted that she could take care of herself.

Most of the time, she could.

Only now, it seemed as if the worst must have happened.

He couldn't say any of this to Aaron, of course. The guy didn't know anything about who he was —or what, more to the point—so Caleb knew he couldn't explain that his demonic gut had told him that going to Laughlin had been a spectacularly bad idea.

No, now all he could do was try to figure out what had happened and what he could do to discover where Delia had gone.

"I'm coming down there," he said.

"Why...are you a P.I. or something?" Aaron replied.

Good thing he was ninety miles away, or Caleb would have been sorely tempted to sock the jerk in the jaw.

"No," he gritted. "I'm her friend. And I'm going to find out what happened to her."

Even as he spoke, though, he thought of someone in Delia's life who actually was a private detective.

Pru Nelson. She might be a good person to bring along, especially since, although she didn't know the whole truth about him, she at least understood that some pretty crazy shit had gone down in Las Vegas over the past few months. Most likely, she wouldn't bat an eye at any possible supernatural involvement, since she already knew about Delia's ghost-whispering sideline and had dipped her toe into some of the freakier stuff like ley lines and energy convergence during the demon-fueled tournament at the Desert Paradise casino.

Also, Pru was Delia's best friend, and Caleb knew she'd want to be involved in tracking her down.

"What's the name of this park again?" he asked.

"Heritage Park. I guess the formal name is the Colorado River Heritage Greenway Park, but no one really calls it that."

Not too surprising. The name was kind of a mouthful.

"Okay. I'll be down there as fast as I can."

"Do you need me to wait here?" Aaron asked, and now he sounded especially reluctant.

"No point," Caleb said shortly. "Delia's already

117

gone. I suppose you can go back to wherever you're staying. You've done enough."

"Hey, I didn't have anything to do with this—"

Caleb lifted the phone away from his ear and pressed the red button to disconnect the call.

Asshole. As far as he was concerned, Aaron Sanchez had *everything* to do with this. If he hadn't begged Delia to go to Laughlin and try clearing the ghost from his grandmother's house, none of this would have happened.

Delia would still be safe.

Caleb made himself drink some water, and then he picked up the phone again and went to his contacts list. Luckily, he'd put Pru's information in there a while back, so it would be easy enough to reach her...especially since it was now the middle of the afternoon and there was no way even a night owl like Prudence Nelson wouldn't be awake and ready to go.

Sure enough, she picked up the phone on the second ring. "Hi, Caleb," she said, sounding friendly enough...but also puzzled, as though she couldn't quite figure out why he'd be calling her, rather than Delia.

"Hello, Pru," he responded. "I have a bit of bad news."

"What is it?" she asked, her tone sharpening at once.

"Delia's missing."

"*What?*"

Pretty much the same response he'd had when he'd gotten the unwelcome news from Aaron. "I guess she went to Laughlin to try to clear a house. The cell reception there isn't very good, so she headed over to a local park to make some calls. Except...her car is at the park, but she doesn't seem to be anywhere around."

"What kind of park is it? Is it someplace where she might have gone for a walk or something?"

"I suppose so," Caleb replied, irritation stirring. Not at Prudence—she'd asked a logical enough question—but at himself for not thinking of that possibility. "I don't know why she'd do that, though. It's pretty hot out right now for a casual stroll."

"And you can't reach her on her phone?"

At least he could answer that query easily enough. "No. I tried multiple times. Texts don't go through, and calls go straight to voicemail."

"Okay, that doesn't sound much like Delia," Pru agreed. "She never ignores calls during work hours."

No, she didn't. In fact, he'd been a little irritated now and then when she'd taken a call while they were together, even though he understood that was part of her business and she needed to be there for her clients.

Which was why he knew she would have picked up her phone this afternoon if she could.

"So you see why I'm worried. I want to go down to Laughlin to look for her...and I was kind of hoping you'd come with me."

Not even a second of hesitation.

"Absolutely," Pru said. "Should I meet you at your house?"

That would probably be the easiest thing. "Do you mind?" he asked. "Or I could come get you—"

"No, it's fine," she broke in. "Just give me a couple of minutes to close out a few things here, and then I'll head right over. Pueblo Street, right?"

"Yes," Caleb replied. He didn't recall ever giving her his address, but Pru was a private detective, after all. It was pretty easy for her to lay hands on information like that.

"I'm going to call an Uber, but I'll be over as fast as I can." A small pause, and she added, "It's going to be okay. We'll find her."

"I know."

They ended the call, and he slid his phone into his jeans pocket, then headed into the kitchen to put a few things together for their road trip. Maybe not the full-on junk food extravaganza he'd first proposed to Delia, but a small cooling bag filled with bottled water, and then a tote from Trader Joe's that he supplied with a bag of chips, some protein bars, and a package of teriyaki beef jerky. They probably wouldn't need most of it, and yet he didn't want to head out without knowing they'd brought some supplies along.

Oh, who was he kidding? He knew he was doing all this so he'd have something to occupy his mind as he waited for Pru and wouldn't keep dwelling on what might be happening to Delia while he was screwing around in the kitchen.

The doorbell rang, and he looked up from the Trader Joe's bag, a little startled. He didn't know exactly where Pru Nelson lived, but he hadn't thought she'd be able to get over here this quickly, especially when she had to wait for an Uber.

He hurried out of the kitchen and went to the front door. When he opened it, though, he saw someone else entirely standing outside.

Ty Carter, the tennis pro and maybe angel. Or half angel. Or whatever.

What the hell?

"What do you want?" Caleb demanded.

"We need to talk," Ty replied, apparently not put off at all by his rough tone.

Well, that was par for the course. Even when all hell was breaking loose inside a casino, the guy never seemed to lose his cool.

Because Caleb already had an idea what all this was about, he didn't bother to argue, but instead stepped out of the way so Ty could come inside.

"Your seer has gone missing," Ty said, and Caleb cocked an eyebrow.

"Is that what we're calling her now?"

"Her powers will continue to grow in strength," the half angel replied. "She doesn't think of herself as a seer, but just as she has begun to see into others' minds, she'll also begin to look into the future."

Too bad she hadn't looked far enough ahead to learn that going to Laughlin had been a very bad idea.

"And I suppose you've shown up here to lend a hand?" Caleb asked.

"Yes," Ty replied. "To be honest, I hadn't thought we'd arrive at this juncture quite so soon. But she's put herself in a place where our adversaries thought it best to move against her."

Caleb didn't bother to ask how Ty knew all this. When you were dealing with angels or part angels or whatever, you had to learn to expect the unexpected.

At least it seemed as if they were on the same side. Never in a million years had Caleb ever thought he'd be fighting on the side of the angels, but he'd been to Hell and knew all too well that throwing in your lot with a bunch of demons was a recipe for disaster.

Mostly, he wished he could have stayed somewhere in the middle and been allowed to live his life without a bunch of complications, but it didn't seem as if the universe was going to grant him that grace.

"Well, I can probably use the help," he said. "In fact, I was getting ready to head down to Laughlin. I'm just waiting for Pru."

"'Pru'?" Ty repeated, even though Caleb had a feeling the guy knew perfectly well who she was.

"Delia's friend, Prudence Nelson," he explained. "I thought it couldn't hurt to have a private investigator along."

Ty didn't reply right away, and something in his expression was almost thoughtful, as if he was pondering this latest development and trying to decide whether he should argue or just let it be.

Apparently, it was the latter, because he nodded.

"She could be of some help."

The doorbell rang again. Since they'd remained in the foyer while they talked, Caleb didn't have to go very far to open the door and let Prudence Nelson in. The last time he'd seen her, she'd had ombre purple hair that was almost inky violet at the roots and had faded to pale lavender at the ends, which had just barely brushed her collarbones. Now, though, it had been dyed a deep forest green, striking against her pale skin and dark eyes. As far as he could tell, she didn't seem to wear anything except black, maybe because that way her clothes would always go with her hair, no matter what color it was that month...or maybe week. He didn't see her enough to know for sure how often she changed her hair. The only thing he did know was that she must either have iron tresses or the world's best colorist, because her shoulder-length locks didn't look fried despite all the torture she must put them through.

She said a brief hello to Caleb, but almost immediately, her gaze tracked to Ty.

"This is Ty Carter," Caleb said. He hated to waste time on introductions, but it would have been rude not to say anything at all. "Ty, this is Pru Nelson, Delia's friend."

"Hi," she said.

"Hello," he replied. For a second, his gaze remained on her face—not long enough to be considered rude, but enough that Caleb couldn't help noticing.

Did the half angel think she was pretty?

Possibly. She actually was attractive despite the crazy hair, thanks to her delicate features and big dark eyes. Not his type—he wasn't into the gamine look—but he could see why she might have piqued Ty's interest.

If that was even the reason for the lingering stare. For all Caleb knew, the half angel was just trying to take her measure and make sure she'd be enough help to justify bringing her along.

Not that it mattered. This mission had been his idea, and he was the one who had the final say on who was included.

"Okay, enough chitchat," he said briskly. "We need to get going. I know where Delia was when she disappeared, so we'll go there first and see what we can find."

"Sounds good," Pru said. For the first time, Caleb noticed that she had a large black canvas satchel slung over one shoulder, and he guessed it probably held her laptop and whatever other supplies she'd thought she might need for the investigation.

"Yes," Ty chimed in. "We should get on the road...before it's too late."

# Chapter Seven

—··《《·☽·》》··—

Pᴩᴜ ʀᴏᴅᴇ sʜᴏᴛɢᴜɴ. Sʜᴇ'ᴅ ᴄʟᴀɪᴍᴇᴅ ᴛʜᴀᴛ she got queasy when she rode in the back seat, and maybe that was nothing more than the truth. Ty hadn't seemed inclined to argue, and they left the house a little before four o'clock, just as rush hour was starting to ramp up.

At this time of year, they'd have daylight well past seven. Still, Caleb couldn't quite ignore the tight feeling in his stomach, the worry that made him push the Range Rover—he'd come to love his Mercedes, but the big SUV was much better suited to taking multiple people along on a road trip— well past the posted speed limit of seventy miles per hour.

If he got a speeding ticket, no big deal.

However, so far he hadn't spied any state troopers, and he prayed his luck would hold, mostly because he was far more concerned about the delay getting pulled over might cause than how much such an inconvenience would cost. And although everyone in the vehicle had stayed pretty quiet while they were within city limits, once they were out on the open road, Pru shifted in her seat so she could look over her shoulder at Ty.

"So...how do you know Delia?"

Caleb couldn't see much of the guy's expression, since he needed to keep his eyes on the road. However, he had to believe Ty hadn't been thrown off by the question.

"She helped me with a house that had a ghost."

Not even a lie, since Ty Carter actually had summoned Delia to a haunted house back at the end of March. True, his real motive had been to see how she worked—and to quietly give her psychic powers a boost—but it wasn't as if there hadn't actually been a spirit involved, one whom Delia had managed to convince to move on to the next plane of existence.

"Ah," Pru said, then paused. Her eyes had narrowed slightly behind the cat-eye sunglasses she wore, and Caleb got the impression that her brain was working a mile a minute. "And that was enough to include you on this rescue mission?"

Ty also hesitated, and his gaze met Caleb's in the rearview mirror. That stare seemed to be asking one very important question.

*How much are you willing to reveal?*

Up until now, Caleb hadn't seen the point in telling Pru anything more than she needed to know. The woman wasn't stupid, however, so he knew she must have realized there were undercurrents here she hadn't yet begun to plumb.

He had no idea what lay ahead of them. At first, he'd been willing to think...well, to hope...that maybe Delia's radio silence was due to a simple misunderstanding and nothing more. After Ty showed up, though, he realized they must be dealing with dark forces yet again.

And that meant Pru could soon be confronted by something that defied explanation.

Unless, of course, she had already realized she was dealing with forces that extended far beyond this plane of existence, in which case she might just roll with it.

"There are a couple of things we need to tell you," he said, then paused, wondering if he should have kept his mouth shut.

Was this a mistake?

He didn't know. The only thing he did know was that sometimes you had to take a leap of faith.

"Like what?" Pru asked. Her lips had pursed just a little, but it seemed she was willing to sit back and listen to what he had to say.

"Well...."

Ty came to his rescue then, saying, "Do you

remember the tournament at the Desert Paradise casino?"

Now she chuckled. "How could I forget? Ley lines and earthquakes and all kinds of weird shit. I got the feeling there was a lot more going on than Delia wanted to talk about, but since we all survived and it kind of felt like no harm, no foul, I didn't bug her about it."

"There was more going on," Ty responded. "Much more. The tournament had been designed as an enormous ritual intended to funnel as much dark energy into Las Vegas as possible. Caleb's intervention prevented that from happening."

Both of Pru's eyebrows lifted behind her sunglasses, and she sent a brief glance over at Caleb in the driver's seat before she returned her attention to the half angel. "What kind of ritual? What was its purpose?"

"I'm not sure," Ty said. "The whole thing fell apart before it reached its endpoint, which is a good thing. But no one summons that kind of power unless they're attempting to do something big."

All of which Caleb had already known. Like Ty, he hadn't been able to determine what Hank Bowers and the rest of the demons or demon-possessed minions had been aiming for with their ritual, although he also realized it had to have been something massive.

The energy had dispersed harmlessly, though... well, except for a small earthquake and some shattered nerves...and, as far as he could tell, no one who'd attended the tournament had realized exactly what had gone on.

Even Aaron Sanchez, who'd been in the thick of it, didn't seem to recall anything about what had happened that fateful afternoon in late March.

Now Pru returned her attention to Caleb. "And you stopped it."

"I did," he replied, now a little embarrassed. At the time, he'd only done what he needed to, acting on instinct because his conscious mind hadn't been able to completely comprehend the forces at work.

"And how were you able to do that, exactly?" she pressed. "This isn't the kind of thing they usually teach in school."

No, it definitely was not.

The only explanation was the truth...incredible as it was going to sound to her.

"It's because I'm a quarter demon," he said simply.

For a second, she sat motionless in the passenger seat, brows drawn together as she seemed caught between trying to decide whether he'd been joking or whether he was just downright delusional.

"That isn't funny," she said, and although she was trying to sound matter-of-fact, he could still catch the smallest tremor in her voice as she pronounced the last syllable.

"I'm not joking," he told her. "My grandfather was a demon from Hell, and my father was half demon. I'm just a quarter, so I'm not nearly as bad as the rest of them."

Once again, Pru shifted in her seat so she could look back at Ty. "Is this some kind of stupid joke the two of you have cooked up?"

"No joke," Ty said calmly. "Caleb is descended from demons, just as he told you. His grandfather was a servant of the demon prince Belial, and therefore among one of the highest orders of demons. That's why he's so powerful, even though he's mostly human."

She shook her head, the deep green strands of her hair shimmering like dark tourmaline in the bright sunlight slanting through the passenger-side window. "So, what...you're a demon, too?"

Caleb couldn't help tensing slightly as she asked the question. Was Ty Carter finally going to come out and say what he truly was?

He should have known better.

"No, I'm not a demon," Ty said calmly, as if he were called upon to answer that question on a regular basis. "Let's just say that I'm someone who has an interest in making sure your friend Delia is safe."

Judging by the way Pru's lips pressed together again, she wasn't too happy with that response.

"He's not going to tell you anything else," Caleb remarked. "Personally, I think he's part angel, but since he won't cop to it, I guess you'll just have to accept that he's here to help."

She crossed her arms and settled against the back of the seat. Something in her expression seemed to signal that she was wishing she could be almost anywhere else, but since she was stuck in a Range Rover heading southbound at roughly eighty miles an hour, she didn't have a lot of options.

"I'm not sure I'm ready to 'accept' much of anything," she said, her tone caustic. "Sure, some weird shit went down at the Desert Paradise, but I'm supposed to believe in quarter demons and part angels and God knows what else?"

"Basically, yeah," Caleb said. He lifted one hand from the steering wheel, palm open. This little trick had been enough to convince Delia he wasn't your ordinary, run-of-the-mill human being, and he had to hope it would work on Pru as well.

For just a second, flames danced on the palm of his hand. Because he wanted them to be harmless, he knew they wouldn't do anything to the Range Rover's interior, or to the woman who currently occupied the passenger seat. They were just for show.

Slowly, Prudence removed her sunglasses and stared at his hand. With the flames now gone, he wrapped his fingers around the steering wheel once more.

"You just...." She shook her head. "How the hell did you do that?"

"Those with demon blood can summon flames," Ty said from the back seat. "It's a talent that can come in useful in some situations."

"More than 'some,'" Caleb replied. "I've used fire to send lesser demons back to Hell, so it's a nice weapon to have in my arsenal. Most of the time, though, Delia and I use her holy water."

"The stuff she gets from Father Bryce for her house cleansings?"

"The same."

Pru returned her sunglasses to her nose. Caleb couldn't be sure whether that was because the glare outside was getting to her, or she simply didn't want him to see her expression clearly.

"But if you're part demon, doesn't it bother you?"

Once again, Ty spoke up. "His demon blood is diluted enough that holy water has no real effect on him."

"Well, that's something, I suppose," Pru said, her tone now positively dripping with sarcasm.

Caleb could see why she'd want to retreat to a tried-and-true defense mechanism. This was all kind of a lot.

Luckily, he always had a few bottles of the stuff on hand, and he'd included it in the kit he'd brought along on this trip, just to be safe. He still didn't know for sure what they were dealing with here, but a little extra insurance never hurt anyone.

"We're telling you this because we don't know what we might be facing in Laughlin," Ty said, and once again, Pru's brows lifted.

"I thought Delia went down there to clear a ghost out of a house."

"She did," Caleb put in. "But since the guy who asked her for the favor is someone who was involved in that mess at the Desert Paradise, we don't know for sure if a regular old spirit is what we're dealing with here...or something much worse."

Pru fiddled with her seatbelt, then said, "I'm surprised she trusted him after everything that happened at the tournament."

*That makes two of us,* Caleb thought. However, since he didn't want Delia to sound like she'd been a complete sucker, he replied, "She saw Aaron's thoughts, or at least enough of them to convince her that no ulterior motives were involved."

"'Aaron'?" Pru echoed. "Aaron Sanchez, that

guy she had me look up before she went on a date with him?"

Even now, Caleb didn't like thinking about that date, although he knew it had come to nothing. "Yeah, that guy. He's fallen on hard times since then, and his family wants to sell the supposedly haunted house and give him a cut. That was why he came to Delia for help."

"And of course she said yes, because she can't resist helping any sad sacks who come across her path."

Caleb wondered if that was how Delia had seen him when they first met. Had she thought he was a sad sack who needed her assistance because otherwise he'd flounder on his own?

He didn't want to believe that. Sure, he'd been more lost than he wanted to admit when he'd come to Las Vegas, and crossing paths with Delia Dunne had felt almost like divine intervention, but....

He set those uncomfortable thoughts aside to be revisited at a later time, well after he knew Delia was safe and he would have the leisure to explore them...if he even wanted to.

"Something like that," he said. "When Aegis Holdings fell apart, Aaron lost his condo, and I guess he lost his job, too, because it sounds like he was pretty much a basket case for almost a week after the Desert Paradise tournament. So of course Delia wanted to help him out."

Prudence tapped her fingers against the knees of her skinny jeans, which were just as black as her tank top and the pointy flats she wore. Unlike Delia, who never seemed to bother with polish, Pru's nails were painted a deep metallic green to match her hair.

"And now she's missing."

"Yes," Caleb replied. It seemed as if Pru was willing to move past the whole part-demon thing and focus on the facts of the matter, and he was damn glad of that. They needed to put all their energies into finding Delia rather than worrying about who was a quarter demon and who was an angel, or whatever.

Prudence looked past him to the spot where Ty sat in the back seat. "And you're just helping out of the goodness of your heart?"

"Delia has certain unique abilities," he said, still with the same utter calmness of voice and expression that made the tennis pro look like some sort of modern-day Buddha.

Well, if the Buddha reincarnated with a ponytail and faded jeans and the face of a *GQ* model.

"Like talking to ghosts," Pru supplied, and Ty nodded.

"That, and a good deal more. She's already begun to hear people's thoughts, but soon she will also be able to catch glimpses of the future, among other things. Gifts like hers will be invaluable in the fight ahead."

Caleb wasn't sure he liked the sound of that. While he'd already guessed there might be some kind of confrontation involved in rescuing Delia, he got the feeling that Ty had been talking about something entirely different, something much bigger than that.

Well, he'd worry about it later. The guy did have a tendency toward pronouncements that might or might not even be provable.

Once again, Pru was silent as she appeared to absorb what Ty had just said. Despite her crazy hair, she seemed like a pretty down-to-earth person, which was probably part of the reason why she and Delia got along so well. However, that kind of temperament also made it a lot harder for her to accept that the universe was much stranger than she could have ever imagined.

"If you're both a couple of supernatural beings, I'm not sure how much help I can be," she said at length.

"That's where you're wrong," Ty replied at once. "You have very useful skills. Just because Caleb has demon blood, that doesn't mean he's omnipotent. We can use all the help we can get."

Noticeably, Ty hadn't made a single comment about his own blood, or whether he himself was also a supernatural being. Just the guy being cagey again, although Caleb couldn't help being a little irritated.

This would have been a lot easier if he'd stopped playing games and fessed up to who he really was.

"Especially because of where we're going," Ty continued, and now it was Caleb's turn to send a questioning glance over one shoulder.

"What about it?" he asked. "I thought Laughlin was just another gambling town, sort of a mini-Vegas on the river."

"The town isn't our concern," Ty replied. "No, it's the river itself. The Colorado River has its own power, a kind of power you may find difficult to deal with. Laughlin does sit at the intersection of two ley lines—"

"Those again," Pru interjected, tone wry.

"—but the river itself has an energy that is diametrically opposed to all things demonic."

Well, that was just great. Here they were, basically flying blind, and now he was supposed to rescue Delia while being handicapped by the Colorado River's energy, whatever that was?

"This just keeps getting better and better," he muttered.

Ty smiled. "It might not be as bad as you think. Your human blood may be enough to buffer you from the draining effects of the river's energy."

Caleb couldn't help noticing how Ty had said,

"May be enough." Nothing seemed to be certain here, and he knew he'd just have to roll the dice and go with it.

But he'd find Delia even if he had to crawl on his hands and knees to get to her.

"Do you know why the Colorado in particular?" he asked. "I know it isn't all rivers, because I spent plenty of time on the White River in Indiana when I was growing up. It didn't have any effect on me."

"I can't say for sure," Ty said. "You might not want to believe this, but I certainly don't know everything. I haven't lived in Las Vegas my whole life, only the past seven years, and I haven't had much need to get out and explore."

"Because you were assigned to Las Vegas?" Caleb asked. He had a feeling the other man wasn't about to give him a straight answer, but he figured he would try anyway.

"I'm not sure if that's the best way to describe the situation."

Of course not. Caleb sent a sideways look at Pru, but now she was staring forward, her expression distracted, as if she was already mentally running through the methods she might employ to track down her missing friend.

And really, that was what he should be doing, too. While he hated to have Ty dodge every single question regarding his past, that wasn't the important thing here. If he wanted to keep his secrets, so be it.

"We're getting close," Pru said as a sign for the turnoff to Davis Dam flashed by.

Yes, they were. He'd looked up the route on his phone, so he knew they needed to keep going but then take the first exit in Laughlin and head north to the park.

They didn't have to cross the Colorado River, and yet Caleb could still sense it as they approached, its strength pulsing in the background like the bass beat of music playing off in the distance. He didn't feel particularly debilitated, but maybe that was because they hadn't gone over the water yet.

With any luck, they wouldn't have to at all. On the other side of the river was Bullhead City and Arizona, and it didn't sound as if any of Delia's business had taken her there.

He followed the signs to Heritage Park, and within a few minutes, they were pulling into one of the parking areas. Sure enough, there was Delia's little white Hyundai Kona, although he noticed that she'd removed the magnetic signs from the front doors that advertised Dunne & Dunne Realty.

That wasn't so strange, though. The whole point of them being magnetic was that she could put them on and take them off as needed...and he guessed she would have wanted to maintain a low profile on this trip.

The spaces on either side of the little SUV were empty—the park didn't look too busy on this hot Tuesday afternoon—so Caleb pulled into the one on the right and turned off the Range Rover's engine.

As soon as he opened the car door, a blast of warm air caught his hair. It was windier than he'd been expecting, but he assumed that had something to do with the way the park sat high above the river, giving a spectacular view of the Colorado as it wound its way past the casinos and restaurants that clustered on its banks.

He wasn't here about the view, though. Pru and Ty had just emerged from the SUV, so Caleb directed his next words to her.

"What should we do first?"

"Let me take a look at the car," she said. "I'll try dusting for fingerprints and see if I can find any that don't look like Delia's."

"You can tell which fingerprints are hers just by looking at them?"

Now Pru grinned, even as she opened up her satchel and started hunting around inside. "Actually, yeah," she replied. "But that's only because I used her as a guinea pig when I was first teaching myself how to do this."

Caleb looked over at Ty, whose shoulders hitched almost imperceptibly.

All right, he'd just stand back and see what happened.

Prudence produced a small vial of powder and a brush from her satchel, and then went over to the driver's door and dusted some of the powder around the handle. "These are all Delia's," she announced after a moment. "Let me check the passenger side."

Again, Caleb and Ty watched as she used the brush to apply the powder to the door. It didn't seem as if she'd found anything of note, because when she looked up, her expression was noticeably annoyed.

"Nothing over here, either. I'll check the back hatch and the rear doors, too."

Those must have been a no-go as well, since Pru came back to the spot where she'd left her satchel sitting on the ground and placed the fingerprint powder and brush back inside.

"All the prints on the car are Delia's," she said, although Caleb had already gathered as much. "I suppose the person who took her could have been wearing gloves, but none of the prints I found are smeared, so I'm not sure about that."

Ty looked away from her to the signage at the far end of the lot, which appeared to show a diagram of the park's trails and amenities. "I'm going to explore," he said. "Maybe Delia didn't stay in the parking lot. It's possible she might have been confronted somewhere else on the park grounds."

The same idea had already occurred to Caleb. "No, I'll do it. You two stay here."

As Ty opened his mouth—probably to protest—Prudence produced a key fob from inside her satchel. "We still need to look inside Delia's car."

And she clicked the fob, and immediately the little SUV's lights flashed.

"You have a key?" Caleb demanded.

"Sure," Pru said easily. "I gave her my backup, and she gave me hers. That way, we each had a little extra insurance in case either of us got stranded somewhere."

"You could have said something about having a key."

She shrugged. "I needed to dust for fingerprints before I looked inside the car."

Caleb glanced over at Ty, who appeared nonplussed.

"Okay, then you two check out the interior of the car. I'm going to wander. Maybe if I'm lucky, I'll bump into someone who saw Delia."

Neither Pru nor Ty seemed too optimistic about the scenario, judging by their dubious expressions, and Caleb had to admit it was something of a long shot. Although there were a few other cars in the parking lot, they hadn't seen a single soul. Anyone who was out and about in the park would be widely spaced enough that there was a good chance they wouldn't have gotten close enough to notice any details about any other people they'd seen.

Although Caleb hoped Delia's coppery hair was distinctive enough that someone might have caught a glimpse of her and would remember the sighting.

Besides, venturing out into the park seemed like a better way to use up some of his nervous energy than pawing around inside her car.

As he went, though, he found his spirits drooping lower and lower. He didn't see anyone around, and the grounds appeared to be meticulously kept, with not a single dropped candy wrapper or soda can to stand out in the landscape. Possibly, that would have allowed him to instantly note anything Delia might have left behind, but he couldn't help thinking that if the park rangers were this neat, they very well could have come along and erased any evidence of her presence here.

If she'd even left the parking lot.

He realized he hadn't seen her at all today, so he had no idea what she'd been wearing when she drove down to Laughlin. She would have gone into the office first, since he knew she had an appointment in the morning, so maybe she was still wearing her usual professional attire of a blouse and skirt and heels.

No, that didn't sound right. Although there had been times when she'd been forced to battle a demon while dressed up, usually she tried to wear something comfortable and practical if she wasn't going to be at the office. She'd probably changed into jeans and flat shoes, most likely sandals, considering how hot it was out here.

So, even if he actually managed to bump into someone along the path, the only description he'd be able to give would be of a slender red-haired woman in her late twenties and not much else.

Great.

He made a loop and then headed back to the parking lot, knowing he wasn't going to find a damn thing out here even if he stayed in the park all afternoon and all evening. The best he could do now was circle back and hope against hope that maybe Pru and Ty had found something inside Delia's vehicle.

That sort of search wouldn't have taken them very long, though. He wondered what they would have found to talk about while he was gone.

The two of them were sitting on the open hatchback of the Hyundai when he approached. Caleb wasn't sure that was entirely respectful, but then again, it wasn't as if park benches had been provided out here in the parking lot.

Also, the Range Rover would have automatically locked itself, so it wasn't like they could have sat down in there, even if they'd wanted to deal with the heat.

"Find anything?" Pru asked, and he shook his head.

"Nothing. No sign at all that she even went into the park. I didn't see anyone I could ask, either."

The low grumble of a motorcycle approached from the feeder road that led into the parking lot. All three of them looked in that direction.

"Great," Caleb muttered.

The motorcyclist was a cop. Not that any of them were doing anything illegal, but still, he tried to avoid law enforcement whenever possible. So far, the identification he'd procured at some cost seemed to be holding up—once he'd used the fake birth certificate to obtain a Nevada driver's license, everything had been golden —and yet he'd rather not stress-test it right now.

Both Pru and Ty got up from their perch on the rear hatch of Delia's SUV. Neither of them looked worried, but then, Ty rarely did. Caleb was a little less certain about how Prudence would act under pressure, although he had a feeling that anyone whose daily routine involved following cheating husbands and collecting evidence on insurance fraudsters probably wouldn't lose her cool very easily.

"This your vehicle?" the cop asked after he'd paused right behind the Kona. He was so typical that he might have come right out of central casting—burly, maybe in his late thirties or early forties, hair cut short, mustache on his upper lip and mirrored sunglasses hiding his eyes.

For just a second, Pru hesitated. Then Ty tilted his head toward her so slightly that Caleb might have imagined the gesture, and she said, "Yes, it's mine. Is there a problem?"

"License and registration, please."

Well, at least he'd said "please." Caleb had no idea what all this was about, although he guessed the park was just remote enough that it might be a tempting spot for people to park and indulge in some illegal substances. None of them had been smoking or even drinking out of the water bottles they'd brought along, but clearly, that didn't matter to the cop.

Pru went around to the passenger side, opened the door, and then fussed in the glove compartment for a moment. When she came back, she was holding the Kona's registration, along with her license and what looked like an insurance card.

Looking as though she didn't have a care in the world, she handed all the paperwork over to the cop.

"Prudence Nelson."

"Yes," she said.

"Your business in Laughlin, Ms. Nelson?"

"I came down with my friends to spend the day here. We thought we'd check out the park before we hit the casinos."

The cop studied the documentation she'd given him for a moment longer before he handed it back almost reluctantly. Caleb strained to see what it said, because shouldn't the officer have called out the obvious fact that it wasn't Pru's name on the registration or on the insurance card?

It was hard to see print that tiny from this distance, but he could have sworn everything was in her name, not Delia's.

His eyes began to widen in surprise, and then he told himself not to react. He knew he hadn't done that, which meant Ty must have cast the minor glamour.

A man of many talents, apparently.

"Have a good one," the cop said. For just a second, Caleb could have sworn the eyes behind those mirrored sunglasses were blank and white, not human at all.

Before he could react—or maybe tell himself he must be seeing things—the man had climbed onto his motorcycle so he could turn it around and head back to the highway.

"That was close," Caleb remarked once the

officer was safely away. Probably better not to mention the eyes, especially since he didn't know exactly what he'd seen.

"More than you know," Ty replied. "He was possessed."

"What?" Pru exclaimed.

A corner of Ty's mouth lifted slightly. "Not by a demon," he said. "By an angel."

Maybe it was the heat, but Caleb couldn't help feeling a little off balance right then. "Angels can possess people?" he demanded.

"Sometimes," Ty said. "This felt like a lower-level angel. We call them the Watchers."

"Guess what they do," Pru put in, her eyes glinting with amusement.

Caleb had the sense she must be quoting from something, but he had absolutely no idea what. "All right, so what's a Watcher angel doing possessing a Laughlin motorcycle cop?"

Ty's shoulders lifted, and he glanced away from them toward the lazy curve of the Colorado a dozen or so yards away. "I already told you that the power of the river is very strong. If someone felt it was in danger somehow, then they'd send out scouts."

"Who would be endangering the river?" Pru asked. Her hands were on her hips, fingernails glinting almost the same deep forest green as her hair, and it seemed clear she didn't want to proceed any further until she had a better idea of what they were dealing with.

For a second or two, Ty's glance slid toward Caleb. "The enemy, of course. The same enemy we've been fighting for millennia."

"The Devil?" she demanded, and now Ty chuckled.

"Oh, he's pretty hands-off these days. No, I meant the other demons who're trapped in Hell. They're always looking for a way to get out of there permanently...right, Caleb?"

Although he hated being put on the spot like that, he knew he had to answer. "Yeah, sure. It's harder than you think, though. They can get out for a few hours or a couple of days...or even months, if they find the right person to possess... but eventually, they always get sent back."

"You haven't," Ty pointed out, and now Prudence stared at Caleb as if he'd sprouted the proverbial pair of horns.

"You were in Hell?" she demanded.

"For a couple of years," he said. "Through no fault of my own, I'd like to point out. I just got caught in the blowback when my father and his half-demon buddies decided to summon Belial to this plane. It didn't go so well for them."

"No," Ty said, "it didn't. And the only reason Caleb made it back was because he was able to piggyback on a recently dead soul who'd been sacri-

ficed to Belial. Those were very special circumstances, though, so I don't think any of them are
going to be repeated any time soon."

Pru didn't say anything for a few seconds.
Instead, she stood there with her hands still planted
on her hips, red-lacquered lips pressed together as
she tried to digest everything she'd just heard.

"All right," she said at length. "So now we're
dealing with both angels and demons. What's
next?"

The park had turned out to be a dead end, and
that meant they only had one lead they could
follow while they were here in Laughlin.

"We talk to Aaron Sanchez," Caleb replied.

# Chapter Eight

———— ·(((· ☾ ·)))· ————

Aaron wasn't picking up his phone, though, and texts didn't seem to be getting through, either.

However, Caleb refused to be discouraged.

"It sounds like the house is a digital sinkhole," he said. "But I have the address. I say we just drive over there and see if he's still around."

"Okay," Pru replied. They were still standing just behind Delia's little SUV, and Prudence glanced back at it before adding, "What should we do with her car? Leave it here?"

"No, we'll take it," Caleb said. "It's obvious she isn't here, and all the signs say that vehicles will be towed if they're left here after the park closes. Whatever's going on with her, I doubt she wants her car to end up in an impound lot."

"Caleb's right," Ty said. "You can drive Delia's

car, and I'll ride with you. Caleb, you can lead us over to Aaron's grandmother's house."

That sounded reasonable enough. True, he supposed Ty could have ridden with him, but it made sense for Prudence to have the protection of someone who wasn't quite human, considering all the weirdness that seemed to be going on around here.

And if Ty had an ulterior motive for preferring to stick by Pru's side, well, Caleb didn't want to get in the man's way.

He told them the address, adding, "It sounded like it's just a few minutes from here."

"What if Aaron isn't there?" Pru asked.

"Then we'll find a place to talk and regroup," Caleb responded at once. "It's not like there aren't plenty of bars and restaurants in this town."

That was for sure. Oh, not with the density you saw in Las Vegas, but still, he guessed they'd be able to find a quiet corner in a bar or lounge or something and plan what they should do next.

In the meantime, they needed to get over to the house that had once belonged to Aaron's grandmother.

Just as Aaron had said, the place wasn't very far. Incongruously, the property was set down in the middle of a bunch of RV parks, although Caleb guessed the house had been here first and the commercial properties had grown up around it.

And there, thank God, was a black BMW that had to be Aaron's parked in front of the detached garage. Luckily, the driveway was long enough that all of their vehicles could easily fit, with Caleb parking his Range Rover next to the Beemer and Pru pulling up right behind him.

She and Ty got out of Delia's SUV and then met up with Caleb so the three of them could head up the porch steps. The house looked as if it was fairly large, probably at least two thousand square feet or more, but even from the outside, he could tell it needed a lot of work. He spied wood rot along the porch ceiling and a couple of the pillars that held it up, and the brickwork needed to be repointed as well.

To be honest, he was kind of surprised that the place had sold at all, even though it had supposedly fallen out of escrow because of its resident ghost and not because of any physical issues with the house.

The other two hung behind a little so he could knock on the front door. A moment passed, and then another.

"Maybe he's on the phone," Pru suggested.

"Or upstairs," Ty added.

Okay, the house was big, but it didn't seem big enough to prevent anyone inside from hearing someone knocking on the door.

"Or maybe he realizes it's us and doesn't want

to talk," Caleb responded, which seemed a much more likely scenario to him. Call it jealousy if you want, but the guy had never struck him as someone with a whole lot of strength of character.

An assessment that some people might have found amusing, coming as it did from someone who could trace his lineage to a demon straight out of Hell, but whatever.

"Maybe he's not even here," Prudence said, and Caleb lifted an eyebrow. "What?" she shot back. "Delia left her car behind, so maybe Aaron did, too. For all we know, those weird angel Watcher things are disappearing people."

"That's not what they do," Ty told her.

"Oh, right...they just watch. My bad."

Rather than look offended at her retort, an amused light danced in Ty's clear blue eyes. "It's possible Aaron was 'disappeared,' as you put it," he said. "But it wouldn't have been angels who did such a thing."

"Let me see if the door's open," Caleb said, figuring it was time to put a stop to the bickering. He knew they were all on edge, but this wasn't getting them anywhere.

As soon as he laid his fingers on the latch, it gave way, and the door swung inward.

"Well, that answers that question."

"I'm not sure we should be trespassing," Pru

told him, her tone now openly doubtful, but he only shrugged.

"Aaron knows we're coming," he said, which was only half a lie. The guy definitely knew he'd been headed down to Laughlin, although it wasn't as if he'd given Caleb an invitation to go inside the house.

Both her well-arched brows lifted. However, Ty interceded, saying, "Caleb's right. Also, I think we need to go in there."

"Some angelic flash of insight?" Caleb asked dryly.

"Something like that."

Even after he opened the door wide and stepped into the foyer, Pru hung back for a moment, clearly reluctant to do anything that might appear remotely illegal. Although he was kind of hazy on how such things worked, he guessed that anyone with a P.I. license needed to be squeaky clean or risk having their credentials revoked.

Well, he'd do whatever he had to in order to smooth out the consequences of their unlawful entry. At least he could claim there hadn't been any "breaking" involved, not when the front door had been left unlocked.

But then she must have realized it was silly for her to have remained standing out on the porch when her two companions had already gone inside

Christine Pope

the house, because she released an exasperated breath and followed them in.

Caleb shut the door behind them. The house didn't look all that different from some he'd seen back home in Greencastle—typical farmhouse with a staircase right in front of them, hugging one wall, and a dining room on one side and a fussy living room or front parlor on the other. As far as he could tell, all the furniture seemed to be in place.

Had Aaron sold it along with the house? If that was the case, Caleb could see why the buyers would have wanted to back out. That stuff was butt ugly.

"Aaron?" he called out. "It's Caleb and a couple of Delia's friends. We didn't find her at the park, so we thought we'd come by and see if you had anything else to tell us that might help us find her."

Absolute silence. Pru had crossed her arms, seeming to signal that she was less than thrilled to be here, and he could see why. Even if you left out the part where they were totally trespassing, something in the house just felt wrong.

Was that the spirit of Aaron's grandmother?

"The energy here is...odd," Ty said, which felt like the understatement of the year.

"That's for sure," Pru replied. "I've been in a couple of Delia's haunted houses over the years, and they were kind of creepy, but something about this place makes the hair on the back of my neck want to stand on end."

"It's definitely psychically charged," Ty agreed. He looked away from them down the hall that appeared to bisect the ground floor of the house. "I need to look at the kitchen."

Without waiting for them to respond, he headed down the hallway. Pru shot Caleb a helpless little glance and then followed their half-angel companion, giving Caleb no choice but to bring up the rear.

At least the wood floors underfoot were nice, although the kitchen itself was an ugly mishmash of nineties-vintage wood cabinets and some truly hideous imitation marble Formica on the countertops.

Pru looked around, a half smile on her lips. "I hope they were selling this place as a fixer-upper," she remarked.

Ty didn't seem to be paying any heed to her words, because he went straight to the cabinets to the left of the sink and opened one of the doors so he could peer inside. "I thought so," he said after a moment. "I could sense it as soon as we entered the house."

"Sense what?" Pru asked. She'd moved closer and had gone on her tiptoes to look inside the cupboard, but because she probably scraped five foot four on a good day, Caleb doubted she could see very much.

"Someone has carved a symbol of protection into the cabinet," Ty replied. "Some call it a witch's knot, but it's actually a form of protection that wards off all evil, not merely those who use magic for evil ends."

Once again, Pru's hands planted on her hips. "So...what...we're dealing with witches now, too?"

She looked less than thrilled by that prospect, and Caleb couldn't blame her. Angels and demons were probably enough for one day.

Ty turned away from the cupboard, the amused expression back on his handsome features. "I don't think we need to worry about witches," he said. "There aren't nearly as many as you might think, although I believe some would have called Aaron's grandmother one. She would have had powers of healing, and she is clearly one of those who used their powers to protect the river and its energy."

"How do you know all that?" Caleb asked. It seemed like kind of a lot to pick up from seeing a single symbol carved into a kitchen cupboard.

"Because we've known for a long time that there were those who guarded the power of the Colorado River," Ty replied calmly. "In fact, it helps to explain why Aaron Sanchez's family would have kept this house for so long. It was only when his grandmother passed and there was no clear heir to take on her responsibilities that the trouble began."

Caleb found himself frowning. "Like Aaron getting possessed by a demon?"

"Yes," Ty said. "If his grandmother had still been around, that would never have happened. Unfortunately, there are those who, for whatever reason, have a vulnerability in their characters that allows them to be exploited by others. Demons seek out those people, of course, because they make easy puppets. We call them vessels, for in a way, that is the thing they're most suited to being."

No wonder Caleb hadn't liked Aaron. It wasn't simple jealousy, but a realization deep down that the man had a fatal flaw running through his soul, the sort of thing that might as well have been a beacon inviting any nearby demons to exploit it.

Then again, his dislike could have simply stemmed from the annoying fact that Aaron Sanchez had gone out for drinks with Delia.

"Well, this particular vessel doesn't seem to be here," Caleb said. "Now what?"

"We need to check the rest of the house," Ty replied. "I'll admit that if he were here, he probably would have heard us and come to see what we were up to, but there's no point in giving up until we know for sure the place is empty. I'll look upstairs. Pru, you can check out the rest of the ground floor.

And Caleb"—Ty's eyes glinted again, a signal that he was probably enjoying himself—"you can check out the basement."

Great. Even though he was a quarter demon and therefore didn't have much reason to be frightened of things that went bump in the night, Caleb had to admit that he'd never been a fan of basements. The one at his parents' house had been converted into extra living space, a sort of man cave with an attached bedroom and bathroom so it had just felt like another level in the home, but he'd never forget the time he'd gone over to a friend's place in sixth grade, and Charlie had suggested they play darts in the basement. That particular cellar hadn't been improved at all, unless you counted the dart board hanging on one wall and the crappy indoor/outdoor carpeting that covered the concrete floor.

However, Caleb had been willing to ignore the complete lack of decor—an eleven-year-old generally wouldn't have given a shit about stuff like that—until a rat scampered right over his foot while he was aiming at the dartboard.

Maybe he hadn't gone running screaming out of the house, but he'd also done what he could to avoid basements ever since then.

However, he was damned if he was going to let Ty Carter see how much this particular assignment annoyed him.

Instead, he replied, "Got it," and headed back to the downstairs hallway, where he'd already noted a door cut into the wall beneath the stairs. Sure enough, once he opened the door, he saw another set of steps leading downward.

His fingers found the switch, placed conveniently next to the door, and he flicked it on. A bare bulb installed in the ceiling responded at once, telling him at least he wouldn't have to make the descent in utter darkness.

As basements went, this one didn't have much to write home about. It only took up about half the footprint of the ground floor, telling him it was probably around five hundred square feet at the most. A ratty plaid couch had been placed up against one wall, and a big, old blocky TV sat on what looked to be a discarded dresser on the wall opposite.

The space was definitely small enough that he could take it in at one glance and realize neither Delia nor Aaron was down here. However, Caleb figured he might as well poke around a bit and see if he could find anything interesting, maybe one of those "witch's knots" that Ty had located inside the kitchen cupboard.

Not that he even knew what one looked like, since he hadn't peered in the cabinet the way Prudence and Ty had, but Caleb guessed that something like that would still look pretty out of place down in a basement full of rejected furniture from the seventies and eighties.

On the far wall was a bookcase. Once he started reading the titles, he thought that maybe Ty had been right about Aaron's grandmother being some kind of witch, since there were lots of titles about plants and philosophy and mysticism. At least half were written in Spanish, so he couldn't say for sure what their subjects were, although he guessed they were probably more of the same.

Still, while all that was interesting, he didn't see anything that looked like a witch's knot—or any other kind of symbol, for that matter. He was just about to head back up the stairs when a small rectangle of white paper on the worn shag carpet caught his eye.

At once, he bent down to pick it up. As soon as his fingers touched the paper, he realized it was actually cardstock, and that what he held was a business card.

*August Sellers, General Manager, Aquarius Casino and Resort,* it read, followed by a phone number.

Why the hell would there be a business card from a casino executive down here?

Probably not because Aaron's grandmother had been a gambler.

No, Caleb remembered all too well how his and Delia's first adversary in Las Vegas had been

Robert Hendricks, a vice president at the Dunes casino, someone connected to a shadowy outfit in Southern California called The Styx Group. Despite Pru's best efforts, they hadn't been able to dig up very much about the company, and so the investigation had been pushed off to the side after they had to deal with the much more immediate problem of Aegis Holdings.

In that case, "Robert Hendricks" had really been the demon Calach, masquerading as a casino exec.

What if this August Sellers was yet another demon, this one reaching out to Aaron because it had recognized the weakness in the man and wanted to exploit it in whatever way he could?

What if this demon was the one who'd kidnapped Delia?

Caleb realized all this was something of a reach, mostly because he had no way of knowing whether Mr. Sellers was even a demon.

Then again, what human being would call himself "August"?

Holding the business card, Caleb hurried back up the stairs. Ty was just coming down the staircase from the second floor.

"I found two more witch's knots," he said. "One in the master bedroom closet, and another scratched into the wall behind the medicine cabinet in the hall bath."

"That's great," Caleb told him. "I found this."

He handed the business card to Ty, who frowned down at it just as Prudence came around the corner.

"I didn't see any of those knots in the living room or dining room," she said. "But there was one on the service porch behind the dryer." She paused there, as if noticing for the first time the card Ty was holding. "What's that?"

"A business card I found down in the basement," Caleb replied. "I'm hoping it might be a clue."

"To what, exactly?" she asked. "I mean, what would a casino here in Laughlin have to do with Delia's disappearance?"

"Maybe nothing," Ty said, but before Caleb could interrupt, he went on, "Or maybe everything. Demons are often drawn to casinos because so many of the seven deadly sins are on full display there. They thrive on that sort of energy. So it's possible this August Sellers is yet another demon in disguise."

Since Caleb had been about to say pretty much the same thing—well, except the part about the seven deadly sins—he only nodded. "I don't know if Delia told you," he said, "but there was a casino exec in Las Vegas who hired her to track me down...except he was a full-blown demon masquerading as a normal person. If demons find

Aaron valuable as a pawn, then it makes sense to me that Aaron might have had a business card from one of them."

Pru stared down at the card for a moment. Then she looked up and smiled.

"Well, it sounds as if we have to pay this August Sellers a visit."

———

She swam up toward consciousness like a diver moving toward the light of the sun flickering through water far overhead. Darkness had been everywhere, but now...

...now when she awoke, she realized she was still trapped in the dark.

Delia still couldn't say exactly what had happened. She remembered driving to Heritage Park, and she remembered getting out of her car. For some reason, she'd been drawn to the cool blue waters of the river just beyond the parking lot, although it had been moving faster than she'd expected, and she'd realized it wouldn't be very smart to stick her toes in.

No, instead she settled for walking on the grass until she found a place where she thought she should stop and call Caleb to let him know she was all right and would probably be heading back to Las Vegas soon.

Just as she'd been reaching for her phone, everything went dark.

Now she realized she was still caught in darkness. She lay on something soft, but her fingers moved over its surface and felt how narrow it was, and she realized it was probably a couch or maybe a chaise lounge rather than a bed. A blanket covered her up to the waist, and she was fully dressed, although the sandals she'd been wearing appeared to have vanished.

What the hell was going on?

"Hello?" she called out—or at least tried to. As soon as the word left her lips, however, it felt as if it had been swallowed up by the same darkness that surrounded her now.

Her heartbeat sped up, although she told herself she needed to remain calm. She still had no idea where she was or who had brought her here—or why it was so very dark, with not the slightest scintilla of light to let her see something of her surroundings—but she appeared to be safe and unharmed.

For now, anyway.

When she tried to push herself off the sofa or chaise or whatever it was that she lay on, though, it was as if she'd been caught in a prison whose dimensions were limited to the piece of furniture that supported her. She could change positions, could lie down or sit up, but she couldn't swing her legs off the edge, couldn't stand up so she might try to explore something of this Stygian prison where she was trapped.

Again, her heart began to hammer away in her chest, and she closed her eyes—not that it really mattered whether they were open or shut—and began doing the breathing exercises she'd learned from a friend who was a yoga instructor.

*Breathe in for four...hold for four...release for four.*

Oddly, that seemed to help a little. Or maybe she was just relieved she had even that much control over herself and her body.

Her pulse had slowed, and she knew she needed to take stock.

All right, shoes missing, but everything else apparently just as she remembered, down to the silver hoops in her ears and the silver ring with its cabochon tourmaline on the middle finger of her right hand. She felt around on the sofa/chaise but didn't find anything that seemed to be her bag.

So, purse gone as well. That meant no phone, no way of getting in touch with Caleb or anyone else who could possibly help.

Which had to be by design, of course.

Because she couldn't get off the sofa/chaise/bed, she had no way of knowing how large her prison truly was.

So...what happened when she got thirsty or hungry, or needed to use the bathroom?

Oddly, though, her body felt almost neutral, as if it had evolved into a state where she didn't need to engage in any of those natural functions.

She wasn't sure whether she should be relieved by that realization...or even more freaked out.

Freaking out wasn't going to solve anything, though. Somehow, she'd gotten in here, and that meant there must be some way of getting out.

She just had to determine what that was, no matter how long it might take.

All the same, she couldn't help sending out a little pulse of thought, a little hope that somehow, somewhere, he might hear her.

*Find me, Caleb.*

# Chapter Nine

—·《〈·☽·〉》··—

THE HOUR WAS GETTING JUST LATE
enough that the casino at the Aquarius was fairly
crowded. Probably not anything close to what it
would be like when dinnertime rolled around and
people decided to go out to eat and then stay to
gamble afterward, but enough visitors wandered
the gaming floor and paused at the bar that Caleb
hoped no one would pay too much attention when
he and Ty and Prudence walked in.

Of course, with that hair, Pru would get
noticed pretty much anywhere she went. He
wondered why she chose such outrageous hair
colors when you'd think a private detective would
want to be much more anonymous, but maybe she
thought that by being so conspicuous, no one
could possibly think she was anything more than a
chick with a penchant for wild hair.

However, nobody seemed to be looking in their direction as they moved through the enormous sliding doors at the entrance of the casino and onto the gaming floor, so that gave him a little hope.

"What's your plan?" she asked in an undertone.

"What plan?" he quipped, and she frowned.

Ty, on the other hand, didn't seem too worried. "I looked up August Sellers when Pru was driving us over here. As far as I can tell, he's still employed by the casino, and it's definitely business hours, so he should be around somewhere."

Maybe that solved a tiny bit of their problem. On the other hand, just because the man was in the building, that didn't mean they could go right up to him and ask him what his business card had been doing on the floor of Aaron Sanchez's grandmother's basement.

Not for the first time, Caleb wondered what he'd done in a past life to get stuck dealing with these kinds of messes.

"I'll handle it," Pru said, and both Ty and Caleb stared at her in surprise. She gave them an almost condescending look as she added, "Private detective, remember? I'm good at talking to people. You two get a drink and let a pro handle this."

She wandered off toward one of the craps

tables, leaving the two men to stand there awkwardly, not sure what to do with themselves.

This was ridiculous.

"I don't know about you, but I actually could use a drink," Caleb said. He'd already spied a bar in the middle of the gaming floor as they came in, so he began walking in that direction.

"I'm not sure that's the best idea—"

Caleb sent a sideways look at the half angel, hoping he'd get the signal. "Let me guess—you don't drink."

"Not usually, but—"

"Well, I wouldn't say this is a 'usually' sort of situation. Besides, the lady said we should get a drink. Don't worry—I'm buying."

And he marched over to the bar, halfway expecting Ty to lag behind or possibly even go in search of Prudence, even though she'd explicitly stated that she could handle this on her own.

Instead, he sighed and sped up his pace so he wouldn't be left too far behind.

"One drink," Ty said as he seated himself next to Caleb at the long bartop. "That's all."

Most of the seats were occupied, but since it seemed as if everyone was absorbed in their individual conversations, he hoped they wouldn't pay any attention to him or his companion.

Still, he kept his voice low as he replied, "With any luck, that's all we'll have time for."

The bartender came over, and Caleb asked what they had on tap. He'd already decided a beer was probably his best bet, mostly because he could nurse a beer for a while and not look too suspicious. Also, a beer had a low enough alcohol content that he wouldn't have to worry about being even the slightest bit impaired. Booze didn't affect him the same way it might someone who didn't have any demon blood in their veins, but he still thought it better to play it safe.

So he ordered a Modelo and was a little surprised to see Ty do the same thing. For some reason, he'd thought the half angel—all right, Caleb still didn't know for sure what Ty was, but "half angel" was a convenient shorthand for now—would order something even wimpier, like maybe a white wine spritzer.

"Do you really think she's going to have any luck?" Ty asked after he'd sipped some of his beer.

The bar was just chaotic and noisy enough, what with slot machines ringing away in the background and a veritable army of cocktail waitresses coming and going, that Caleb had already guessed no one was paying any particular attention to them. However, he noticed how Ty hadn't spoken in any specifics and knew he should do the same.

"Hard to say," he said, then had a swallow of Modelo. Maybe it wasn't particularly high-octane, but it sure felt good going down after wandering around outside in the heat. "She's definitely good at digging up stuff online. I just don't know for sure how effective she is at talking to people face-to-face. Then again, she's been working as a P.I. for at least the past five or six years. If she sucked at it, I doubt she would have been able to keep going that long."

Ty appeared to think this assessment was a valid one, since he nodded and drank some more beer. The whole time, though, he kept scanning the casino floor, as though he halfway expected to see August Sellers or maybe some of his lackeys walk through at any time.

"Are there any here?" Caleb asked, and one of Ty's eyebrows tilted slightly.

"Any what?"

"You know...people like me."

Caleb knew better than to say the word "demon" out loud.

For a moment, Ty didn't reply. Then he shook his head. "Not that I can tell. However, there's a lot of chaotic energy here. It's hard to pick out anything in particular."

Well, that was true. Although Caleb was used to the frenetic vibe inside casinos by now, he thought there was something extra here, an edge to the atmosphere that he hadn't experienced before. It thrummed at the edges of his perception, making him just slightly off balance.

Good thing he'd already decided on only the one beer and nothing else.

The half angel continued, "And you feel it, too, don't you?"

"Yeah," Caleb replied. "What is it?"

Ty tilted his head in a direction that was probably southeast, although it was hard to tell for sure. "The river. Its energies are difficult for de—for people like you to handle. It's a little easier for you because you don't have as much of that blood in you, but you can still feel it."

That was for sure. Caleb found himself hoping their little foray here wouldn't require them to actually cross the Colorado River, because he wasn't sure whether he could handle having all those millions of gallons of psychically charged water flowing right under his feet.

"Good thing I didn't have any plans to go jet-skiing."

The half angel actually grinned, then picked up his pint of beer again and took a sip. "Do you ever take anything seriously?"

Well, there was a question. Caleb knew he could be serious when the occasion warranted—he knew his feelings for Delia were no joke, even if he still didn't have any idea what to do about them— but he also thought there was no point in being all doom and gloom, either. Sometimes a little levity was what you needed to get through the day.

"When the occasion warrants it," he replied. "But it's good to know that I should steer clear of the river, just in case. Let's hope Mr. Sellers hasn't taken Aaron out on his houseboat or something."

"If he's even here at all," Ty said. "Just because you found that business card doesn't mean there's a direct connection with what's been going on. For all we know, Aaron was just trying to sell the man a house."

That thought hadn't even crossed Caleb's mind. However, he was forced to reluctantly admit that Aaron Sanchez was a realtor—albeit one who'd just gotten fired from the agency where he worked—and some kind of real estate transaction was the most likely explanation for why Aaron would have had August Sellers' business card.

"What about the Watchers?" Caleb asked next, and Ty shrugged and reached for his beer.

"They won't intervene," Ty said. "That's not their place. But I know they've noted our presence here and are standing back to see what we do."

Which, at the moment, wasn't much of anything. But they were here now, so they needed to wait and hear what Pru had to say.

She came by about ten minutes later, long after Ty and Caleb had exhausted any topics that might safely be discussed in public. Since she was practically beaming, he hoped that meant she had some good news to share.

However, she tilted her head toward them and then away from the bar, indicating she wanted to talk someplace a little more private.

Fine by him. He was just getting to the point where he would have needed to order another beer anyway, and he would have rather avoided doing that.

The two men followed Pru through the casino and off to a little alcove away from the crowd. Possibly, one time it had housed a series of pay phones, but now it was utterly empty except for a single forlorn-looking trash can.

"So, August Sellers was here today," she said.

"'Was,'" Ty repeated, not looking very happy.

"Yes," she said. "But that's fine, because I found out from one of the servers in the Cove Bar that he's having a private party on one of the Laughlin River Cruise boats."

This didn't sound like particularly good news to Caleb. "And?"

She sent him a withering look, one which all but said out loud that he had an appalling lack of vision. "And that means he's going to be away from the casino and in a place where it'll be easier to see what he's up to. In fact, Jacob said he could probably get us on board."

Ty's expression grew even more disapproving, if possible. "Jacob?"

Pru didn't quite roll her eyes, but Caleb got the feeling that she wanted to. "He works at the Cove Bar...but he's also going to be serving at the private party on the boat. When I told him that August Sellers denied my old, sick mother's claim to her winnings at the craps table and that I needed to get in his face to get her the money she's rightfully owed, Jacob agreed to smuggle us all onto the cruise."

Okay, Caleb had to admit Prudence had earned some points with that flabbergasting lie. "And this guy believed you?"

"Of course," she said, and fluttered her eyelashes at him. He didn't think they were fake, but they were impressively long and lush. "I guess ol' August has a reputation for being a real tight-ass. So now we can get on the boat and see what he's up to...because we all know he's not having this river cruise for shits and giggles, right?"

Probably not. Or rather, Caleb couldn't think of any good reason why the casino's general manager would suddenly want to head out on a cruise on a Tuesday night when he'd probably gone on similar cruises multiple times in the past.

"You think he might have Delia hidden on the boat?" Ty asked, and Caleb wanted to smack himself for not thinking of that first.

"Maybe," Pru replied. "It would make a pretty good hiding place. And it would be a place where he could question her without anyone hearing them or interfering."

Caleb didn't want to contemplate the terrible notion of the woman he cared about being questioned by someone who might or might not be a demon. "Okay, that makes sense," he said. "What time is the cruise?"

"The boat leaves the dock at seven," she responded. "The crew needs to be there no later than six-thirty."

Since it was only a little after four, that meant they still had plenty of time to kill.

Good thing, because he definitely wasn't looking forward to setting foot on that boat. As soon as Pru had brought up the possibility of going out on the water, he'd been wracking his brains, trying to figure out the best way of dealing with what felt like an impossible situation.

He had no idea whether the solution he'd come up with would even work, but he had to try something. Otherwise, he might be less than useless once they were out on the water.

"We need to find a drugstore," he said, and both Pru and Ty stared at him, clearly confused.

"Why?" she asked.

"Because I need to buy some Dramamine," Caleb replied.

When they met Jacob, the guy who'd agreed to smuggle them onto the boat, Caleb immediately saw that this was probably just as much about earning brownie points with a girl he thought was cute as it was about getting some kind of justice for her fictional mother. The guy looked less than thrilled to learn that her two "friends" were men only a little older than she was, but at least he didn't try to tell them that they couldn't come aboard.

No, he only pointed to the closet where the uniforms were kept and said they needed to put some on so they wouldn't stand out too much. Pru had already warned Caleb and Ty about this, so they quickly switched out their T-shirts and jeans for dress pants and white shirts and bow ties.

She, on the other hand, had gone shopping in one of the casino's stores and had come back out with a tight-fitting sheath dress and high-heeled black sandals. A couple of hairpins allowed her to pull her siren-green hair up into a twist, and when she emerged from the bathroom, she looked like an entirely different woman.

"Impressive," Caleb said. "I guess you've watched a lot of James Bond movies."

Pru stuck her tongue out at him, thereby ruining the impression of subversive elegance. "Well, when Jacob told me there'd be some high rollers from the casino in attendance along with the casino execs, I figured that was my chance to get glammed up rather than having to look like a working stiff like you two."

A pained expression crossed Ty's face, but he only said, "In a way, that's good. It'll give the three of us more opportunities to fan out on the boat and see if we can learn more about the real reason for this cruise."

Caleb thought he'd seen a flicker of admiration in Ty's features when Prudence appeared in her evening attire, but it was certainly gone now. No, he was all business.

Which was fine. If Ty wanted to moon over Pru Nelson, he could do it when they weren't trying to figure out where Delia had been spirited away to.

"How are you doing?" Pru asked, and Caleb gave a stiff nod.

"I'll survive."

He'd taken a couple of Dramamine and put on some of those anti-seasickness elastic wrist bands for good measure, even though he knew his real problem with the river wasn't the motion of the waves but the power the water itself contained. The medication helped, but he could still feel the river's energy pulling at something deep in his chest, like a constant low-grade headache he couldn't quite shake.

Well, he supposed it could have been worse... even if it could also have been a whole lot better.

"Okay, let's get out there," he said, and did his best to quell the flicker of unease in his gut. It wasn't so much that he might be confronting a bunch of demons...he'd slid a couple of bottles of holy water into the pockets of his dress pants as he changed, just to be safe...but more that he was going to have to walk out there and pretend he knew what he was doing when he'd never had a food service job in his life.

He had no idea whether Ty did, either, but at least he'd been working as a tennis pro for the past few years and knew how to deal with the public. And although Caleb didn't have a clue as to Pru's work history before she became a private detective, he wouldn't have been surprised at all to learn she'd waited tables while attending college and playing bass in Delia's band.

Not that it really mattered, since Prudence got to play a high roller tonight, not a waitress.

She went out first, and then Jacob—a gangly guy around twenty-five who never would have had a chance with her—pointed Caleb and Ty toward the bar.

"It's pretty easy," he said. "They're only serving champagne tonight. All you have to do is pick up a tray and circulate with it, then come back and get a fresh one—and drop off any empties—after you're done."

Okay, that didn't sound too hard. Caleb had been having nightmare scenarios in his brain of serving a room full of people who wanted a million substitutions or a bunch of stuff on the side, just like how one of his girlfriends in college used to order her meals whenever they went out to eat.

That relationship hadn't lasted very long.

He picked up a tray and Ty did the same, and then the two of them headed into the cabin.

It looked larger than Caleb had expected, partly because of the large windows that made up the bulk of the walls. Outside, the sun was long gone, and although a faint orange glow lingered on the horizon, it didn't do anything to interfere with the brilliant, multicolored lights of the casinos and the hotels reflecting off the waters of the Colorado River.

Looking at the view, his stomach tightened again, but he told it—and his sometimes troublesome demonic blood—that he didn't have time for any of that crap tonight. No, he needed to focus.

People were dressed up, but not in an over-the-top sort of way, the women in cocktail dresses, the men in dress shirts and pants, although ties and jackets were in short supply. It was really too warm for that sort of thing; even with air conditioning pumping through the cabin's vents, the doors that led out onto the deck stood wide open so people could come and go as they pleased, and warm air flooded the space.

Pru had shown him on her phone what August Sellers looked like, so Caleb knew he was looking for a tall, blond man with dark eyes and brows that were much darker than his hair. Maybe he bleached it, or maybe that was his natural coloring.

That didn't matter. What mattered was that their quarry was naturally distinctive enough that Caleb knew he'd be able to easily pick him out of a crowd.

Except...he didn't see the guy, even though he circled the cabin several times, letting people clear his tray of champagne glasses and then bringing back the empty flutes so he could pick up a fresh batch. No one here seemed to have any worries about partying hearty on a Tuesday night, but he supposed a lot of them weren't exactly the type to be holding down a nine-to-five job.

"Anything?" he murmured to Ty when they came back for new trays of drinks, and the half angel shook his head.

"I haven't seen him. And even though the water's energy is playing with my senses a little, I still haven't gotten the feeling that any of the people in here are anything more than regular human beings. If there are demons around, they're not in this room."

Caleb had come to that same conclusion.

Had this whole thing turned out to be a colossal waste of time?

Just as he was about to pick up yet another tray, Prudence appeared out of the blue and murmured, "Sellers and his buddies are downstairs on the lower deck. They've convened in a private room."

Well, that didn't sound sketchy at all.

"Do you know why?" he asked, and she shook her head.

"No, but I doubt it's for anything good. We should go check it out."

Caleb sent a quick glance around the cabin, but Ty was on the far side, which meant there was no way to go fetch him without looking far too obvious.

No, the half angel would have to keep up his waiter masquerade while Pru and Caleb headed down to the lower deck.

"Come on," she whispered, then gestured for him to follow her.

The narrow stairs led down to a deck that the boat's passengers probably were never meant to see. It was strictly utilitarian on this level, from the plain LED lights mounted on the wall to the brushed steel floor beneath their feet.

Not that Caleb cared. He wasn't here to go sightseeing.

A rumble of voices came from a partially open

door at the end of the hall. Why the people inside hadn't closed it all the way, he didn't know, although he assumed it was probably because everyone else had been told to stay far away.

And when the guy paying the bills told you to do something, you followed his orders.

Pru paused so she could slip off her high heels. "Too noisy," she told him in an undertone he had to strain to hear. "Take yours off, too."

Caleb really didn't like the idea of padding around here in sock feet, but he knew she was probably right. They had to approach with the most stealth they could manage if they wanted a chance to hear—and hopefully see—what was going on inside that room.

So he bent down and unlaced the dress shoes he'd been given, then tied the laces together and hung them around his neck. "Okay?" he whispered.

Pru nodded. With one hand, she gestured for him to follow her.

They crept down the corridor, pausing every few steps to make sure no one in the room ahead seemed to have heard them. The voices continued, though, and because just enough sound from the DJ and the general murmur of conversation upstairs seemed to filter down through the floor, Caleb guessed it wouldn't be easy to hear him and

Prudence approaching unless they really screwed up and sneezed or something.

Thanks to the covering noise, they reached the door without incident. Pru inclined her head, seeming to signal that she thought Caleb should be the one to look inside. That made sense, if only because he was taller and would have a slightly better vantage point.

And also, since he was part demon and she wasn't, if anything truly sketchy was going on inside, he'd have a better idea of recognizing it for what it was.

The cabin wasn't very large. Standing at the far side was a man he recognized as August Sellers, tall and thin and blond. Gathered around him were four more men of various heights and sizes and ages, all of them in dark suits.

And sitting in the middle of that circle was Aaron Sanchez.

His head was tilted back, and his blank eyes stared at the ceiling. Caleb couldn't tell if he was drugged or in a trance or what, but his mind was clearly elsewhere.

August Sellers nodded, and one of the men standing in the circle stepped forward, then lifted Aaron's arm. Unlike the others, he was dressed casually, in jeans and a pale blue polo shirt and tennis shoes—much the same sort of outfit he'd been wearing when he'd come to Caleb's house to ask for help, except for the color of his shirt.

Sellers gazed around at his followers...Caleb couldn't really think of them in any other way...and then he raised a hand and pressed one long, thin finger against Aaron's arm, tracing a pattern as he went.

A dark shape appeared against Aaron's warm brown skin, not exactly like the sigils Caleb had seen on the demon-controlled participants in the Desert Paradise poker tournament, but close enough that he knew it must be something similar.

Something designed to control.

"You will keep watch," August Sellers said. "You will not allow anyone to come near. The psychic must be left undisturbed."

The psychic? Was Sellers talking about Delia?

"I will keep watch," Aaron repeated in a monotone.

What was it that Ty had said about the man? That he was a vessel, someone easily manipulated and controlled by dark forces?

Well, Caleb was definitely seeing obvious evidence of that dubious quality right now.

Next to him, Pru shifted. "What's happening?" she whispered.

Caleb gave a violent head shake, hoping his vehemence would be enough to let her know this was not the time for conversation. True, she'd spoken in a very soft whisper, one that barely reached his ears, but....

August Sellers' head went up, reminding Caleb of his old dog Riley when he'd smelled something on the wind.

"Someone is out there," he said clearly. "Get them."

Time to go.

Caleb grabbed Pru by the arm and all but hauled her down the corridor. From behind him came the clatter of leather-soled shoes on metal.

Yep, those things were pretty loud.

Speaking of which—

He lifted the shoes from around his neck and imagined the pair aflame, then hurled them backward. Although he couldn't stop to look, an explosion and a set of shouted curses from behind him told him the shoes had done their work.

They'd also let him know that those men must have also been enslaved the same way Aaron Sanchez just was, rather than actually being demons, because otherwise, they surely would have thrown a few retaliatory fireballs of their own.

"What the actual fuck?" Prudence gasped.

"Just keep going," he said.

They'd reached the stairs, so he was able to throw a quick look over one shoulder to see what was happening before they started heading up to the main deck. Smoke swirled in the passageway, but it cleared soon enough to reveal a tall figure moving straight for them.

August Sellers.

He lifted a hand.

Okay, *really* time to go.

They were about a third of the way up before the fireball smashed into the stairwell. Caleb clung to the handrail and saw that Prudence had had the presence of mind to do the same. In fact, it looked as if she was hauling herself up purely through arm strength, since the stairs immediately behind her had given way.

Screams and the sound of shattering glass came from the main cabin, and the boat began to list to one side.

Starboard? Port? Caleb had no idea. The only thing he did know was that throwing fireballs around on the lower decks was apparently not a great thing for hull integrity.

They emerged near the kitchen and almost bumped into Ty, who stared at them in consternation.

"What the hell is going on down there?"

"They were putting some kind of mind-control sigil on Aaron Sanchez," Prudence said, her voice still not much more than a gasp. "And then they saw we were there and started chasing us."

"And I'm pretty sure August Sellers is about to

appear at any moment," Caleb put in. "So we need to get out of here."

Ty's mouth compressed, but it seemed clear he knew they didn't have time for any arguments. "All right. This way."

He led them through the chaos in the main cabin—the music had stopped, but people were running this way and that, not sure where they should go—and out onto the deck. This part of the boat felt lower, as if it had already begun to sink.

Well, Caleb had been standing just under this section when he threw those shoe-bombs at their pursuers.

"What now?" he said, looking all around.

But this wasn't the *Titanic,* and he sure didn't see any lifeboats.

"We jump," Ty said calmly. "We're only a few hundred feet from shore. It's an easy swim."

Under normal circumstances, sure. Caleb had grown up with a pool in the backyard, and he got in at least a hundred laps most days in the pool at his new house as well.

That wasn't ordinary water out there, though.

No, it was the Colorado River, filled with the kind of energy that didn't seem too friendly to a being such as he.

Not that they had too much time to argue. August Sellers had just emerged from the cabin, a shadowy figure behind him that might or might not have been Aaron Sanchez.

"And where do you think you're going?" Sellers demanded.

"Jump!"

A pair of strong hands hit Caleb squarely in the back, and the next thing he knew, he'd gone right over the railing and into the strong, cold current of the river.

Some of it went into his mouth and he choked, thinking it tasted like battery acid. Almost at once, he began to flounder...

...and then a bubble of glowing white light surrounded him, somehow shielding him from the worst of the water's energy.

*Swim,* came Ty's voice in his mind. *Head for the Nevada shore.*

Luckily, that was easy enough to see, thanks to the lights of the casinos shining in the water. He began to move in that direction, his body remembering the effortless side stroke he used every morning in his pool, even when his conscious mind couldn't completely think of what to do.

From behind him came the sound of splashing, and he thought he saw Prudence and Ty swimming after him. She also seemed to know what she was doing, but he thought that Ty was sticking close to her, just to be safe.

The rocky shore arrived sooner than Caleb had expected. He dragged himself onto solid land, gasping and coughing, and the bubble of white light Ty had summoned disappeared as if it had never been.

A moment later, Pru came ashore as well, followed by the half angel. Behind them, sirens blared as other vessels converged on the cruise boat, which looked to be partially engulfed in flames but didn't seem to have sunk any further.

"They'll be able to save it," Ty said briefly. "Is everyone all right?"

Caleb nodded. "Thanks for the assist."

Prudence pushed a strand of wet green hair—looking for all the world like seaweed—off her forehead. "Thank God we kicked off our shoes earlier."

True. The sandals she'd been wearing had fastened around the ankles and his had laced up, so they would have been difficult to get rid of while swimming.

"What now?" he asked.

She looked over at the shimmering towers of the hotel casinos, their lights glaring in all colors of the rainbow against the night sky.

"We find a place to crash and regroup," she said. "Come on—let's get out of here before Sellers figures out which way we went."

And she began to trudge away from the waterline toward the nearest hotel...not the Aquarius, Caleb noted with relief.

Since he couldn't think of a better idea, he decided to follow her.

# Chapter Ten

— ·‹‹‹·☾·›››· —

"Why Aaron?" Prudence asked. "What's so special about the guy?"

Caleb wanted to reply, *Nothing much,* but he knew that wasn't entirely accurate.

It seemed the guy made a great servant for demons, whatever else his other shortcomings might be.

The three of them were sitting in the living room of a suite they'd rented at Harrah's, which happened to be the hotel whose beach was the spot where they'd scrambled ashore. Luckily, Caleb had transferred his wallet to his borrowed pants, so it wasn't as if he didn't have his credit cards with him. Maybe the front desk clerk had looked sideways at their dripping clothes, but no one was going to argue too much when you were willing to spend five grand a night for a hotel room.

This one had two bedrooms and a large sitting area in between. Although Caleb wasn't totally thrilled to be sharing a bedroom with Ty, it just made sense that they would take the room with two queen beds rather than the one with the king, so Pru could have her own space.

And now that they'd all changed into the shorts and T-shirts and other items they'd scrounged at the surprisingly well-stocked store by the lobby, they could really sit down and plan what they should do next.

"So...." Prudence began, then paused. With most of her makeup erased by her dip in the river and her dark green hair pulled back into a scrunchie she'd also bought in the shop in the lobby, she looked about thirteen years old, like she was having a sleepover at a friend's house rather than crashing in a cushy suite with a couple of not-quite-human guys. "August Sellers was messing with Aaron because he's a vessel?"

"Yes," Ty replied. "The inherent weakness in his nature makes him the perfect servant for a demon...or someone being controlled by a demon." He glanced over at Caleb, who was sipping from a glass of water and thinking he should have ordered a six-pack from room service. "Did you get a clear idea of what exactly August is?"

Caleb leaned forward and set the glass down on the coffee table. Since the table appeared to be made of plastic or some kind of composite, he wasn't going to worry about a coaster. "Not really," he said. "Things happened pretty fast, and the whole time, he was just far enough away from me that I couldn't get a good read on the guy. But since he managed to chuck a fireball at us as we were running up the stairs, I'm pretty sure he must be a real demon, not just someone who's possessed. The guys he had working for him didn't seem to be demons, though, so I suppose that's something."

Ty steepled his fingers and pressed them against his chin. He looked positively Spock-like in that moment, and Caleb repressed a smile.

"Why do that to Aaron, though?" Pru asked. "What's Sellers' endgame?"

"Demons always like to have servants," Ty replied. "In this case, though, I think August Sellers —or whatever is pretending to be him, more to the point—wants to subvert Aaron precisely because his family is connected to the river. I'm still not sure what Sellers' ultimate goal is, but the more servants he has to help him reach it, the better."

"Sounds like I need to do a little more research," she said, and got up from the club chair where she'd been sitting so she could fetch the satchel that carried her laptop and other essentials. Since all those items had been left behind in their cars, it had been easy enough to move the vehicles over here once they were checked into Harrah's.

Or rather, even though Caleb had been utterly on edge as they hurried over to the parking lot at the Aquarius to retrieve his Range Rover and Delia's Hyundai SUV, no one seemed to have paid them any attention. If August Sellers had been actively looking for them, he must not have thought they'd have the brass balls to sneak onto his hotel's property and drive off in the cars they'd left behind.

MacBook Pro in hand, Pru returned to her seat and opened the laptop's lid. A burst of quick typing, and she said, "Found something on the boat fire. Sounds like the local fire department is attributing the issue to an electrical problem that sparked a fire on the lower deck."

"Well, I suppose that's one way to explain away a couple of fireballs," Caleb said with a grin.

Her mouth quirked as well. "They had to come up with something plausible, I guess. Anyway, the people at the fire department were able to have the boat towed back to the dock, and everyone got off okay."

Including Sellers and his new lackey, Aaron Sanchez, Caleb supposed. Demons were usually pretty good at landing on their feet.

Still, he was glad to know that none of the ordinary people on the boat had been hurt. He had no idea why they'd been on the guest list, but he had a feeling they were mostly innocent bystanders.

"People rarely want to see what's right in front of their faces," Ty remarked. "What about August Sellers?"

Pru began typing again. "Looks like he started working at the Aquarius about three years ago." Her eyes narrowed, and she typed a little more. "He went to UNLV and got a master's in business administration. After he graduated—more than twenty years ago now—he worked at various casinos in Las Vegas and Reno before he got the job at the Aquarius." She looked up from the computer, something in her expression almost defeated. "It seems like a pretty normal resume to me."

"Well, it would," Caleb said. "If Sellers is like Robert Hendricks, then he would have been a normal enough person before the demon took over."

"And clearly, he hasn't said or done anything to rouse anyone's suspicions," Ty added. "I'm sure the demon possessed him precisely because he was someone in a position of power here in Laughlin, a man who could come in very useful...especially if he avoided attracting any attention."

Her fingers stilled on the keyboard, and she seemed almost restless, as if she wished she could be doing something else but wasn't sure what.

"I could try digging some more," she said, although she was already frowning. "Except I don't really want to try anything like that when I don't have access to a secure connection. I'm using my phone as a hotspot, since I obviously don't want to be connected to the hotel's wi-fi, but I don't think that's secure enough, either. The last thing I want is to set off some alarms that would let August Sellers know we're looking into him."

Caleb hadn't even thought about that, but he'd be the first to admit that he wasn't exactly a cyber-security expert.

Whereas Pru had to delve into sensitive information all the time, and therefore she knew which precautions she needed to take.

However, a thought occurred to him.

"I can reach out to Jim Whitaker, the P.I. who helped me out during that whole Desert Paradise mess," he said. "He was the one who figured out that Paul Reeves' carpet cleaning business was just a front, so maybe he'll be able to dig up something incriminating about August Sellers."

Pru closed her laptop, looking resigned. "That's probably a good idea. I don't think I should be taking the risk right now. Yeah, I have a VPN installed on this computer, but it's still not as secure as my setup at home."

He had to believe she knew what she was talking about, so Caleb didn't bother to try convincing her she should do some more research. There weren't any clocks in the sitting room, but

Caleb noted as he got out his phone that it was almost nine-thirty. Probably too late for a phone call, and he hoped Jim would be less inconvenienced by an email.

Typing it out on his phone felt way more laborious than sending a text, but eventually he had the thing written and then sent it. As he put his phone back in the pocket of his shorts, he said, "Okay, that's taken care of. I doubt he'll get back to me before tomorrow morning, though."

"It's fine," Ty said. "There probably isn't much else we can do tonight, anyway. Besides, I doubt you'll be able to find much. Any demon given the charge of trying to subvert the river's powers would be one with a good deal of power and self-control. He isn't the type who would let anyone around him know he wasn't the same person he used to be."

And that meant they'd probably have a hard time trying to figure out exactly when the real August Sellers had disappeared and the demon currently inhabiting his body had taken over.

This just kept getting better and better.

They were all moodily silent for a moment, and then Pru sat up a little straighter, as if she'd decided there wasn't much else they could do at the moment and they needed to focus on something that might actually be productive.

"Tomorrow we should probably do some real

shopping over in Bullhead City as soon as the stores open," Pru suggested. "The stuff we got downstairs will hold us over tonight, but if we're going to be stuck here for a couple of days or even longer, then we're going to need some real clothes."

Caleb hated to waste his time on something so trivial, but he knew she was right. Driving back to Las Vegas and picking up some of their actual possessions would take far longer than just going across the river and seeing what they could find on the Arizona side of the Colorado.

A few hours ago, he wouldn't have been so unconcerned about the prospect of crossing the river. Now, though, after getting actually dunked in the Colorado and living to tell the tale, he figured he could probably roll with whatever the river tried to throw at him.

"Let me check what's there," he said, and got his phone out again. Although he didn't expect to find a Nordstrom or a Neiman Marcus or anything, he was still glad to see there was a Kohl's. That was a few steps up from having to go to Target or Walmart.

He relayed this information to the other two, and Pru nodded. "That works. So we'll just plan to be up early so we can be there as soon as they open at nine." She stopped there, expression turning worried. "I should probably call Linda, though."

Linda Dunne, Delia's mother. Under other

circumstances, Caleb might have said there was no reason to let Delia's family know what was going on, not when no one on this fun little expedition to Laughlin even had a clear idea as to how to even find her, but the two women ran a business together, and Linda needed to know that her daughter wouldn't be available to honor any appointments she might have tomorrow...or the next couple of days.

He really hated not knowing how long all this could drag out.

"You don't think it's too late to call?" he asked.

"Maybe a little, but since this is kind of an emergency, I don't think she'll mind."

Caleb couldn't really argue with that. Or at least, he hoped Linda would recognize the need to get in touch with her tonight, but at the same time also understand that this was just about making sure Delia's clients were taken care of, and not because Linda's daughter was in any immediate danger.

That they knew of, anyway. However, Caleb tried to tell himself that she must have been taken because August Sellers thought she was valuable in some way. Hurting her would be counterproductive.

Although Caleb hated to think of the situation in such stark terms, he also knew he had to look at this the way a demon might. They were extremely transactional beings.

Pru got out her phone and navigated to her contacts list. Through all of this, Ty had looked on with mild concern, as though he knew these were details they needed to handle but wasn't too worried about getting involved with any solutions they might come up with.

"Hey, Linda?" Prudence said. "It's Pru. No, I'm fine. It's just—"

A pause, and Caleb guessed that Linda had interjected something before Pru could continue. But then she spoke again.

"Delia's down in Laughlin on some business that's taking her longer than she'd planned. Her phone's acting up, and that's why she asked me to contact you. I—"

Again, she went quiet. Most likely, Linda was asking why her daughter had been able to get in touch with Prudence but not with her.

"No, she emailed me. She knows I check my email all the time but that you often don't look at yours after you're done at work."

Caleb had no idea whether that was true or not. Then again, Pru had known Delia and Linda for a lot longer than he had, so he had to believe she was much more familiar with their habits.

"Right, right," Pru was saying, which seemed to be a signal that Linda had decided to believe the story. "So if you could contact her clients tomorrow morning and let them know they need to reschedule, that would be great." Another pause, and this time Prudence frowned slightly, as though she wasn't sure what would be the best way to respond. "Um...maybe Friday?" she replied. "Yes, okay. Thanks—I'll let Delia know you're taking care of it. Have a good evening."

And she pulled her phone away from her ear and put it down on the coffee table.

"All handled?" Ty asked.

"As much as it can be," Pru replied. "I got Linda to push everything until Friday. I hope that'll be enough time."

Caleb wasn't so sure about that. Tomorrow was Wednesday, and that would only give them two days to get all this straightened out.

A lot could happen in forty-eight hours, though. He was pretty sure if someone had told him on Sunday that two days later he'd be sitting in a hotel room at Harrah's in Laughlin—accompanied by a half angel and a private detective, no less —he would have burst out laughing.

There was nothing funny about Delia's disappearance, however. They didn't have any hard evidence that August Sellers was behind all this, and yet Caleb had to believe he was the responsible party.

Innocent people generally didn't start lobbing

fireballs just because you happened to be in a section of a boat that was supposed to be off-limits to passengers.

"And once we're done with our shopping tomorrow, I think we should go back to Alba Sanchez's house," Ty said. "We didn't really perform an exhaustive search of the place, and there could be something we overlooked, some detail that might give us more information as to the Sanchez family's connection to the river and exactly how they were guarding it."

Caleb supposed a return visit to the house could be useful. On the other hand, he couldn't stop himself from wondering if Ty was grasping at straws, trying to grab hold of something useful because he wasn't really sure what to do next.

In a way, the notion was oddly comforting. At least it meant the half angel wasn't omnipotent.

Not that Caleb had ever thought he was. If he wanted to be completely honest with himself, he knew that Ty's aura of calm confidence could be just the wee bit irritating, so realizing that the half angel didn't have the answer to everything made Caleb feel better about life.

Of course, he'd feel much better if any of them had some real answers to what was going on, but he knew the only way through this was to take everything one step at a time.

Even if they might have felt like the tiniest of baby steps.

"Then I suppose we might as well go to sleep," he said. "We've got a long day ahead of us tomorrow."

Pru stared at him as if he'd just suggested they go skinny dipping in the Colorado River. "It's not even ten o'clock yet."

Right. He'd forgotten what a night owl she was. Too bad—she'd just have to suck it up and get with the program, as Max Robbins, his high school football coach, might have said.

"And we need to be at Kohl's at nine sharp tomorrow," he reminded her. "So take an Ambien or whatever, but we're going to sleep now."

"I don't use sleeping pills," she said primly. Before he could respond, she added, "But I think I saw some chamomile in the basket of tea at the coffee station in my room, so I'll make some of that."

Well, at least she was trying. "That should work."

He got up from the sofa, realizing that their escape from August Sellers had pulled a few muscles he hadn't noticed at the time. Oh, well. A good night's sleep should take care of that.

Ty rose as well. "See you in the morning," he told Pru, then headed over to the room he was sharing with Caleb.

"Good night," she responded, looking resigned.

"Night," Caleb said, and they both went to their respective rooms.

He kind of doubted it would be a good night, but that was okay.

Tomorrow, they were going to find Delia.

# Chapter Eleven

— ‹‹‹‹ ‹ ☾ › ›››› —

SHE HAD NO IDEA OF HOW MUCH TIME WAS passing…or whether it was even passing at all. This dark room with the soft chaise lounge beneath her might as well have been in an entirely different dimension, one placed far outside the world she knew. And even though it felt as if she had been here for a hundred years, she still wasn't hungry or thirsty, had no need to go to the bathroom.

A blessing, maybe. However, even though she wasn't experiencing actual thirst, she thought she could really use a drink right about now.

A very strong one.

And as much as she racked her brains and tried to dredge up even the smallest, most insignificant detail, she couldn't seem to remember a single thing about her abduction. She'd been walking back to her car—had even gotten close enough to spy the little white Kona waiting for her as she wound her way down the path that led to the parking lot—and then everything had gone black. As far as she could tell, no one had been anywhere near her. She hadn't seen anyone, hadn't heard anything.

Yet here she was.

Obviously, trying to retrace her steps wasn't going to help her any, which meant she needed to come up with some other way to get out of here. Earlier, she'd sent a tendril of a thought beaming outward, imploring Caleb to find her. However, she hadn't meant anything much by it, had only wanted to feel as if she was doing something, even if it proved to be a futile gesture.

All the same, she couldn't help wondering if these strange powers that had begun to awaken might help her in ways she hadn't yet imagined.

So far, she'd been more of a receptor, hearing Aaron's thoughts in her mind. Why he'd been able to make such a connection with her, she wasn't sure, but maybe the circuit worked both ways.

Of course, she had no intention of reaching out to Aaron, even though his mind—so far, at any rate—seemed to have been the most transparent to her. He might have been able to help, but she knew that Caleb was the one person who would have both the motivation and the means to come to her rescue.

She had no idea how to go about doing such a thing, though. It wasn't as if she'd gone through some sort of apprenticeship with a Jedi master to help her gain control of her abilities.

No, this would have to be trial and error.

Well, if time didn't exist here, then it wouldn't matter how long all this might take.

Even though it was just as dark with her eyes open as it was with them shut, she went ahead and closed them anyway. No need to focus on anything at all except her breathing and the soft sound of her breath moving in and out, gentle and yet as sonorous as waves spilling across some secret shore.

Something about water....

She couldn't say why, but for some reason, her mind filled with an image of the Colorado River as she'd seen it from one of the overlooks at Heritage Park, moving slowly but purposefully through the dry, golden landscape. It had a rhythm of its own, one that spoke to her with the strong sureness of its current and the way it rippled in the sunlight.

The river. Yes.

Delia had no idea where the thought had come from, but it surfaced nonetheless.

*They need you to connect them to the river.*

Who were "they"?

Well, whoever had kidnapped her and put her in this strange prison, one that definitely wasn't your ordinary basement oubliette. Why they thought she had any particular abilities when it came to the Colorado River, she had absolutely no clue. Sure, she'd always enjoyed the outings her parents had taken her on when she was a kid and they'd gotten a houseboat on Lake Havasu or had come here to Laughlin for a quickie weekend on the water...or the one memorable time when she'd gone to Southern California and got to see the ocean...but it wasn't as if she'd ever had any particular affinity for bodies of water.

Pru was the Pisces, not her.

Still, the conviction remained that whoever was behind all this, they needed her for a particular reason that involved the river.

Something connected to these weird powers of hers?

Maybe. Delia couldn't think of a single other reason to kidnap her. She was just an ordinary real estate agent with a fairly humdrum life...as long as you left out the part where one of her closest friends happened to be part demon.

Was there some connection to Alba Sanchez's house? The ghost had tried to communicate something about guarding the place, although, because the communication had consisted of only a word or two at a time and nothing about the context of those words, Delia believed she'd missed out on the actual meaning of that exchange.

Still, there had to be a reason for the strange

symbols she'd found scratched into the kitchen cupboard and the master bedroom closet...not to mention the huge, glowing one that had appeared to her briefly as she stood there and stared at it in astonishment.

And although she didn't have any idea where she was, at the very least, she could try to communicate that she was still alive, although trapped someplace very strange. Caleb had always made it sound as if he didn't know as much about the supernatural and the world of demons as he probably should, considering his heritage, but still, he might very well have a better idea of what this strange void was than she did.

Also, she had to believe he must have come in search of her. She'd agreed to regularly check in, and although she had no idea how much time had passed since she was abducted from the parking lot at Heritage Park, she still knew Caleb wouldn't have waited too long before he set out to discover what had happened to her.

What she needed to do now was visualize him and send all her thoughts to the person she saw in her mind. While she'd never been very good at meditating, she knew she excelled at creating pictures in her head, something that came in very handy when walking into a space in a house and seeing how it might be updated or renovated.

So...Caleb Lockwood. Dark blond hair that was

always a little bit messy and overgrown, although she guessed he paid a lot for cuts that would allow it to look like that. Dark, strong brows and equally dark eyes, with lashes to match. Those cola-brown eyes were usually dancing with mischief, just as his mouth was almost always curved in one corner, as though a smile was just waiting to break out.

Well, maybe she shouldn't be thinking about his mouth. She needed to focus now, and not be distracted by what it might feel like to have those lips pressed against hers.

Now, though, she had a clear image in her mind, and she held it there as best she could, even as she focused every ounce of purpose and need and strength into a single thought.

*Caleb, I need you to hear me.*

---

He was just in the middle of trying on a pair of Levi's—more for form's sake than anything else, since he'd worn the same size of 501s for years—when he heard Delia's voice.

*Caleb.*

Bewildered, he paused with one leg in the 501s as he looked all around him.

Crazy, right? Like Delia Dunne would be hanging out in the men's dressing room of a Kohl's in Bullhead City.

That voice had been so clear, however, that he couldn't quite shake the feeling she was somewhere close.

"Delia?" he ventured.

"Did you say something?" came Ty's voice from a couple of dressing room stalls down.

"No," Caleb said quickly.

Maybe Ty believed him, and maybe he didn't. The important thing was that he didn't say anything else, and apparently returned to trying on his own set of clothes.

Time to go at this in a different way.

*Delia?* he thought. Doing so felt foolish, even though he knew she was psychic and that reaching out mentally was just as valid a way of communicating with her as any other.

Also, he so very badly needed to believe she was okay.

*I'm here.*

That mental voice sounded exactly like her, the pitch just a little low, smooth and friendly, the sort of voice he could see some early morning radio shock jock having as his female sidekick.

*Where is "here"?*

*I don't know. It's dark. I'm sitting on something that feels like a bed, but I can't see anything, and I can't move.*

*Can't move?* he thought back, his mental voice sharpening. *Are you tied up?*

*No, no. Just that I can't leave this bed or chaise or whatever it is. And I'm not hungry or thirsty, even though I should be.*

He had to admit that sounded weird. However, at least she wasn't bound, although her description of her current prison didn't exactly reassure him.

*Do you know what happened?*

Although he couldn't see her, he got the impression that she shook her head.

*I can't remember anything, Caleb. One moment I was in the park, and the next I was here.*

It was probably too much to expect that she might be able to provide at least a single clue about who her kidnappers were. However, her description of her current prison made him think August Sellers or some other demon must be involved, since it certainly didn't sound like a place that was bound by the usual rules of physics.

*Don't worry,* he told her. *I'm in Laughlin with Ty and Pru, and I know the three of us will be able to figure this out.*

*That's good. Whatever's going on, I think it has something to do with the river. I —*

And just like that, the mental contact was gone. It almost felt as if he'd been holding hands with Delia, and then something or someone had pulled her away.

He wanted to cry out to her, but he knew that wouldn't do any good. No, she was hidden from him again, but at least he knew she was alive.

"Ty?" he called out.

"Yes?"

"I hope you're done trying on clothes," Caleb said. "Because we need to talk."

---

They'd driven his Range Rover to Kohl's—Caleb didn't think it was a very good idea to use Delia's Kona, even if Ty could flex his angelic powers to make it look as if it was registered to Pru—so the three of them were huddled together now in his SUV, their bags of new clothes and shoes safely stashed in the cargo section.

"Sellers must have her bound somewhere close," Ty said, and Pru raised an eyebrow.

"I thought Caleb said she wasn't tied up."

"Psychically and spiritually bound," he replied briefly. "It sounds as if her mental voice was strong, though, so I have a feeling she's still somewhere in Laughlin."

That was something of a relief. However, it wasn't as if Laughlin was some tiny burg with just a couple of hundred residents. An exhaustive search would take a lot of time.

"Also," Ty went on, "she said this had something to do with the river. We already know that Alba Sanchez and her family were connected to it somehow, so I think we should stick with our original plan of going back to her house."

Failing any other concrete evidence, that did seem like the best thing to do. Except....

"What if Aaron Sanchez is hanging around the place?"

"I doubt he would be," Pru said, sounding very definite.

"Why not?"

"Because as far as he—and the demons who're controlling him—is concerned, the house has already done its job. It helped to trap Delia, and that's what this is all about, right?"

Yes, it did seem as if Aaron had lured her to Laughlin for the express purpose of getting her close enough that the demons could grab her and put her in the supernatural prison where she was being held. All the same, Caleb couldn't help thinking there were some holes in the story.

"If Aaron was already under August Sellers' control, then why would he have bothered to put another binding sigil on the guy?"

Ty didn't look too concerned by the question. "Those bonds have to be refreshed occasionally. Also, if Sellers is somehow trying to gain control of the river's power, performing such a ceremony while actually out on the water would only give the ritual that much more strength. But I think Pru is right. The house has served its purpose as far as

Aaron Sanchez is concerned. He isn't living there, so I don't think he'll be anywhere nearby."

And it was probably better to do something other than sit in a Kohl's parking lot and keep arguing. On that particular Wednesday morning, the place wasn't very crowded, but still, it might look kind of suspicious for them to keep sitting there.

"Okay," he said. "Quick detour to the hotel so we all can change, and then we'll head over to Alba Sanchez's house."

———

It did feel better to get into his new clothes. Even in the heat of the summer, Caleb wasn't a huge fan of shorts, so putting on the 501s he'd just bought—the prewashed kind, since they certainly didn't have time to wait for him to send them off to the laundry at Harrah's—and a plain burgundy T-shirt made him feel a lot more like himself.

Ty was also wearing jeans and a T-shirt, while Pru had bought black skinny jeans and a sleeveless black top with some interesting lace and pintucking, sort of like a goth Victorian grandmother. However, while her green hair might get a few sideways looks, Caleb thought that overall they were pretty unremarkable, and not anyone people would remember moving through the crowded lobby at Harrah's and out to the parking lot.

Once they got to the neighborhood where their destination was located, they had to wait a minute or two, since someone pulling an enormous trailer maneuvered out of one of the trailer parks just as they approached Alba Sanchez's house, but after that annoying interruption, they were able to pull into the long driveway that led to the detached garage. Caleb was glad of all the trees that surrounded the property, just because someone driving past and sending a quick glance toward the place probably wouldn't even notice his big black Range Rover parked back there.

That was the only thing he'd allow himself to be glad about, though. He hadn't liked going inside the house the first time, and he doubted he was going to enjoy it any more during the second go-round.

"How are we even going to get in?" Pru asked.

"It wasn't locked last time," Caleb pointed out.

And they hadn't locked up when they left, figuring that doing so would only alert Aaron that someone had been trespassing inside.

Ergo, chances were that the house would still be wide open.

When he put his hand on the knob to the back door, though, it wouldn't turn, signaling that at least this entrance had been secured.

"Well, we didn't check this door last time," Pru said reasonably. "Maybe it was always locked and we just didn't know."

"Guess we'll have to try the front," Caleb said, but Ty frowned.

"No, that would be far too visible. Let me open it."

He moved past Pru and Caleb and put his hand on the knob. Immediately, the door swung inward.

"Nice trick," Pru commented as they all went inside the service porch and then moved into the kitchen. Everything looked just like it had the day before, which seemed to be a signal that no one had entered the place during the intervening hours. "I guess you can always switch to a career as a cat burglar if the whole tennis pro thing doesn't work out."

Ty's expression grew pained, but he didn't bother to answer. Instead, he said, "We need to look for more witch's knots. If you find one, don't touch it—just make a note of its location."

"And what is this supposed to prove?" Caleb asked. "We already know that Alba Sanchez was some sort of witch."

"A *curandera*," Ty corrected him. "Subtle difference. More importantly, I'm almost positive she was someone whose charge was also to guard the river in all ways possible. If we find more of the knots concentrated in a particular spot, then that might point to the place where she and others like her conducted their rituals. Such a location would be valuable to August Sellers because of the power concentrated there."

Pru didn't look terribly convinced by all this, and Caleb knew he wore a similarly doubtful expression on his face. But—even though he didn't like to admit it to himself—he realized that Ty knew a whole lot more about this sort of stuff than he did, and that meant they needed to follow his lead.

"All right," Caleb said. "I guess I'll go back to the basement."

Even though he really didn't want to. Sure, his explorations down there yesterday hadn't turned up any rats or oversized spiders or anything else too frightening, but he could still happily live out the rest of his life without ever having to set foot in another cellar.

However, it felt way too squirrelly to send Pru or even Ty down there just because he would prefer to avoid the place. Better to get this over with.

"All right," Ty said. "Today, though, I'll stay downstairs, and Pru can check the second floor. It's possible either of us might see something the other person overlooked."

She still didn't look too convinced, but she didn't offer any arguments. "Okay," she replied. "I'll see what I can find."

They all went their separate ways, with Caleb

once more heading down the basement stairs. At least this time, he knew what awaited him—namely, some pretty gross shag carpet and a few pieces of furniture deemed too ugly to occupy the upstairs but not so useless that the Sanchezes had wanted to throw them out.

Too bad there wasn't some 1970s-vintage faux wood paneling on the walls to match that shag carpet, because at least that way he could have tried pulling some of it off to see if any witch's knots were concealed on the plasterboard behind it. But the space hadn't been improved even that much, although someone had once painted the cinderblock with a creamy white paint in an attempt to brighten up the place.

As far as he was concerned, they hadn't been too successful.

He dutifully made his way along the walls, looking for the faintest of scratches that might indicate one of the puffy, cross-shaped symbols might have been etched there. So far, he hadn't found a damn thing, and he began to think this whole expedition had been a fool's errand.

Shouldn't they be looking for Delia instead?

Unfortunately, they had absolutely no clue as to where she'd been hidden, so maybe it made more sense to follow up on one of the few leads they had here in Laughlin.

His gaze moved to the bookcase. Yesterday, he'd

inspected the titles of the volumes lined up on those shelves, but he hadn't lifted any of the books out of the way to see what might be hidden behind them.

After he'd removed several rows of books, though, he was pretty sure there weren't any sigils hidden there, either. The whole time, he'd felt the odd energy of the house pressing down on him, heavy and somehow sullen, but it didn't seem quite as oppressive as it had been yesterday.

Was that because he was getting used to it, or had his dip in the Colorado last night blunted some of the river's effects?

He hoped it was the second option, if for no other reason than he had no idea whether he might have to cross the river again, or maybe even go out on another boat, and it would be great if being around the body of water didn't make him feel like he was suffering the mother of all hangovers.

When he started to replace the books on the shelves, the bookcase seemed to shift slightly. This whole time, he'd thought it was a built-in because there didn't seem to be any space between the back of the bookshelf and the wall itself, but now he wondered if it had been placed that way precisely to create such an impression.

Fingers flying, he started to remove all the books again, placing them on the floor enough out of the way so they wouldn't take up the space he needed to move the bookcase itself. Once they'd been removed, he grasped the thing on each side and shifted it about six inches to the left.

Carved into the cinderblock wall was a huge witch's knot, one almost as tall as he was. As he stared at the thing, it seemed to shimmer with energy, pulsing with a soft golden light.

Bingo.

He backed away and headed over to the base of the stairs.

"Ty? I found something!"

Almost at once, the half angel poked his head in the doorway.

"What is it?"

"A witch's knot as big as I am. You and Pru need to get down here."

Ty disappeared, presumably so he could go upstairs and fetch Prudence. A few minutes later, the two of them came hurrying down the basement steps.

"Wow," she breathed as she came farther into the room and saw the glowing knot Caleb had uncovered.

"That's...impressive," Ty said. He walked toward the knot, and it seemed to glow brighter and brighter the closer he got.

"Why is it there?" Pru asked. "Is it guarding something?"

"That's my guess," he replied. "The trick now

is to let it know that we don't mean it any harm and that it's safe to let us pass."

"Pass where?" Caleb asked. "That's a solid cement wall."

Ty's mouth lifted at one side. "Is it?"

He now stood only a few inches from the glowing knot. For a moment, he remained where he was, appearing to contemplate the thing, and then he lifted one hand and reached out toward it.

Light flared away from the wall toward his outstretched fingers and then ran down his arm. He didn't flinch or make a sound, so Caleb guessed the golden glow wasn't painful in any way.

Or maybe Ty had a very high tolerance for discomfort.

A few seconds passed, and then the light traveled back into the knot. It pulsed again...and immediately afterward, a dark doorway yawned in the wall.

"What the hell...?" Pru breathed.

"I was hoping I would find something like this," Ty said. "Like I told you earlier, Alba and the other guardians would have needed a secret place to conduct their rituals. No one would have ever realized this was here. The knot would have kept those who wished ill upon the river far away, and the bookcase that hid this spot would have prevented anyone in the family from wanting to investigate further. Let's go."

He stepped into the passageway, then paused and looked over his shoulder when it seemed clear the other two weren't too eager to follow.

"We need to see where this leads," he said.

Pru's crimson lips pressed together. "I'm not a huge fan of enclosed spaces."

Neither was Caleb, but he thought he could handle that part okay. No, his big problem was the prospect of the passage being filled with rats, just like the scene in that old Indiana Jones movie where the tunnels under Venice were just choked with rodents.

"There's nothing in here that can harm you, Prudence," Ty said, and his gaze moved toward Caleb, even as he pulled his phone out of his pocket so he could turn on the flashlight function. "Nor you, even though your kind normally wouldn't be allowed in this place."

*Your kind?* echoed in Caleb's mind, but he knew Ty hadn't meant the words in a cruel way. No matter how you sliced it, Caleb understood that he was always going to be a quarter demon, so he just needed to accept that reality and move on.

"Then let's get this over with," he said, and inclined his head toward Pru. "Come on—it doesn't look as if that passageway is too small. Ty's standing straight up in it."

Yes, he was, even though his head nearly brushed the ceiling. But since he had a good ten inches on Prudence, if not more, she definitely didn't have anything to worry about.

She still didn't look too thrilled. However, she didn't argue, but only followed Caleb over to the passageway, her mouth still tight.

Once they were past the cinderblock walls of the basement, their surroundings became packed soil with timbers placed every so often to keep the tunnel from collapsing in on itself. The air felt and smelled damp, something he hadn't encountered in Nevada too often.

Well, the Colorado River wasn't very far from here, maybe a quarter-mile at the most.

They walked for what felt like a hundred yards or so, although he hadn't been counting. Abruptly, the passageway opened up into a cavelike space, but Caleb guessed it was just as manmade as the tunnel they'd traversed.

Carved into the walls at what he guessed were the four points of the compass were more of the witch's knots. Although they'd been relying on the small beam from Ty's phone to guide them along, there was no need for that light here, since the chamber was illuminated by the warm glow emanating from those knots.

"Yes, this is the place," Ty said. He moved a few paces farther into the earth-walled room, and his blue eyes narrowed for a moment, as if he was trying to sense something. "It's a portal, something the Sanchez family would have had every reason to protect."

"'A portal'?" Pru echoed as she looked all around the chamber. "I don't see any doors."

Ty smiled, although there didn't seem to be anything indulgent in his expression. "A portal between worlds...a doorway between realities. The barrier here is very thin, which is why I think August Sellers wanted to use Delia to find this place."

"What does he want to do with it?" Caleb asked.

The half angel now looked almost condescending. "Think about it. What is one overriding goal that almost all demons share?"

Well, that was easy enough. "They want an easy way to get to Earth."

"Exactly. And if August Sellers found out about this spot, then I think his powers would be sufficiently strong to open a portal and bring as many of his friends here as he likes."

Pru had stepped toward Ty, her face a study in confusion. "I thought the demons were already here," she said.

"Some of them," he replied, his tone still gentle. "There are always a few who find their way to this plane. But unless they work very hard at it, they can't stay very long. With this portal open, hundreds or even thousands of them could come through...and remain here for as long as they liked."

She swallowed, and Caleb guessed she was beginning to understand the implications of having hordes of demons free to roam around the planet. Probably not completely, just because she didn't have the same knowledge of demon-kind that he did, but enough so she could see this would be a terrible outcome.

"What can we do?" she asked.

"It's more what Delia can do," Ty said. "She has to work as hard as she can to prevent August Sellers from fully tapping into her powers. The longer she can block him, the better the chance that we can find her before Sellers locates this place."

Easier said than done. Caleb hated this sensation of impotence, of knowing Delia was out there somewhere but having no idea as to her true location.

She was strong...and yet he knew she wouldn't be able to hold out forever, not with a powerful demon bending his will upon her.

He looked away from Ty, his gaze scanning the chamber where they stood. It seemed very plain, with those four knots engraved into the walls its only real decoration.

But....

"I think there's something funky with that one

knot over there," he said, and tilted his toward the witch's knot that he thought was supposed to designate true north. "The center of the design is glowing brighter than the other ones."

"I think you're right," Pru said. "They're all bright enough that I've been trying not to look at them directly, but it's definitely a little different."

Ty was closest to the engraving in question, so he moved over to it and placed his hand against the brilliant flare of the circle at the center of the knot. It flickered...and in the next moment, a folded piece of paper fell in his hand.

"What is it?" Caleb asked as he and Pru went over to see what the half angel had found.

"A map of some sort," Ty replied as he unfolded the paper. It wasn't parchment or anything so fancy as that, only what looked like a large piece of art paper, since one edge appeared slightly rough, as if it had been torn out of a sketchbook or something. "Look—it's the Colorado River here in Laughlin. It has several spots that are starred."

"Why?" Pru asked, leaning closer so she could get a better look at the thing. "What's so special about those places?"

"I'm not sure," Ty said, and his brows drew together as he inspected the map once more. "There's no legend or anything to show what these stars mean, or why they're different sizes. I suppose the people who made it—and anyone they would have left it to—would already know."

"Then how helpful is it?" Caleb demanded. He was getting tired of half-clues and hints. He wanted something concrete, damn it.

"Well, it's a piece of information we didn't have a few minutes ago," Ty replied calmly. "And if I can take some time to analyze it, maybe I'll be able to figure out why those particular locations are starred. It's clear this was made long before Laughlin was really developed, since there's nothing here to show where any of the casinos are located."

So maybe they could set a current map of the city next to this one and see if there were any correspondences.

"Is there anything else here?" Caleb asked, and Pru glanced around the chamber.

"Nothing that's noticeable," she said. "But we should probably take another good look, just to be safe."

Ty refolded the map and secured it in his pocket, and for the next couple of minutes, the three of them moved around the earthen chamber, feeling the walls, inspecting the ground underfoot to see if anything in particular stood out.

Nothing.

"I think the map was left here for whoever the next guardian was supposed to be," Ty said.

Caleb wondered who that was. Definitely not Aaron.

"Does that mean the portal's been unguarded this whole time?" he asked, and Ty nodded, looking worried...unusual for him, since he usually gave off the impression of a Zen master slumming as a surfer type.

"It's well-hidden, so that helps, and the witch's knots are still doing their jobs. Eventually, though, they'll need to be refreshed—just like August Sellers had to refresh his binding on Aaron Sanchez —so they won't hold up indefinitely."

The news just kept getting better and better.

"But someone has to step in at some point," Pru said, her voice tight with concern.

"They do," Ty said. He paused before adding, "And it seems that right now, Delia is the best candidate for that particular job."

# Chapter Twelve

—·‹‹‹·◌·›››·—

As much of a relief as it had been to talk to Caleb, to realize he'd somehow heard her in his mind and that this dark room that held her captive couldn't keep her thoughts imprisoned, the place felt even more like a gaping hole in the world once their connection had been cut off.

Had her captors found out she was speaking with him and intervened to break their contact?

Maybe, although Delia thought it just as likely that the connection had been severed because she didn't have the mental capacity to keep it going any longer.

Once again, what she didn't know about these gifts of hers seemed almost overwhelming.

On the other hand, she'd managed to hold a psychic conversation that felt as if it had gone on for at least a minute, maybe longer.

And that seemed to tell her she was getting better at all this, almost as if something deep in her subconscious knew things her waking mind didn't.

She moved on the bed or chaise or whatever it was, scootching backward until her shoulders touched a wall.

All right, that meant this place had some actual physical boundaries, wasn't just a featureless void hiding in some strange dimension with no actual relation to reality. This cheered her, especially since she knew that before her talk with Caleb, she hadn't been able to move enough to feel the wall or even know it was there.

Did that mean whatever spell was holding her here had begun to weaken, if only the smallest bit?

In another time, she might have laughed at herself for entertaining the notion that magic and spells were even a real thing. But she'd seen too much over the past couple of months to ignore the simple truth that the universe was a much more complicated place than she'd ever imagined.

If the spell was weakening, then she needed to do whatever she could to continue to push against it.

With enough pressure placed on the enchantment, it might finally shatter altogether.

Focus.

She breathed in and out. This time, though, she didn't close her eyes.

No, she wanted to see whatever she could.

A wall behind her. A bed beneath her.

And it was a bed—a daybed, she realized, with a padded back and padded head- and footboard, which was why she hadn't been able to tell whether it was a chaise lounge or a regular old bed. The upholstery was nubby beneath her fingers, and even though she would have said she couldn't see a damn thing in there, somehow she knew the fabric was dark blue, almost navy.

Okay, that was something. Possibly not the most important piece of information in the world, but it told her that she was already perceiving far more than she had a few hours ago.

She stared into the darkness, and somehow knew she was trapped in a small room about ten feet by twelve, the size of a standard bedroom.

Was she in someone's house?

At once, she dismissed that idea. This couldn't be a normal bedroom because it didn't have any windows—or a closet, she realized. On the far side of the space was a single door.

If she were somehow able to get up from the daybed and walk over there, would it open?

No, she told herself. It had two deadbolts in addition to the lock in the doorknob. Even if she somehow made it over there, she'd never get past all those locks.

Or…would she?

It was a novel concept, realizing that she truly had no idea what she could or couldn't do. Someone she doubted she'd be able to Hulk out and smash right through the thing, and yet maybe there was something she could do with her mind to get the door unlocked.

Could the same powers that allowed her to talk to Caleb using only the force of her thoughts be enough to somehow slip inside those locks and move the tumblers so the door would open on its own?

A tempting idea. She just didn't know whether it would work.

Probably better to start with baby steps...literally.

She shifted again and knew she was getting close to the edge of the bed. When she tried to swing her feet over so she could stand up, however, it was as if they'd hit some kind of weird rubbery barrier.

"Ouch!"

Yes, that was her voice. She'd heard it, and she knew she'd uttered the syllable out loud because whatever spell was holding her here on the daybed had—up until now, anyway—kept her silent.

Not being able to get off the bed was something of a setback. But knowing she hadn't been utterly silenced helped a little to remove the sting from that failure.

"I'm here," she said aloud.

Just two words, but they were enough to tell her that one "ouch" hadn't been a fluke.

She sat cross-legged on the daybed and did a little more deep-breathing. Oddly, she experienced just the faintest twinge of hunger.

That would have been a relief, except she knew if she was starting to feel hungry, then she'd probably soon be thirsty as well. And if her body woke up much more, then she was going to be seriously bemoaning the lack of a bathroom around here.

Still, it was another crack in the spell, and that had to count for something.

Then she closed her eyes for a few seconds and caught a flash of an image.

She knew she'd never seen the man before. He was tall and thin, with pale hair and a face that was attractive in a bony, beaky sort of way. His dark gray suit was obviously expensive, but it still hung on him, although she couldn't say for sure whether that was because he'd recently lost weight or because he couldn't be bothered to get the thing properly tailored.

He stood behind a desk in what appeared to be a fancy office, with a spectacular view of the Colorado River hundreds of feet below. However, the big, expensive desk of burled walnut didn't hold a computer or a phone or anything else that you might have expected in such a setting.

No, a black cloth covered the surface, and on that cloth a series of small crystals, all red and black, had been placed in a pattern Delia didn't recognize but somehow still felt wrong, as if its proportions were just enough off that they managed to hurt her eyes. A bowl about a hands-breadth across held some kind of dark liquid.

The man reached into the bowl with one finger and withdrew it, then smeared the reddish liquid... blood, she was sure...across the surface of a hunk of what she thought was either onyx or obsidian.

Almost at once, her temple twinged, and she reached up and pressed a hand against her head.

Great, was she getting a migraine now on top of everything else?

Again, the man dipped his finger into the bowl of blood, and this time he smeared it on a reddish crystal that she didn't recognize. Garnet, maybe?

Now it felt as if something had pinched her forehead, and she winced. At the same time, a strange dizziness descended, and she was suddenly very glad that she hadn't been able to get up from the daybed and start exploring her prison. If she'd been standing when that wave of vertigo hit, she might very well have fallen right over.

Would anyone have come to her rescue if she'd cried out?

Doubtful.

The vertigo disappeared as suddenly as it had

come. In her mind, the man reached for a black cloth and wiped the traces of blood from his fingertips.

Realization flared, bright and painful as that twinge in her forehead had been.

Oh, dear God.

He wasn't a man.

He was a demon in disguise, just like Robert Hendricks had been…just like some of the players in the Desert Paradise poker tournament. And the ritual the blond man had been conducting was designed to tap into her powers.

That was why she'd been caught here. So he could milk her brain whenever he liked.

But for what purpose? She'd told Caleb it was because of the river, but she still didn't understand exactly why.

The man went to the window and looked out. Across from the building where he stood was a tall white tower with hundreds of windows, their mirrored glass blinding in the sun.

However, not so blinding that she couldn't see the logo spelled out in what would probably be garish neon at night.

*Aquarius.*

The hotel had two towers, so the blond man—demon, she reminded herself—must be standing in one of them.

And although she couldn't say for sure how she

knew, Delia understood that was where she was imprisoned now. Not in a hotel room, but in some secret chamber below the casino floor. Possibly a vault, or maybe just a storage space. That would explain why it didn't have any windows, why it was so utterly black in here.

Gritting her teeth, she pushed against the rubbery membrane that had kept her trapped on the bed. It seemed to stretch and stretch—and then it broke with a rebound that somehow made her ears ring, even though everything had remained utterly silent inside her prison.

One foot touched the floor, and then another. It was cool under her bare feet, definitely not carpet. Some kind of linoleum, though, because it didn't feel hard enough to be tile.

As soon as she stood up, the room seemed to spin around her, and she put a hand down on the bed to steady herself. A few breaths, and the dizziness was gone.

Her fingers trailed along the daybed until they found the wall. It was cool and smooth but definitely seemed to be drywall, again affirming her suspicion that this was an interior room on one of the hotel's sublevels.

She walked about ten paces and then hit a corner. That was fine—if nothing else, it seemed as if the room was about the size she'd thought it would be.

Just as she was about to start measuring the next wall, a flood of images hit her brain—an older woman falling to her knees and gasping, hands at her throat as if something was choking her. Another woman, but much younger, maybe around Delia's age, hurrying out of an apartment with suitcases in both hands, throwing frightened looks over her shoulder as she went.

A horrible accident on a lonely highway, one vehicle looking as if it had somehow managed to wedge itself under a semi.

No one in the car could have survived that impact.

*They needed us gone,* rang through her mind, and Delia looked around in horror, even though there was nothing to see in that black, black room.

*Who needed you gone?* she wanted to ask, but she knew she wouldn't get an answer to that question. What she'd just experienced had been echoes of trauma, stray energy that had hung in the air around Laughlin, even though the people she'd glimpsed were now long gone.

But she'd seen those echoes...and she thought she knew what they meant.

Or at least partially. She couldn't say for sure why the river was so important to the blond demon in her vision, but she guessed that he or his minions had driven out or killed anyone who'd been trying to protect it.

And she knew without knowing how she knew that the older woman must have been Alba Sanchez, the river's last guardian.

*House...stays.*

Those words had been utterly cryptic when Alba's ghost had uttered them. Now, though, they'd taken on a new meaning.

The house was crucial in all this, but again, Delia couldn't quite grasp that piece of the puzzle. Why could her gift show her some things and not others?

Because she wasn't a god or an angel or a demon. She was a human woman with a strange talent, and that meant it didn't always do what she wanted it to do.

But even if she wasn't an angel or a demon, she knew that Ty and Caleb were...or at least, possessed enough supernatural heritage that they could do things she couldn't.

And they were looking for her.

They had to know about the blond man.

They had to know she was trapped somewhere beneath the Aquarius.

Delia flattened herself against the wall, trying to stand as steadily and quietly as she could. She didn't know if this was going to work, but she had to make the attempt anyway.

*Caleb, I'm being held beneath one of the towers of the Aquarius hotel.*

# Chapter Thirteen

— ·((·۞·))· —

CALEB STARED AT TY, WHO LOOKED imperturbable as usual, standing there in the middle of the earthen chamber, the map they'd just discovered in his hands. "Delia can't be a river guardian, or whatever you want to call it. She has a life in Las Vegas."

The other man's shoulders lifted almost imperceptibly. It sure seemed as if he didn't care whether Delia was forced to uproot herself from everything she knew and everyone she loved just so she could babysit the Colorado River and make sure a bunch of demons didn't turn it into their personal playground.

"I don't think that's anything we need to worry about right now," Pru cut in. "We need to find her first."

"And stop whatever Sellers is doing," Ty agreed.

"But at some point, someone will need to step in and pick up the reins so the river doesn't remain unguarded. It's too powerful...and too vulnerable... to trust that fate will protect it."

"Okay, fine," Caleb said. The first order of business was to find Delia. After that, well, they'd figure it out as they went.

"We should go back to the hotel," Prudence said. "I want to look at this map next to a modern one to see if these stars make any sense."

Considering they didn't have any other real plans of action, her suggestion appeared to be the best thing to do for now. Ty guided them out of the chamber with its four guardian witch's knots, along the narrow corridor that connected it to the basement at Alba Sanchez's home, and eventually back upstairs.

They locked the back door behind them and got in Caleb's Range Rover. The drive over to Harrah's didn't take very long, less than ten minutes, and they made a quick detour into the gift shop to see if they could find any maps.

Luckily, the shop had both guidebooks with maps and even the old foldout kind—"great for when your nav craps out on you," the clerk helpfully said—so once the three of them were back in their suite, it was a simple enough task to get out the hand-drawn map Ty had found in the hidden chamber and lay it out on the table in the dining area next to the one they'd just bought.

The twists and turns of the river were easy enough to follow, so it didn't take too much work for them to line up the maps and take note of the correspondences.

"There's one right up by the dam," Pru said, a slender finger tipped with chipped green nail polish tracing the line of the Colorado River. "And another at the park."

"Both power spots," Ty responded, his expression thoughtful. "I think whoever made this map was calling out the places where their protective spells would be the most powerful."

"And another on the Arizona side of the river where there's that little carve-out with the island," Caleb added.

Pru leaned over the maps, dark eyes intent as they scanned the two side-by-side documents. "And a big one right beneath the Aquarius Hotel."

No wonder Caleb had felt buzzy and strange when he'd entered the place. At the time, he'd simply thought it was the power of the river acting on him, but now he knew it must have been something much more than that.

"With the final one down at Big Bend State Park," Ty finished.

Pru straightened and pushed a lock of dark

emerald hair away from her face. "Great, so we know that these are power spots, and we know where they're located. What are we supposed to do with any of this?"

A very good question. Although Caleb knew he had a particular set of gifts—and understood that Ty probably possessed many more, even if he hadn't yet revealed all of them—none of this was going to help them locate Delia.

Unless, he supposed, they went to one of those "power spots" and somehow used its energy for a form of divination. He hoped Ty knew how to do something like that, because he sure as hell didn't.

Even as the half angel opened his mouth to reply, Caleb instead heard Delia's voice.

*Caleb, I'm being held beneath one of the towers of the Aquarius hotel.*

Immediately, he responded, *Delia, are you all right?*

No answer. Somehow, he got the impression that she'd used every reserve of energy she had to get out that one blast of thought.

It had been enough, though.

He looked over at Pru and Ty, both of whom were staring at him, their expressions mirroring a sort of identical concern that might have been almost humorous if the situation hadn't been so dire.

"I know where Delia is," he said.

Pru blinked. "How?"

"I just heard her in my mind. She said she's under one of the towers at the Aquarius Hotel."

In any other sort of circumstances, saying such a thing out loud probably would have prompted an uneasy chuckle from the other party, along with a query as to whether he was feeling all right.

Now, though, Ty and Pru both understood they were working with forces that couldn't always be easily explained.

In fact, Ty gave a nod, as if this bit of information had provided an important piece of the puzzle.

"Of course," he said. "We just discovered that the hotel was built on top of one of the river's power centers. Even though demons have a difficult time with the river's energy, if August Sellers has been able to harness it somehow—even partially— then he would have been able to create an effective prison somewhere on the hotel's grounds."

"Delia said she was under the hotel," Caleb told him, and the other man shrugged again.

"Then we'll have a better idea of where to start."

"How will we know which tower, though?" Pru asked.

Again, a valid question...although Caleb thought he already knew the answer.

"Sellers would want to keep her close," he said. "So I'm pretty sure she must be underneath the tower where his office is located."

"Let me check on that," Pru said.

She pulled her laptop out of her satchel, which she'd slung over the back of one of the chairs in the dining area. A few seconds of typing, and then she gave a satisfied nod.

"All the corporate offices are in the north tower," she announced. "So I guess we know where we're going."

Yes, now they knew where they were headed... even if Caleb had absolutely no idea what they'd do once they got there.

---

They'd been to the Aquarius just the day before, but it still felt as if a hundred years must have passed since then. Now they knew where Delia was—well, a ballpark idea, anyway—and Pru thought she had a notion as to what they should do next.

"I'm sure the lower levels are off-limits to guests," she said. "Most of the time, though, those sorts of places only have keycard access, which should be easy enough to circumvent."

"How?" Caleb asked. They'd gotten a table in a corner at the Cove Bar, figuring they needed to have some sort of base of operations, although they knew better than to order anything stronger than some iced tea or soda. "Or do you have some computer hacking experience I don't know about?"

For all he knew, maybe she did, although he'd mainly gotten the impression from Delia that Pru's main private detective superpower was knowing which databases to access to find a particular piece of information. None of it was illegal, but quite a few of them required a P.I. license before you could go poking around in there.

"Unfortunately, no," she said. "I was thinking of something a little more hands-on."

"Such as?" Ty responded. His expression was both dubious and wary, as if he'd guessed what she was probably up to but was sort of hoping it might turn out to be something different.

"Ye olde 'bump and snatch,'" she said. "I dated a guy for a while who was a pickpocket. You would not believe how much money he made off tourists who were careless with their purses and their wallets."

Caleb grinned. "Oh, I can guess. Considering how crowded the streets in Las Vegas usually are, he probably did around low six figures, right?"

She smiled back at him, pointedly ignoring the outraged look on Ty's face.

Well, angels—and half angels—tended to be a bunch of goody two-shoes.

"Sometimes more than just 'low,'" Pru replied. "He had a fence who would help him get rid of the watches and the jewelry. You'd think a person would be smart enough not to be walking around in a crowd wearing a Rolex worth twenty-five grand, but people's cluelessness continues to amaze me."

"And the plan?" Ty asked, now sounding positively testy.

"I'll go out in the casino and look for people wearing lanyards. If they're ID-ing themselves that way, then I'll know they must work for Aquarius's corporate offices in the north tower. All I have to do is brush by one who looks like they're really not paying attention, and *voilà!* I'll have instant access to the lower levels."

She stood up then and straightened the hem of her shirt.

"Be careful," Caleb warned her. "The last thing we need to deal with right now is bailing you out for petty larceny."

Her dark eyes flashed with amused scorn. "I know better than to get caught. You two hang out here—this shouldn't take me more than ten, fifteen minutes tops."

After delivering that reassurance, she headed out of the bar and into the casino proper. Once she was gone, Ty sent Caleb an annoyed glance.

"We shouldn't be letting her do this."

Funny how he thought they were "letting" Pru Nelson do anything. "She's a big girl," Caleb said, then drank some of his Coke. Mostly, he avoided soda, but today he thought he could use the extra jolt all the sugar provided. "It sounds like she knows what she's doing. Besides, do you have a better idea? Can you just magic one of those key cards off one of the employees so Pru doesn't have to stoop to petty larceny?"

"Different types of intervention have different...consequences," Ty said, his expression a mixture of annoyance and concern. "Bypassing technology is one thing. Taking something directly from a person crosses another line entirely."

"Right," Caleb said. "Wouldn't want you to break your angelic code of honor."

Rather than respond, Ty only looked away, his gaze scanning the bar as though he feared someone might be paying particular attention to them. As far as Caleb could tell, though, everyone there appeared to be occupied with their own pursuits, drinking and laughing and having a nosh, since it was right around lunchtime.

If they'd been here for a happier reason, he might have ordered a plate of nachos. However, he had a feeling such a suggestion wouldn't get a very positive response. Also, they'd all had a big room service breakfast before they headed out to Kohl's earlier, since they hadn't known what they might be facing and had thought it would be better to lay down a good base just in case they wouldn't be eating again for a while.

"Relax," Caleb said in a murmur. "No one here could give two shits about us."

"That you know of," Ty returned in an equal undertone.

"Do you sense any demons?"

The half angel paused for a moment, as if performing a scan of the room, and then he shook his head. "No, everyone here seems to be exactly as they appear."

"Well, then."

Caleb relaxed against the back of his chair, although he, too, was more conscious of time passing than he would have liked. What if Pru got caught? Sure, he had plenty of money to bail her out, but he had to believe that if she was arrested for petty larceny, her private detective license might be in danger. He didn't want her to get into that kind of trouble, even if she was trying to help them bust Delia out of her hidden prison.

He and Ty lapsed into an uneasy silence, each of them sipping at their drinks and trying to act as if all this was perfectly normal.

Before Caleb's tension could ratchet up to levels where he'd start to regret all the caffeine and sugar he was consuming, Pru reappeared. Since she was wearing a big shit-eating grin, he had to believe she'd been successful in her errand.

"Got it," she said as she slid into the booth. "Took a little longer than I thought—I guess a bunch of people must have melted away for lunch or something. Also, I specifically wanted to lift the thing off someone who looked as if they were headed out of the building for a while. That way, we'll have more time before they realize it's missing."

It seemed as if she'd tried to cover all the angles.

"Perfect," Caleb said. "What's next?"

"Well, I pulled up some blueprints of the building while we were driving over here," she replied. "The corporate offices are all up on the twentieth floor, so at least Sellers should be pretty far away from the scene of the crime. From what I was able to tell, it looks as if there's a bunch of storerooms on the third sublevel, which I'm guessing is where they must have stashed Delia. We just have to figure out which storeroom they hid her in."

"That does narrow it down," Ty said. "Good work, Pru."

A tinge of color might have touched her cheeks. "Just doing my job," she said lightly. "Anyway, because it's lunchtime, there are probably fewer people roaming around down there. The main thing I'm worried about is the security cameras. They're all over the place on the public levels, and I have to believe they've got the lower floors covered, too."

"That's fine," Ty responded at once. "I can take care of those."

Caleb raised an eyebrow. "And that won't mess with your code of conduct or anything?"

The half angel's eyes might have narrowed just the slightest bit. "I'm doing this to keep us safe," he said. "I'm not breaking any laws by making sure we're blurred out of any footage that might capture us."

Pru's mouth pursed, but she must have decided to leave it alone, since she only commented, "Then it sounds as if we have all the bases covered. Let's do this thing."

They all got up from the booth, and Caleb laid a twenty-dollar bill down on the table even though their entire tab had only been a little more than half that. Still, they'd been taking up a prime seat while they conducted their business, and he thought it only fair to leave a little thank-you for the wait staff.

After all, it wasn't their fault they worked for an organization that apparently was headed by a demon in disguise.

Since Pru appeared to have memorized the layout of the casino, they let her take the lead. She guided them to a regular elevator and descended one level, and then gestured for them to follow her through a door at the end of a corridor that appeared to have some restroom facilities but nothing else.

As they went—after pausing so she could tap her stolen key card against the lock next to the door —she sent a significant glance up at a reflective half-globe on the ceiling, a covering that obviously concealed a camera. Ty gave her a nod in return, seeming to indicate that he was taking care of the hotel's surveillance.

Sometimes, it was good to have friends in high places.

The hallway on the other side of the door was much less flashy, the walls painted a pale gray, the close-pile carpet underneath a darker shade of the same dull color. That was all right, though—they weren't here for the décor.

"There's a stairwell at the end of this hallway," Pru said, still pitching her voice low even though Caleb guessed that Ty was making sure the security system wouldn't pick up anything they said. "I figured it would probably be safer to take the stairs, although there's also a cargo elevator."

"No, the stairs are better," Ty replied. "Less obtrusive."

Caleb supposed that was one way of looking at it. So far, they hadn't seen anyone else on this level, which meant Pru had apparently been correct in her assessment that a lot of the corporate employees probably took lunch around the same time.

They came to a landing with a door. Affixed to the wall next to it was a small sign that announced it opened onto Sublevel 2.

"Looks like we came to the right place," Caleb remarked, then went ahead and opened the door.

Just beyond was another hallway that appeared to be identical to the one they'd just left. Well, the architects and the designers had probably decided there wasn't much point in trying to make these lower levels visually appealing when this section of the hotel was off-limits to the public. However, he could see how the corridor made a sharp turn at either end, telling him that the stairs must have opened onto the first hallway and that there were probably more stacked beyond what they could currently see.

"Which way?" he asked, and Pru shrugged, looking uncertain for the first time.

"I'm not sure," she said. "I mean, most of this level is storerooms, so they could be holding Delia anywhere."

Caleb glanced over at Ty, who appeared equally flummoxed.

"I'm not sensing much of anything," he said. "Or rather, I can tell spells of concealment have been cast down here, but it almost feels as if they're coming from everywhere at once, so I can't really narrow it down."

Great. Caleb had also felt the slow pulse of some sort of energy as they descended into the bowels of the hotel, although he'd thought it was just his demon senses picking up the energy of the river, now only fifty or so yards away.

And maybe that was all it had been. He and Ty were unlike enough that it was entirely possible they would sense and react to the energies here in very different ways.

"Then I guess we just need to be methodical about this," Caleb said. "Let's start with the hallway in front of us, and if we don't find anything there, then we'll move on to the next one and so on. She's got to be in here somewhere."

At least, that was what he hoped. Yes, he'd heard Delia's voice in his mind telling him she had been hidden under one of the towers at the Aquarius, but what if their assumption that it would be the same one where August Sellers had his office turned out to be wrong? There could be an entire complex identical to this one hidden under the south tower, and they'd have to start all over again.

If the keycard Pru had stolen would even work over there.

Caleb told himself to stop borrowing trouble. It seemed far more likely that Delia was here somewhere, and that all they had to do was keep their cool and they'd eventually find her.

However, as they tried each doorway along the first corridor—it seemed Ty didn't have a problem using his angelic powers to unlock a door, even though he drew the line at pickpocketing—they found absolutely nothing of any use. Brand-new furniture still swathed in plastic, pallets of similarly unused plates and glasses, other rooms that held stacks and stacks of chairs, most likely for when banquets and weddings were held here, other rooms with furniture that had been sent down to storage after being deemed too banged-up to be used by the guests any longer...yeah, they found plenty of that.

But no Delia.

"On to the next," Pru said, her tone falsely cheerful, and they went around the corner to the next hallway.

In there was only more of the same, and tension began to creep into his back and gut.

What if she really wasn't here?

Now both Ty and Pru were beginning to look grim, and Caleb could tell they were thinking the same thing, that maybe they'd assumed way too much and that she might actually be hidden under the other tower.

But then they came around a corner...and saw

Aaron Sanchez standing guard in front of a door in the middle of the next hallway.

# Chapter Fourteen

—·《《·◦·》》·—

I T   W A S   H A R D   T O   S A Y   W H O   L O O K E D   M O R E
surprised—Aaron, or Caleb and his companions.

"What—what are you doing here?" Aaron
stammered.

"We might ask you the same thing," Caleb
replied. "I have a feeling you're not hanging out in
front of that door just so you can enjoy the
scenery."

The other man blinked at him, his expression
suddenly vague.

"He's under a spell of control," Ty murmured.
"The sigil is working on him so he does exactly
what August Sellers wants."

Right...there was that black mark on the back
of Aaron's left forearm. Anyone looking at it
would probably think it was just a tattoo, but

Caleb and Ty and Pru all knew it was something much more than that.

"I need to watch the door," Aaron said, still in that robotic tone, and Prudence frowned.

"Is the demon who's controlling him watching through his eyes?"

Good question. To Caleb's relief, though, Ty shook his head.

"I don't think so. Aaron's just doing what he was told. To turn him into an actual spy would take a much stronger enchantment than the one I'm sensing here."

That was something, Caleb supposed. It would have really sucked to have made it down here without being detected, only to have Aaron start beaming their presence back to his lord and master.

"So...what're we supposed to do?" Pru asked.

Ty crossed his arms, while Aaron continued to stand there, his expression now almost stupidly blank. Had that moment of shock when the trio appeared in front of him been his true personality emerging for just a second before August Sellers' spell descended again?

Maybe. Caleb didn't have a lot of experience with this sort of magic, so it was hard for him to say what was or wasn't possible.

"I'm sure the binding spell attached to the sigil ensures that Aaron will fight to the death to protect this door if necessary," Ty said. "That means we can't just try to push him out of the way, because he'll go on the attack."

"I can take him," Caleb responded—to his mind, the comment wasn't bravado, since he had a couple of inches and probably twenty-five pounds on the guy—but the half angel shot him an annoyed look.

"You may think that," Ty said, "but you don't understand what a spell like this does to a person. He will literally bite your ear off...or worse...if that's what it takes to keep you from going through that door."

That didn't sound great, but Caleb refused to be concerned. "Not if I blast him with a fireball first."

"Can we stop all the macho posturing for a sec and figure this out like logical people?" Pru's voice practically dripped acid. "Nobody's fireballing anybody. For one thing, even though Ty's messing with the cameras to keep them from seeing us, throwing fire around is sure to set off a smoke alarm somewhere."

Which Caleb thought the half angel could also silence, although he realized doing so would be dangerous, especially if Delia really was hidden behind the door Aaron had been guarding. None of them wanted a fire to get out of control down here.

"Do you have any bright ideas?" he demanded.

Pru looked over at Ty. "This isn't really my field of expertise. There has to be some way around the spell, though, right?"

He rubbed his chin. "Hard to say. August Sellers seems like a fairly high-level demon, and since Aaron is a vessel, that makes any enchantments cast on him even more difficult to dispel. But...."

The words trailed off as the half angel appeared to ponder their options. Then his gaze seemed to sharpen, and he nodded as if to himself.

"It could work," he said, and Pru set her hands on her hips.

"What could work?"

Ty looked over at Caleb. "We could use your blood to circumvent the effects of the obedience spell that currently controls Aaron Sanchez."

Immediately, Caleb raised his hands. "Whoa— blood magic? I don't think so."

Not that he even knew precisely what was involved in that sort of enchantment. But if it included getting blood out of him by some means or another, he was definitely not on board.

"Don't be a baby," Pru told him, ignoring the way he bristled at her comment, then returned her attention to Ty. "So...what's involved?"

"It's not that difficult," the half angel replied, and now his lips wore something that looked suspiciously like a half smile.

The bastard was enjoying this, wasn't he?

"If it's so easy, we can use *your* blood," Caleb said.

The slight smile didn't budge. "That won't work, I'm afraid. My blood will only set off an alarm and let August Sellers know that something is seriously wrong with his servant. Yours, on the other hand, is just demonic enough to keep Sellers from realizing what we're up to...but also human enough to disrupt the spell."

Great. It wasn't that Caleb had a problem with the sight of blood, but he didn't much like spilling his for a trick that might or might not work.

"How much blood?" he asked, knowing how suspicious he sounded.

"Not much," Ty assured him. "Only a few drops."

All right, that was a little better, especially since he'd been imagining the half angel opening a gash in his arm and letting the blood pour all over that damn sigil August Sellers had left stamped on Aaron's skin.

Through all of this, the man had been standing there with a distracted expression on his face, almost as if he was listening to a song only he could hear. The heated conversation of the three interlopers in front of him didn't appear to have fazed the guy at all.

In a way, it was kind of fascinating...but also creepy as hell.

"Then let's get it over with," he said. "This had better work, though."

"It should," Ty replied.

Caleb couldn't help noticing that he hadn't said "it will."

*Nice way to hedge your bets, Ty.*

However, this was the only plan they had at the moment, and every minute they stood here arguing was another minute that Delia remained trapped only a few feet away.

Feeling resigned, Caleb asked, "What do I need to do?"

"Nothing," Ty said. "I'll make a small cut on your palm, and you'll hold it over the sigil on Aaron's arm. Once the blood hits it, that should be enough to break the spell."

Yet another "should." Rather than call the half angel on his equivocation, though, Caleb only extended his hand. "Do your worst."

Ty shook his head, although he also reached into his pocket and pulled out a keychain with a small Swiss Army knife attached. He extended the blade and made a precise cut, barely half an inch long, on the rounded flesh just below Caleb's thumb.

Immediately, blood began to well up. As both Pru and Ty looked on, he took a step toward

Aaron, who now appeared vaguely alarmed, as though he wasn't sure whether he should interpret such a move as a threatening gesture or whether he should just let it go.

Before the other man could react further, Caleb extended his palm over the sigil on Aaron's arm. Blood dripped down on the strangely sinuous symbol, blurring it so its shape was no longer recognizable.

At once, Aaron stared at him, his expression one of utter confusion. "Where...what...?"

"You're underneath the Aquarius hotel," Caleb said crisply. "You don't remember coming here?"

"No...." Aaron shook his head, as though doing so might clear some of the fog that had clearly descended. "I don't remember anything after last night." He paused there, brow furrowing. "If it was even last night. What time is it?"

"It's a little after noon on Wednesday," Pru supplied, and Aaron stared at her in shock.

"It's not Tuesday anymore?"

"Nope," Caleb said cheerfully. As far as he could tell, the blood had worked. Of course, his palm had continued to ooze through all this, which was a little annoying.

But Prudence, who'd had her satchel slung over her shoulder this whole time, only reached inside the bag, scrabbled around for a second or two, and then pulled out a miniature first aid kit. "I told you that you didn't need to be such a big baby," she said as she pulled out a small antiseptic pad and a couple of alcohol wipes.

"And you could have told me you were carrying around a first aid kit in there," Caleb returned, and she shrugged.

"So...what are we all doing here?" Aaron asked.

Caleb held back a wince as Pru dabbed at the cut on his hand with one of the alcohol wipes, but since she immediately slapped the pad on top and made sure it was properly secured, he figured he'd let it go.

"We were hoping you could tell us that," Ty said. "You don't remember anything at all about what happened last night? How did you get off the boat when it caught fire?"

Aaron sent the half angel a blank stare. "What boat caught fire?"

Demon control was a hell of a drug. "August Sellers had you on his private river cruise last night," Caleb said, then pointed at the blood-smeared sigil on Aaron's arm. "That's where you got that. He's using it to control you."

Aaron blinked and stared down at his forearm as if he'd never seen it before. "I don't remember. But...."

The words drifted away into the air, and Caleb sent a sideways glance at Ty, who hitched his shoulders but didn't appear ready to offer any explanations.

Pru, on the other hand, didn't seem too worried about stepping in. "But...what?" she said. "Do you remember maybe a little bit?"

Brow furrowing, Aaron said, "It's really hazy...."

"We don't mind a little haze," Caleb told him. "Even the smallest piece of information could be helpful."

A second or two passed while Aaron stood there, forehead still furrowed in thought. "I remember a room. There were other people in it."

"Demons?" Caleb asked, recalling the group he'd seen gathered around while August Sellers painted that sigil on Aaron's arm.

"No...other people like me."

"Other vessels?" Ty demanded. He, too, was frowning, so it seemed as if this piece of news wasn't a welcome one."

But Aaron only sent him a blank look. "What's a vessel?"

Prudence released an audible sigh of exasperation. Ty, however, only kept his gaze fixed on the other man. "Someone susceptible to demon magic, like you."

"Oh." Aaron hesitated, and his shoulders lifted ever so slightly. "Then I guess they were like me. Some of them had a mark like this on their arms."

And he tilted his head down toward the sigil imprinted on his flesh.

"That's not good, right?" Caleb said, looking over at Ty.

"Not really." The half angel had kept his gaze fixed on Aaron the whole time. Now he asked, "Do you know how many of them there were?"

"Um...four or five?"

He didn't sound very certain, but Caleb had a feeling that if they pressed him on that particular point, he wouldn't be able to provide much more information than he already had.

Ty also seemed to realize further questioning wouldn't be very helpful, because he also let out a breath and said, "So it seems we'll have some vessels to worry about, on top of however many demons or demon-controlled humans August Sellers has in his cabal."

Pru didn't even blink. "Are they going to be a problem?"

"Maybe." The half angel rubbed a hand against his chin, expression now thoughtful. "It depends on how strong a hold Sellers has on them. We were able to break the spell on Aaron, so it's possible we might be able to do the same for the rest of the people he has in his thrall."

"What, by throwing my blood bombs at them?" Caleb definitely didn't like the sound of that. Yes, getting the few drops they'd needed to disrupt the sigil on Aaron's arm hadn't been too big a problem, but he wasn't sure he wanted to do the same thing over and over again.

Especially since he was pretty sure that Sellers would figure out what they were up to and do whatever he could to stop them before they were able to unenchant more than one or two of the other vessels.

"If necessary," Ty replied. Before Caleb could say anything in response, though, he went on, "Although I'm not sure that's going to help much. Sooner or later, Sellers will realize that Aaron is no longer under his control, and I'm sure he'll be able to guess why—and alter the existing spells so they can no longer be broken by part-demon blood."

"Then that means we need to work fast," Pru said, then returned her attention to Aaron. "Do you know why you were guarding this door?"

He blinked. "Um, no. I just got the idea that I should be here for a while."

A truly insidious spell, Caleb realized, since it seemed designed to make its target believe that all their actions were of their own choice, rather than suggestions implanted there by a demon with his own motivations.

"But it's okay if we look inside that door, right?" Pru persisted, and the frown returned to Aaron's brow.

"I don't know...this is Aquarius Hotel property, isn't it?"

She set her hands on her hips, dark eyes intent on the man's face. Caleb decided it would be better not to interject, since it seemed as if she knew what she was doing. For all he knew, she was using the skills she'd burnished while getting confessions out of men who'd cheated on their wives or people who were out perfecting their golf game when they were really supposed to be on bed rest, thanks to a workman's comp injury.

Or maybe not. He still didn't know exactly how hands-on Prudence was when working on one of her cases, although she'd already amply proved that she could handle herself in a crisis.

No wonder she and Delia were best friends.

"Do you work for the hotel?" Pru asked, her tone pointed, and the furrows in Aaron's brow deepened.

"Um...no."

"Then what does it matter to you whether we look inside that room or not?"

He shoved his hands in his pockets, expression now mildly panicked. Although Caleb still wasn't sure exactly how these things worked, it sure seemed to him that the spell had some lingering hooks in the guy. Maybe not enough to completely erase his free will, but sufficient to make him second-guess anything that went against the original instructions he'd been given.

"Um...."

Pru cocked an eyebrow, and that seemed to be enough to make Aaron Sanchez fold.

"I guess it doesn't matter," he told her, and even stepped partially out of the way so he was no longer blocking the door handle. "But I'm pretty sure it's locked."

Since Ty had already shown that door locks were no big deal, Caleb wasn't too bothered by that weak caveat. "It's fine," he said. "We can take care of it. Right, Ty?"

"Not a problem," the half angel responded. He moved closer to the door and touched a finger to the handle. Even from where he stood, Caleb could hear an audible *click*.

His heartbeat sped up just the slightest bit. He could tell himself until he was blue in the face that his worry over Delia was the same concern he would have shown toward anyone in his circle if they'd disappeared unexpectedly—all right, his "circle" consisted of Delia, Ty, and Prudence and no one else, but still—and yet he knew his concern was deepened by the realization that he wanted Delia to be much more than merely his friend.

Even if he wasn't sure whether he'd ever have the guts to tell her that.

The door opened out into the corridor where they all stood, and the space inside appeared utterly black —much darker than a simple windowless room probably should have. A chill inched its way down his back.

Something about the chamber felt utterly wrong, much worse than the odd, pulsing energy of the Colorado River.

"Another spell," Ty said briefly. "One that put this place outside time and our plane of existence."

"If it's not on our plane, then why can we see it?"

"Because it protrudes into our existence enough that we can still detect something of its shape and form."

That explanation made about as much sense as the organic chemistry class Caleb had struggled through his senior year of college. Anyway, he wasn't here to discuss the physics of the situation.

"Delia?" he called out.

"She can't hear you," Ty said. "The whole reason she was placed in here was to keep her out of our reach. However, I'll do what I can to disrupt the enchantment."

He raised his hands, and a white glow enveloped them, slowly moving outward until it surrounded his entire body. Pru's mouth dropped open slightly—she might have seen him use his powers here and there, but nothing as obvious as this—but Ty wasn't paying any attention to his audience.

With the white glow still surrounding him, the half angel took a step into the room, then paused, as if he was taking a read on the spell and doing his best to think of the most efficient way to neutralize it.

Caleb wasn't sure exactly what happened next, but the white light expanded outward abruptly, making it look as if a supernova had gone off in the space. Out of reflex, he lifted a hand to shield his eyes, while Pru did the same.

Aaron, on the other hand, continued to look into the room as if nothing strange had happened.

When Caleb lowered his hand, he could tell everything had changed. While it was still dark in there, it appeared to be an ordinary darkness, one where he could pick out the occasional detail, thanks to the light filtering in from the corridor outside.

And when Ty touched the light switch next to the door, everything was thrown into sharp relief—a daybed with a padded head and footboard, a small table.

A pair of women's sandals lined up neatly next to the table, with a brown leather purse sitting next to them.

"She's not here," Pru said, her face taut with worry and disappointment.

Caleb could relate. He was so sure they'd find Delia trapped inside the room.

But....

"No," he replied, "but she was here. She told me she was sitting on a daybed, and I'm pretty sure those are her sandals and her purse."

He didn't like the idea of her wandering around barefoot or being without her cell phone, although he supposed he should be somewhat relieved that the room they'd found pretty much matched the few details she'd been able to tell him about the place where she was being held prisoner.

"So...where is she now?" Pru asked, her voice tight with worry.

Caleb had moved closer to the bed as he was speaking. Now he was close enough that he could bend down and retrieve Delia's purse and her sandals, which were a pair of low wedges made of brown leather. He straightened, and they dangled by their straps from one hand.

"I have no idea," he said heavily.

# Chapter Fifteen

—·((‹ · ☽ · ›))·—

SHE'D FELT CALEB OUT THERE SOMEWHERE, his energy coming across to her like the warm glow of a campfire seen against a distant hillside. Every time she tried to contact him mentally, though, it felt almost like she was smashing up against a brick wall, as if someone had learned about the manner in which they'd been communicating and had found a way to block it.

A demon, she assumed. No one else would have the power to do something like that.

She sat cross-legged on the bed, feeling increasingly hungry and thirsty—and also as if she really needed to go to the bathroom. Those physical urges seemed to be an indication that the spell holding her in place wasn't quite as strong as it had once been.

Or maybe her captor had decided to torture her a little by bringing her enough back into the world that she could experience sensations that had been previously blocked.

Once again, she tried to get off the bed, but the rubbery membrane seemed to be keeping her effectively trapped.

Well, this was just great.

Delia tried her best to explore her options, but she really didn't have many. Only to sit there and wait...and hope she succumbed to thirst before she peed the bed.

Panic fluttered in her gut, although she knew freaking out wasn't a very good game plan. Again, she tried to reassure herself that she must have some value to her captor, or he wouldn't have gone to all these lengths to make her his prisoner.

Which sort of reinforced the notion that he was having some fun tormenting her, but would get down to brass tacks eventually.

A strange weariness came over her, and she found herself uncrossing her legs and lying flat against the mattress, her hands crossed on her chest. As soon as she closed her eyes, she was gone.

---

She awoke on a very different bed, one that looked as if it was located in some sort of luxury hotel room. The blackout drapes were drawn, so she couldn't tell what time of day it was.

Carefully, she lifted one hand. That seemed to work just fine, so she sat up. Nothing appeared to have prevented her from doing that, either, and she figured she might as well go for broke.

She swung her legs over the side of the bed.

Shock coursed through her—but not enough that she didn't realize she needed to get to the bathroom, stat.

All but running, she hurried over to the bathroom and took care of business. Once that was handled, she returned to the main part of the room. It was large but not a suite, as far as she could tell.

"Hello?" she ventured, feeling foolish. Then again, whoever had trapped her in this place obviously had supernatural resources at their disposal, so maybe it wasn't so strange that they might be able to hear her.

No reply, though.

Fine. At least she was able to get up and walk around. Several bottles of water sat on the dresser, so she went over and popped one open and drank half of it in a single large gulp. Soon enough, she'd finished the rest of the bottle and unscrewed the cap on another one.

Thirst satisfied, she opened the mini-fridge and took a look inside. It seemed well-stocked, and she got out a can of macadamia nuts and opened the lid. Sure, the list of prices inside the fridge announced that the nuts were eight bucks, but she didn't care much about that.

*They can bill me,* she thought.

There didn't seem to be much else in the room, as far as she could tell. Whoever had brought her here, they hadn't seen fit to bring her sandals and purse along, which irked her even though she knew she had plenty of other things to worry about.

Although she realized it would probably be an exercise in futility, she couldn't help making her way over to the door and trying it. The thing was firmly locked, telling her she wouldn't be going anywhere.

All the same, she wasn't about to give up that easily.

"Help!" she shouted through the door, and pounded on it with her fists. "Someone kidnapped me and locked me in here!"

However, the sound of both her voice and her fists seemed strangely muffled, as if something was wrong with the acoustics in the room.

Or, more likely, whoever had put her in here had placed some kind of spell on the door to prevent her voice from carrying more than a few inches. Delia knew it was weird to acknowledge spells and magic as if they were part of her everyday life, not much different from the cell phone she used and the car she drove, but she couldn't really ignore them anymore, not after being trapped in that black void of a room...not without knowing she herself possessed powers she would never have even imagined a couple of months ago.

For just the briefest second, she contemplated the windows hidden behind those heavy drapes, but she knew even if they weren't enchanted, they'd been designed to never open—and probably were reinforced to ensure any hapless gambler who'd just lost his life savings wouldn't decide the best way to fix his problems was to take a step out in midair.

Assuming she was still in Laughlin, of course, and this hotel wasn't located in L.A. or New York... or Shanghai, she added with a grim mental grin, thinking that city's history perfectly suited her current situation.

She went to the window and pushed the drapes aside, then looked down. Immediately below was a wide open space with some tennis courts and the flat roofs of what she guessed were a couple of restaurants, while off to her right was the wide, slow-moving blue of the Colorado River.

And right across from her was a tower she guessed was identical to the one in which she stood, with "Aquarius" spelled out near the top.

Well, now at least she knew where she was...and

she couldn't help being relieved that she hadn't gone very far after all.

Since it didn't look as if she was going to get out anytime soon, though, she had no idea how valuable that information even was.

Her situation had improved a lot, though. She had access to food and water—okay, not the best food in the world, but at least they weren't starving her—and she could move around normally, wasn't trapped on that funky daybed.

She popped another macadamia nut in her mouth and drank some more water, then headed over to the closet. Maybe they'd hidden her sandals and purse in there rather than leaving them out in the room.

What she found, though, wasn't her favorite pair of Cole Haan wedges and her beloved brown leather Sak tote.

No, it was a full-length dress completely covered in sequins in shades of blue and green, something that shimmered like mermaid scales when she pulled it out of the closet.

What, was the demon planning to take her to dinner and a show or something?

No matching shoes or other footwear, though, which seemed to be a signal that the dress wasn't going to get an outing at the lounge downstairs.

Weirder and weirder.

Delia crossed the room and picked up the

phone on the desk. After her experience with the door, she was none too sanguine that the phone would be of any use, but she had to try.

As soon as she lifted it to her ear, though, she heard a fast busy signal, the kind of thing you might get when all the circuits were overloaded, like after a natural disaster or something.

Not that she thought Nevada was on fire or anything close to it. No, it seemed her captor wanted the space to retain all the normal trappings of one of the Aquarius's higher-end rooms, but at the same time make sure she had no way to communicate with the outside world.

Which sort of begged the question as to why he hadn't kept her trapped in that black hole with the daybed rather than bringing her here.

Since she doubted she was going to get any answers soon, she went back over to the fridge. The mini bottles of wine were tempting, but she knew she needed to stay sharp.

She got out a bottle of Perrier and a snack-size packet of Wheat Thins, then took her haul over to the bed and sat back down.

About all she could do now was wait to see what her captor had planned for her.

---

"Now what?" Caleb asked.

They'd left the hotel proper and taken up positions at the Outback Steakhouse on the Aquarius's grounds, mostly because that felt like they were still close by while giving them a more neutral space to discuss strategy. He and Ty and Pru had discussed whether to leave Aaron to his own devices or have him stay close so they could keep an eye on him, and Ty and Prudence had won that argument, mostly because they'd pointed out that they had no idea what Sellers might do to the guy if they just left him down there on the sublevel where Delia's former prison was located.

"I know he's kind of a tool," Pru said, "but I know I wouldn't forgive myself if it turned out we could have protected him and didn't."

That was why he sat at the far end of their booth now, munching on bits of a blooming onion and looking as if he didn't have a care in the world. As far as Caleb could tell, the sigil was still exerting just enough influence that Aaron wasn't entirely himself yet, but in a way, that was kind of a good thing.

This lightly mind-controlled Aaron was a lot more good-natured.

Ty tapped his fingers against the side of his water glass. Smarting with the disappointment of not locating Delia, Caleb had gone ahead and ordered a Foster's to soften the blow, but it seemed the half angel wasn't going to lower himself to drink a beer with his lunch.

"I'm not sure," he said, his tone heavy. "I have to believe that Sellers kidnapped Delia because he has some specific purpose for her in mind, but I don't know when it's going to happen. If it was a full moon tonight—or better yet, the dark of the moon—then I'd say he was waiting for that. But it's just a little past a quarter right now and doesn't have any particular strength of its own."

Caleb didn't bother to ask how Ty knew the exact phase of the moon. Some people seemed to pay attention to that sort of thing, and if the moon's energy at any given time affected magical rituals, then he supposed it was somewhat valuable information.

"Maybe it's not the moon," Pru said. She also had avoided alcohol and was instead drinking some sparkling water with a slice of lime. "Maybe it's just that Sellers needs it to be dark before he does...well, whatever he's planning on doing."

Rather than shoot down that idea, Ty gave a thoughtful nod. "That makes sense," he replied. "He waited until it was dark before he took all the human vessels on that boat cruise so he could mark them with the sigils. I can see how he would want to use the powers of darkness to make his ritual that much stronger."

"And even if we don't know exactly how he's

going to accomplish it, I think he must be trying to open a portal and bring his demon friends over," Caleb said. "It's the only logical explanation for all this bullshit he's been pulling."

Prudence frowned and pushed at the slice of lime in her glass with the end of her straw. "But I thought he didn't know where the portal was located."

"He doesn't know where the one we found is located," Caleb corrected her. "That map we discovered has power points all up and down the river, including the one right beneath the Aquarius. Maybe he found that one and is planning to have some kind of ritual there."

"I can see that," Ty said. He ran a hand over his chin, eyes narrowing slightly as he appeared to work at the problem. "The portal near Alba's house is stronger, if the relative size of the stars we found on the map is any indication, but if Sellers somehow manages to rope Delia into the ritual, that might not matter. She could be enough to complete the circuit...and strengthen it."

That didn't sound good at all. "Then we have to stop him," Caleb replied. "I've spent time in Hell, and believe me, you don't want a bunch of demons rampaging around Nevada."

"Or anywhere else," Pru remarked darkly. "The question is, where's the portal? Somewhere down in the sublevel where we were poking around?"

"I doubt it," Ty said. "Too much interference from manmade materials. It would need to be like the chamber where we found the map, something carved out of the earth itself. And it would have to be as close to the river as possible, just because Sellers would want to utilize Delia's connection to it to make her contribution more powerful."

As far as Caleb could tell, the only good thing about all this was that Delia was clearly important to the demon, so he probably wouldn't do anything to hurt her.

At least, not until the ritual was over, which made it even more urgent that they find her before all this went down.

"Maybe there's a tunnel somewhere," he suggested. "You know, sort of like the tunnel we found that connected Alba Sanchez's basement to the map room. Sellers could have made it lead off the lowest sublevel and hidden the entrance or something."

Ty picked up his glass of water and drank as he pondered that proposition. "I suppose it's possible. A high-level demon would be able to make sure something like that stayed concealed, so even if the hotel's employees were conducting ordinary busi-ness down there, they wouldn't necessarily see anything strange."

Expression resigned, Pru said, "Does that mean we're going back down to the sublevels? Because I honestly don't think that's the best idea in the world."

"Why not?" Caleb replied, and she raised an eyebrow, as if she couldn't possibly believe he was that dense.

"Because it's now after one o'clock. The person I lifted that keycard from has probably reported it stolen, which means hotel security would have already deactivated it. And if I were running things around here, I'd know our system might have been compromised, and I'd post security guards wherever there's a door controlled by one of those card locks. They might just be the Aquarius's version of rent-a-cops, but they're still going to be a lot harder to get past than the normal unmanned security measures."

Right. Caleb had honestly forgotten about that aspect of the situation, mainly because it had been so easy to get into the sublevel that he hadn't thought about any future complications that might crop up.

"Well, I can still go back in," he said. "I can tele-port, remember?"

Pru stared at him, nonplussed. "What about the rest of us?"

"I can, too," Ty said.

She worked her jaw, clearly not thrilled with either of them. "Yeah, but I can't. What am I supposed to do—sit in the bar and drink mai tais and babysit our little friend here?"

Caleb thought there were worse fates, especially since Aaron seemed pretty docile at the moment. He continued to work away at the blooming onion in the middle of the table and, in fact, had consumed far more than his fair share, mostly because the rest of them had been too preoccupied with their conversation to take more than a few cursory bites of the appetizer.

"Basically, yeah," he replied.

"No way," she returned. "Maybe I don't have all your superpowers, but—"

"But nothing," Ty cut in, and she shot him an angry glare. "You've done a lot to help out, and neither of us wants to discount that. Now, though, I think we're coming to a point where it's better—and safer—for you to stand back."

She was silent for a moment. Caleb could practically see the way she wrestled with her thoughts, with the knowledge that, as smart and capable as she was, she still didn't have the kind of supernatural abilities that would assist her in a face-off with a demon master and his minions.

"I don't like feeling useless," she said.

"You're not useless," Caleb responded at once. "We wouldn't have gotten anywhere as far as we have without you. But you need to keep an eye on Aaron, and—"

"And what?" Pru asked, dark eyes still glinting with a hard, angry light. "What if the big boss demon asserts control over him again? How am I supposed to handle that? It's not like I'm going to have Caleb with me to bleed all over him again and get him to settle down."

"You use this," Ty said calmly, and set a small plastic bottle down on the table in front of her.

Caleb recognized it all too well. He and Delia had deployed the same bottles in their previous confrontations with demons.

Holy water.

It seemed Pru knew what it was as well—probably since Delia had been using the stuff in her ghost-whispering business long before she got tangled up with demons—because she released a breath and then reached out and deposited it in her satchel.

"If I use that, won't the boss demon know the gig is up?"

"He'll already know that," Caleb said, "because we'll be in his face, trying to rescue Delia and stop him from completing the ritual. This is just insurance to keep Aaron from joining the party."

Again, Prudence was silent for a moment, most likely because she was trying to come up with a convincing argument as to why she should stick with them and not get left behind. It didn't seem as if she was successful, since she replied, "Okay, I get it. I don't like it...but I get it."

"We'll have lunch," Ty said. "And then you should probably take Aaron back with you to our suite at Harrah's—to keep him out of the line of fire," he added hastily, since her eyes had begun to glint with annoyance again. "It's neutral ground, and you should be safe there."

Again with the "should."

But Caleb understood that even Ty was trodding on some unfamiliar ground here, and he was just doing his best to make sure everyone involved made it out of this alive.

"And we'll reconnoiter," he said, and the half angel nodded.

"We need to locate the portal before nightfall so we have enough time to make a real plan of attack. But whenever we do find it, we'll need to stand back and wait until the ritual begins."

Now it was Caleb's turn to raise an eyebrow. "Don't you think we should block the guy before he gets up a good head of steam?"

Unfazed, Ty stared back at Caleb and said, "If we do that, then we might miss our chance to rescue Delia. Until she's actively participating in the ritual, August Sellers will keep her elsewhere. Moving too soon only lessens our chances of getting her away from him."

Man, Caleb hated it when Ty Carter made sense.

"I don't like it," Caleb replied.

"You don't have to like it," Ty said. "You just have to be willing to do whatever's going to result in August Sellers being taken out of the equation and Delia rescued. This isn't about us. It's about her."

And that, Caleb realized, was a fact he couldn't really dispute.

# Chapter Sixteen

—·‹‹‹·⚜·›››·—

Sometime around two-thirty, a room service cart appeared in the middle of the hotel room where Delia was trapped. She'd been sitting on the bed, watching TV—it wasn't as if there was anything else she could do to pass the time, although she'd taken the world's shortest shower to freshen up after reassuring herself that she was utterly alone in the room—when the cart suddenly materialized.

She'd been startled, of course, although she also told herself she should be used to this sort of thing by now. Or rather, even though she'd never seen a room service cart show up out of nowhere before, it was pretty far down the list of crazy shit she'd had to deal with lately.

After she paused the show she was watching, she got up from the bed and walked toward the cart, knowing she probably looked like someone approaching a wild animal, not sure whether it would attack.

However, the thing looked completely ordinary...and she swore she could smell the rich, beefy aroma of a French dip drifting out from under the silver dome that covered the food.

She reminded herself that her captor would have had plenty of opportunity to do all sorts of terrible things to her before this, and she sort of doubted he would have used room service as the means of her destruction.

Or maybe he'd decided she wasn't so useful after all, and he thought that poisoning her with some kind of tempting meal was the most amusing way to dispatch her.

Quickly, she lifted the cover from the plate. Sure enough, a French dip sandwich and a little bowl of au jus sat there, accompanied by a pile of delectable-looking shoestring fries lightly dusted with parmesan and parsley.

Her stomach rumbled. Maybe the macadamia nuts and the Wheat Thins had shut it up for a while, but her body seemed to think it could really use a good helping of protein.

And she'd eaten the stuff out of the minibar and hadn't suffered any ill effects.

For a second, she stood there, inhaling the

sweet, sweet aroma of the sandwich and fries...and then she resolutely set the cover back in place.

As good as it all smelled—and as hungry as she was for some real food—she didn't dare take the chance. The stuff from the minibar had still been in its factory packaging, while the late lunch that had appeared out of nowhere could have been tampered with by almost anyone.

"I'm good, thanks," she said aloud, just in case her captor was eavesdropping on her. She'd checked the room for any hidden cameras...Pru had taught her how to do that a while back after she'd talked about getting an Airbnb in Tahoe for a long weekend at a time when horror stories about secret cameras in vacation rentals had been making the rounds on the internet...but as far as Delia had been able to tell, the place was clean.

Then again, a demon or whoever her captor might be probably was someone who didn't have to rely on something as mundane as spy cameras.

Trying not to inhale too deeply—she knew the scent of the French dip would linger in the air for a while, even with the cover in place—she headed back over to the bed, picked up the remote, and turned HGTV back on.

Caleb and Ty sent themselves back into the sublevel and to the same stairwell they'd used to descend to the room that had once held Delia. They'd agreed on that location because they both knew it well enough, and also because the stairs had seemed pretty much deserted, and they didn't think there was too high a risk of bumping into any Aquarius employees there.

That appeared to be the case now as well, since Caleb didn't see anyone around when he and Ty appeared.

"All the way down to the bottom?" he asked, and Ty nodded.

"Yes. Any tunnels would have to branch off from the lowest level."

They kept heading down, past the landing that would have allowed them access to Sublevel 3, and then past Sublevel 4, until the stairwell terminated at a final landing that opened onto the lowest level of the underground facilities.

Even though it looked exactly the same as the level where they'd found Aaron guarding Delia's erstwhile prison, something about the place gave Caleb the creeps. He glanced over at Ty, who nodded.

"Yes, I feel it, too. It's not quite the same energy as the portal near Alba Sanchez's house, but it's similar. I think we must be getting close."

"Where do you think Sellers would have

hidden the tunnel?" Caleb asked. "Walls...or floor?"

"It could be either," Ty said. "But let's walk the perimeter first, and then if we have to, we'll start searching all the different hallways."

Which could take a while. Then again, they had almost six hours until night fell, so it wasn't as if there wasn't plenty of time available for exploring.

Even though every passing minute felt like a century.

By unspoken agreement, they both headed to the right, moving slowly so they could absorb the energies of the space. That was what would betray the location of the tunnel or passageway, not any visible evidence. August Sellers would have made sure that the ordinary employees who came down here wouldn't find anything of note...well, unless they were psychic or something.

The whole time, Caleb could sense the way the portal's energies pulsed in the background, although they weren't slow and steady, but rather had an odd, almost staccato beat, as if their natural rhythm had been perverted somehow.

No big surprise, not when Sellers must have been meddling with those energy signatures to make them more suited for opening a gateway into Hell.

"Will it go back to normal after all this is over?"

Caleb asked Ty in an undertone. It sure didn't seem as if anyone was observing them, and of course, Ty would be interfering with the security cameras to make sure there was no trace of their passage, but it still seemed wise to keep their voices down.

"I hope so," the half angel replied, also speaking in a near-murmur. "I haven't encountered anything like this before, so I can't say for sure."

While Caleb would have preferred a more definitive answer, at least Ty hadn't said that the portal would be damaged forever. Maybe the river's energies weren't in sync with his demonic blood, but the Colorado was still a source of natural beauty and vitality, and he would have hated to think it was permanently defiled by the demon's meddling.

They fell into silence again as they continued their circuit. This wasn't really the time for small talk, so even though the quiet felt a little uncomfortable, Caleb didn't try to come up with a topic that might have kept the conversation going.

The wrongness in the background seemed to strengthen, that odd rhythm beginning to feel like the whining buzz of a fly trapped in a room, drilling into his eardrums. If their mission hadn't been so urgent, he would have been tempted to tell Ty that they needed to get the hell out of there.

Of course, he didn't.

Then the half angel stopped suddenly and pointed at the floor beneath their feet. "Here," he said.

"You're sure?" Caleb asked. As far as he could tell, this particular section of industrial carpet didn't look any different from the rest of the sublevel they'd already surveyed.

"It feels wrong."

Caleb couldn't help lifting an eyebrow. "Dude, this whole place feels wrong."

Ty gave a reluctant chuckle. "Okay, you're right about that. But the wrongness feels concentrated here."

He knelt and spread his hands over the section of carpet he'd indicated. A faint glow surrounded his fingers, not nearly as bright as the illumination he'd called to himself in the chamber where they'd found the map.

However, it appeared to be effective enough, because the outline of a square about a yard on each side began to glow in response.

"Help me pull it up," the half angel said, and Caleb knelt as well so he could lift the square of flat carpet out of the way.

Sure enough, below the concealing square was a metal door with a recessed handle in the middle. If anyone had walked directly across it, they might have sensed a slight depression in the floor, and yet Caleb had the feeling that not many people even came to this level beneath the hotel.

He began to reach for the handle, but Ty laid warning fingers on his forearm.

"Not yet," he said, and Caleb sent him an annoyed look.

"I thought the whole point of this little expedition was to locate the tunnel that leads to the energy point."

"And we have," Ty replied calmly.

Caleb wasn't all that convinced. "We found a door in the floor. I wouldn't exactly call that incontrovertible proof that it connects to the spot we're looking for."

"Oh, it is," Ty said. "I can feel it. The tunnel heads east for about twenty or thirty feet and ends in an open space. I'm sure that's where we'll find Delia...when the time comes."

"And you got all that from just touching a door handle?"

"I did." He reached over and took hold of the square of carpet they'd just removed, then slid it back into place and ran a glowing finger all around its edges. Once he was done, you couldn't tell it was any different from the rest of the dark gray indoor/outdoor carpet that covered the floors in this sublevel. "The more we tamper with this, the greater the chance that August Sellers might be able to detect that someone was here and found his secret passageway. Much better to go back to the hotel room and wait it out."

That plan sounded awfully anticlimactic, but Caleb had to reluctantly agree that Ty was right. The longer they hung around here, the more risk they ran of someone coming along and discovering a couple of interlopers in a place where they had no business being.

And when he glanced down at his watch, he realized they'd spent more time down here than he'd thought, since it was now almost four o'clock. Still a good ways to go until nightfall, especially at this time of year, but it could have been worse.

"All right," he said. "Let's go back."

---

It was getting dark, Delia realized as she went to the window to look out and see what the world was doing. She'd spent most of the afternoon watching TV, although she'd gotten up and done some yoga poses in between shows, just enough to keep her blood flowing and her body ready for whatever might come next. From time to time, she'd gone to the door and pounded and yelled—not because she thought it was going to do any good, but more because she refused to give up that easily.

And when she'd gone into the bathroom one time, she'd come back out to see that the room service cart with its uneaten lunch had vanished as mysteriously as it had appeared.

Right now, she was sort of regretting that decision, since snacking on nuts and crackers and even some wedges of Laughing Cow hadn't been enough to really quell the gnawing hunger inside her. After all, it had been more than twenty-four hours since she'd eaten any real food.

Well, it couldn't be helped now. The sun had disappeared past the western horizon, and the lights from the casinos shimmered across the dark waters of the Colorado River. It should have been a beautiful sight, but for some reason, Delia shivered and pulled the drapes shut again.

When she turned around, a strange man was standing in the middle of the room.

He was very tall, maybe as much as six feet four, and also thin, his black suit seeming to hang on his nearly skeletal form. Pale hair was pulled away from his angular face and bound into a tight ponytail at the nape of his neck.

And the eyes that met hers had a reddish glow in them, telling her he wasn't quite as human as he appeared.

"Hello, Delia," he said, casual as though they'd just run into each other at a cocktail party. "It is time."

Those words made an additional frisson of fear run down her spine, but she lifted her chin and met his gaze as squarely as she could. "Time for what?"

"You'll see soon enough," he replied. "You need to get changed."

She looked down at the wrinkled jeans and sleeveless top she wore. Yes, she'd taken a quick shower earlier and done what she could to finger-comb her hair, but she was still a rumpled mess.

However, she couldn't figure out why the stranger...clearly a demon in human guise...gave a damn what she looked like.

"Who are you?" Delia asked. She didn't think he'd provide her with a straight answer, but it seemed kind of rude that he knew her name and she had no idea who he was.

"You may call me August," he said. "Now, go change. The gown is hanging in the closet. I will wait out here."

After delivering that command, he went over to the desk, which was placed a few feet away from the dresser, and sat down on the chair placed in front of it.

What would he do if she refused?

Judging by the flicker of red she'd glimpsed in his eyes, nothing good.

Because it seemed wiser to play along for now and hope that an opportunity for escape would present itself sooner rather than later, she raised her chin and marched over to the closet, removed the gown—which looked as if it had been designed to grace a red carpet and not as a component of whatever horrible ritual "August" had planned—and then went into the bathroom and locked the door.

That flimsy lock wouldn't have kept even a regular human out if they were determined enough, let alone a demon, but the spurious security measure made Delia feel a little better.

What didn't make her feel good at all were the gown's spaghetti straps. No way in the world could she wear her current bra under that, and she hated the idea of feeling so exposed, even if the dress did have cups sewn into the lining to provide a little support. She supposed she could have kept on the bra—she sure as hell didn't care what she looked like—but she had a sneaking suspicion that if she emerged with exposed straps and maybe even the edge of her undergarment showing around the low neckline, the demon would only order her to return to the bathroom and not come out until she was wearing the gown the proper way.

So she quickly slid off her bra and hung it from the brushed nickel hook on the back of the bathroom door, then slipped the dress over her head. It somehow felt heavier on her body than it had when she'd only been carrying it, and it clung to her in ways she wasn't sure she liked. She worked out and kept herself in shape and liked wearing clothing that fit her well, but she still wasn't into garments that stuck to her like a second skin.

Not that her personal preferences mattered a damn right now.

The gown was beautiful, though, even if she didn't feel comfortable wearing it, and although it was probably foolish to think such a thing when she had much more important matters to worry about, she kind of hated how her hair and makeup...or, more accurately, lack thereof...definitely didn't match the dress.

Since there wasn't much she could do about her appearance, she hung her blouse and her jeans on the hook next to the one that held her bra.

Would she be able to come back and retrieve them?

Somehow, she didn't think so.

When she emerged, August rose from the chair where he'd been waiting for her. "Much better," he said. "Although not quite there."

He didn't do anything so obvious as snap his fingers, but in the next second, her long red hair had been scooped up and arranged into an artfully messy bun, and shoulder-duster earrings hung from her ears. She caught a glint of deep green and guessed they were probably emeralds.

"That's a nice trick," she commented. "I bet you'd clean up getting people ready for the Oscars."

The demon didn't even blink. "I would not

waste my time on such a frivolous endeavor. But now that you're ready, we can go."

He walked over to her, and although Delia's first instinct was to back away, she guessed he wouldn't put up with that sort of nonsense. Again, she reminded herself that she needed to play along so she could wait for the right opportunity to escape.

Even if she wasn't sure whether that opportunity would actually come along.

Cold fingers clasped her forearm, and she tried not to flinch. Shouldn't a demon's touch be hot?

Caleb's fingers were always warm.

But he was only a quarter demon, and much more human than not. Thinking about him then made her wish more than ever that he was here, because she was pretty sure he'd make short work of August. The guy might be acting like he was in charge, but Caleb had demolished other demons, and she had no doubt he'd take care of this one, too.

She tried again to call out to him with her mind. Unfortunately, the same spell that had prevented her from using the phone or allowing anyone to hear her cries for help seemed to have blocked that ability as well.

August smiled, showing teeth that were too white...and too sharp.

"We will go now."
In a blink, they were gone.

# Chapter Seventeen

— ·《《· ☾ ·》》· —

MORE THAN EVER, CALEB WISHED HE'D come to Laughlin with Delia for a little change of pace, maybe a chance to rent a boat and go out on the river—even though he knew spending an extended amount of time on the Colorado probably wasn't a good idea for him—or just have dinner and catch a show.

Maybe finally gather his courage enough to tell her he was glad to be her friend but that he wanted a whole lot more.

Instead, he was back in the fifth sublevel below the Aquarius, watching as Ty pried up the section of carpet that concealed the tunnel leading to the chamber where August Sellers would be performing a ritual intended to open a portal to Hell.

Well, the tunnel that supposedly led there. Ty

seemed very sure about the whole thing, but because he hadn't allowed them to explore when they came here earlier in the day, saying they needed to be careful not to tip their hands, Caleb had no idea whether the half angel's assessment of the situation was correct.

This time, though, Ty actually did open the door, which revealed a pitch-black passageway with a metal ladder secured to one wall.

"Probably for the people who dug it out," he said as he and Caleb began to make the descent. "Sellers would have hired workers to do the job and then either erased their memories...or simply erased them."

"What, he couldn't just snap his fingers and make it happen?" Caleb asked. Oddly, the lower they got, the more illumination he detected, as if there was a light source farther down the tunnel they currently couldn't see.

"Doing so would have required an enormous amount of energy," Ty replied. "Much easier for him to hire mortals to dig the tunnel."

Fair enough. Caleb was still finding his way around what demons could or couldn't do. He might have grown up around other quarter demons and had half demons like his father as part of the mix as well, but all of them had been focused on making sure no one would ever be able to tell they were anything more than regular mortals. They weren't trying to do anything flashy, other than live the lives of wealth and privilege that had been set up by their progenitors, the demon princes who had come to this plane to serve Belial.

By that point, they'd reached the bottom of the vertical tunnel. There, it turned forty-five degrees and stretched out straight ahead of them before opening into a chamber about a hundred feet or so from where they stood.

That was the source of the illumination...but it didn't come from any lights fastened to the walls or roof of the earthen room, one that was similar in dimension to the one beneath Alba Sanchez's house.

No, the brilliant glow was coming from Delia Dunne.

She hung in midair, eyes closed, hair pulled up into the sort of carefully messy do that usually still took hours to accomplish. Her slim form was encased in a fabulous gown of shifting blue and green sequins, and long, glassy emerald earrings hung down to nearly her shoulders.

In short, she was absolutely spectacular...and completely terrifying.

"What's going on?" Caleb whispered to Ty, who had also stopped in his tracks to stare at the spectacle in front of them.

"He's using her as a power source," Ty

murmured in reply. "With her psychic abilities fueling the ritual, it will be very powerful."

No shit. Caleb realized then that Delia wasn't alone in the chamber. He couldn't see August Sellers from where he and Ty stood, but he noticed that four other men were ranged along the walls, all of them wearing the same somehow stupefied yet beatific expression Aaron had plastered on his face before they snapped him out of his spell...and all of them with the same sigil of command inked onto their forearms.

"What about the army of goons?" Caleb asked next. "Am I going to have to bleed all over them, too?"

Maybe Ty's mouth quirked just a fraction. "It's an easy way to break them out of the spell. But since we're not worried about alerting August Sellers as to what we're up to—he'll know we're here to disrupt the ritual as soon as he spots us—I think holy water will be the easiest way to dispatch those men. It should break the hold those sigils have on them, and once they've woken up, they'll be of little use to Sellers."

All that sounded encouraging...up to a point. There were still a lot of them, and if they decided to stay and fight, they could be a real problem.

But they had to get Delia out of there before Sellers drained her dry...or opened his damn portal to the underworld. Luckily, her little SUV had had nearly a full case of holy water back in the cargo area, as though she'd loaded up before she headed down to Laughlin, not sure what she would find.

Now her forethought might be the thing that saved her. Well, along with an assist from Caleb and Ty, her otherworldly posse.

By unspoken agreement, they inched toward the chamber where Delia still hung suspended in the air, looking like a gorgeously oversized Christmas ornament. Caleb had never seen her like this before, and despite his worry that Sellers and his minions might outmatch them, he still thought she was the most beautiful thing in this world...or any other.

"I'll go after August," Ty said in an undertone. "You take care of those men and do what you can to snap Delia out of that trance."

Would she awaken if he kissed her, like some latter-day version of Sleeping Beauty?

As appealing as that mental image was, Caleb knew better than to try anything like that. If he ever did have the luck to kiss Delia Dunne, he wanted to do it when she was in full possession of all her faculties.

And while he could have protested and said he'd take on August Sellers, the truth of the matter was that Ty probably had more experience with this sort of thing. Better to have an angel battle a demon...especially if that left Caleb free to rescue Delia.

"Got it," he murmured.

With their plan in place, the two of them continued to move forward. Now they were only a few feet away, and Caleb could finally see August Sellers.

He stood at what was the northern compass point of the chamber. Just as in the one under Alba Sanchez's house, this earthen room also had sigils carved into the walls in the four cardinal directions, only this time, they weren't witch's knots—designed to keep evil magic at bay—but copies of the same sigil of command that had been drawn on the forearms of all his minions.

Were those symbols exerting some sort of additional control? What if the holy water Caleb carried in a bag hastily purchased in the Aquarius's gift shop wasn't enough?

Too late to voice those worries to Ty, because the half angel's body suddenly flared with light, and he stepped into the ritual chamber, blazing like a miniature supernova.

"You will not do this!" he thundered. "I command you with all the power of the Lord God Himself, and all the strength of the choirs of angels, and the voice of Christ Himself!"

And he raised a hand and threw what looked like a blob of pure energy at the demon.

However, August Sellers only lifted a hand in reply and smacked the glowing white orb to one side, rather like someone deftly deflecting a volley-ball. "You'll have to do better than that," he sneered. "Do you think I care about the power of your God? I have tapped into the energy of the river that flows so near us, and amplified it with the gifts of the woman I now command. Tell your Jesus or your God—or your angels, I suppose—to come here and stop me, for there is no way you will ever be able to do such a thing yourself...half angel."

Well, that answered one question. Caleb couldn't do much with that interesting piece of information, though, because just as the demon stopped speaking, his minions seemed to awake from their stupor and came rushing toward the spot where Caleb stood.

Luckily, he already had a vial of holy water in each hand, their lids popped and the liquid inside ready to go. He splashed it into the faces of the first two who approached him and they recoiled, clawing at it as if it was acid.

After that first violent reaction, though, they both blinked and looked around as if they had no idea where they were.

To be fair, they probably didn't.

"Exit's that way," he said, and inclined his head

toward the tunnel that led to the fifth sublevel and the real world.

"Thanks, man," the first guy said. He looked like he was barely old enough to drink, with the kind of muscles he would have gotten from long hours at the gym.

No wonder Sellers had wanted him for a lackey. He could probably put someone right through a wall.

"Don't mention it," Caleb replied, since two more of the minions were coming straight toward him.

The first pair made their escape down the tunnel. Out of the corner of his eye, he saw that Ty had apparently decided it wasn't worth his time to waste any further words on the demon, and instead was hurling ball after ball of white light at Sellers.

However, each one seemed to bounce off an invisible barrier, one that shimmered like black glass. Was the disguised demon really that powerful? Caleb was pretty sure any one of those light balls would have knocked out any of the other demons he'd encountered.

But they hadn't been drawing on the power of the river, amplified to crazy levels by Delia's burgeoning gifts.

Which meant the connection between them— however August Sellers had brought it into being —must be destroyed as soon as possible.

First, though, Caleb needed to splash more water on the lackeys as they rushed toward him.

The next one reacted the same way the first guy had, which was to blink and look confused, and then run for the closest exit.

The last guy, though, didn't seem to want to wake up from his trance. Eyes still blank, he went straight for Caleb with his arms outstretched, clearly intent on wrapping them around his throat.

Well, that wasn't going to happen.

He brought his knee up straight into the man's groin. That seemed to bring him out of his trance the way the holy water hadn't, because he went down like a ton of bricks, moaning and doing his best to curl into a fetal position.

Okay, he was definitely awake now...and would probably follow the rest of his compatriots as soon as he was able to stand again.

Behind Caleb, Ty and August continued to battle it out, lobbing their respective energy weapons at each other, but it didn't seem as if either one was gaining the upper hand.

Stalemate, unless Caleb could do something to tip the balance.

He moved closer to Delia, still suspended in midair, her oval face as serene and lovely as a Renaissance Madonna. There had to be something he could do to wake her up from her trance.

Throw holy water at her, the way he had with

Sellers' minions? No, she wasn't a demon, but she appeared to be controlled by one, the same way those clueless men had been.

Caleb pulled another vial of holy water out of his bag, reflecting that if he was going to keep getting dragged into fights like this, he should probably have some kind of bandolier setup made for the things, maybe like one of those rigs he'd seen waitresses wear in a couple of bars he'd visited since his arrival in Las Vegas, where the women had bottles of their current pour hanging from their waists in holsters and a bunch of shot glasses loaded in leather straps that crossed over their chests. It would be more efficient than what he was currently doing.

But since they hadn't had the time to buy a specialized rig like that, he'd just have to make do with what he had.

"Sorry," he murmured under his breath. Yes, this was necessary, but he still didn't like the idea of splashing Delia full in the face with a bunch of water.

Desperate times and all that.

He removed the cap and threw the entire contents of the vial right at her. It should have hit her face and hair...and maybe some of the chest that was more exposed by the sequined gown than he'd ever seen before.

That was some seriously spectacular cleavage.

The water never reached her, though. Instead, it splashed onto some sort of barrier, sort of like the one that seemed to be shielding August Sellers from Ty's attack, only this one shimmered white as the holy water hit the surface.

Shit.

Caleb stared at the barrier in consternation. If it had been created by the demon, then it should have shattered into nothingness the second the holy water made impact. That it didn't...

...well, that seemed to tell him Delia herself was the one who'd created the barrier that currently protected her.

And that meant the usual methods weren't going to work.

"Delia!" he shouted at her. "You have to drop the shield!"

From behind him, August Sellers released the kind of cackle that only a demon could produce. "You're wasting your time," he called out as a crackle and hiss indicated that yet another of Ty's energy blobs had been absorbed with the dark magic that appeared to have made him all but invulnerable. "She can't hear you. She can't do anything except give me the power I need to make sure the portal opens."

"How are you going to manage that?" Ty countered. He sounded breathless, and Caleb had to wonder how much this battle against the demon was taking out of the half angel. No one had limitless stores of strength, and it appeared pretty clear that Sellers was trying to wear Ty down until he didn't have any fight left. "It seems like you're a little distracted right now."

"Fool," the demon shot back. "I'm not going to open the portal."

He paused there, and his eyes glowed red and his teeth seemed to sharpen as he smiled.

"Delia is."

# Chapter Eighteen

— ‹‹‹ ‹ ۞ › ››› —

THE ENERGY OF THE RIVER SEEMED TO flow all around her. Delia drifted within it, feeling as suspended in its power, its strength, as if she'd been floating in its actual water.

Why had she been so frightened when August brought her here?

This was beautiful.

Everything was beautiful.

He'd told her she only needed to speak to the river, to hear it in her mind the way she could hear other people's thoughts. The river would show her the way to open the gate and let all of August's friends in.

He'd seemed lonely when he told her he wanted his friends to be here, that it had been too long since he'd been surrounded by others of his kind. Delia thought she could understand that, since she'd sensed the same loneliness in Caleb, a man who had no one else truly like him in this world.

Caleb.

Was that his voice she heard now?

No, she must be imagining things. All she was supposed to do was float on the river's currents of power, letting them show her where she should reach out and open the passageway between two worlds.

In fact, she thought she could see the gate shimmering off in the distance. It wasn't open yet, had only begun to materialize, but soon enough, it would yawn wide, and all of August's friends would come through.

But then she thought she heard Caleb again.

"Delia! *Delia!*"

Her eyes flared open, and she saw she was suspended in midair in a room whose walls were made of earth. Off to one side, Ty Carter seemed to be in the battle of his life with August, wild scatters of white energy splashing everywhere.

Alarm flared in her.

She was supposed to protect August, wasn't she?

"Delia!"

Then she looked down and saw Caleb standing a few feet away from her, handsome features tight with worry, that one lock of dark blond hair falling over his forehead just as it always did.

The sight of him somehow made her come back to herself, as if seeing his face had awoken the deepest, truest part of her.

Of course.

She wasn't supposed to be helping August. He was a demon. He'd kidnapped her, kept her suspended outside time until he was ready to use her to further his own ends.

But Caleb....

He'd come here to save her, just as she'd prayed he would.

She reached out, and her fingers touched an invisible barrier. Of course—August had guided her in creating it, but because it had come from her, she should be able to remove it just as easily as she'd brought it into being.

When she focused on doing so, however, nothing seemed to happen. The barrier continued to shimmer around her, even as she did her best to imagine it crumbling away to nothing.

Maybe this was one time when she needed some help from a friend.

*Caleb....*

His head went up at once, so she knew he'd heard her.

And then there was the welcome sound of his voice in her mind.

*Delia! Are you all right?*

*Hanging in there,* she thought back at him, and he grinned, that flash of white teeth she knew she'd never get tired of.

*Ready to get down?*

*Yes,* she replied. *But I think we need to do this together. We need to think of the barrier dissolving and floating away into nothing. Can you do that?*

*Absolutely.*

He moved closer and placed his hands against the barrier, and Delia did the same. She couldn't feel his fingertips, but somehow she sensed the way the shimmering veil seemed to shudder, as though something had struck it.

Good.

*I think it's working,* she told him. *Keep going.*

Another shudder, stronger this time. A flash at the corner of her vision told her Ty and August were still going at it, and she prayed they'd stay occupied until she was well out of this containment field or whatever you wanted to call the invisible wall that surrounded her.

And then the barrier shivered away into nothing, falling apart into shiny specks like a handful of glitter thrown on the wind.

Caleb's fingers closed on hers, strong, reassuring.

Real.

"Thank God," she said, and knew the words

had come out almost as a sob. "How did you know where to find me?"

"A bunch of supernatural detective work," Caleb replied. He continued to hold onto her hands, almost as if he feared she would disappear again if he let go.

Somehow, she didn't mind too much. However, she also knew she couldn't allow herself to get distracted. "We have to work fast," she said. "I think the portal is already starting to open."

At once, his brows drew together. "Where?" he demanded, looking around as if he expected to see a gateway opening on the other side of the earth-walled room where they stood.

"It hasn't touched this plane yet," she replied. "But it will soon if we don't stop it." She paused there, trying to think of the best way to describe what she was feeling. "It's like a wound in the fabric between worlds, and it's getting bigger. August is using the river's energy to tear it open, but if we—"

A roar of fury from across the room cut her off. August had broken free from Ty's hold and was advancing on them, his human façade finally cracking. Otherworldly fire blazed in his blood-hued eyes, and the air around him seemed to shimmer, almost as if he gave off as much heat as a furnace.

"You will not interfere!" August snarled, raising his hands. Dark energy crackled between his fingers and blazed here and there pure red, like magma breaking through a volcanic crust. "The gateway had already begun to open, and there's nothing you can do to stop it!"

Caleb stepped in front of Delia, as though he intended to use himself as a shield, but she moved to stand beside him instead. "We'll do this together," she said, her voice firm.

At least, she hoped it sounded firm. Inside, she was shaking like the proverbial leaf, although she couldn't say for sure whether that was because she was scared shitless or because her body was merely reacting to being released from the binding spell.

The demon's power bore down on them, inexorable as an approaching tsunami, but Delia reacted instinctively, raising a shield not so very different from the one that had held her suspended in the air only a few minutes earlier. This time, though, she knew she was firmly in control, with the last dregs of August's dark magic ebbing away, and dark fire bounced off the invisible barrier. She had no clear idea how she'd done it, but desperate instinct had somehow shaped her chaotic new abilities into something useful.

"Nice work," Caleb commented, still wearing that same fierce grin. "But we have to focus on that portal."

Delia closed her eyes, reaching out with her newfound abilities beyond the earthen chamber.

There—she could feel it now, a ragged tear in reality itself, growing wider with each passing second. Through it, she sensed something vast and hungry pressing against the boundary, eager to break through.

"It's almost big enough," she murmured. Better not to advertise what she'd learned too loudly, just in case August didn't know exactly what was happening with the portal. "Caleb, we have maybe minutes before—"

August lunged toward them with inhuman speed, reminding Delia of nothing more than those frightening "fast zombies" from the *28 Days Later* films. Somehow, Ty managed to intercept him, and the two of them slammed into the earthen wall hard enough to make dirt rain down from the ceiling.

"Now would be good!" Ty called out, face taut with effort and strands of hair coming loose from his ponytail. Bony fingers tight around his arms, August Sellers snarled, baring teeth that were now nothing close to human, and instead looked like the fangs of some terrible creature of the ocean's depths.

Delia's mind raced as she fought to come up with a solution to an utterly unprecedented situation. How could they seal something that existed between dimensions? She was just a real estate agent with a few special powers, not one of the Avengers or something.

Self-defeating thoughts like that wouldn't help, though. She needed to focus on a solution, no matter how crazy it might seem.

Looking away from Ty, she saw the curving patterns carved into the packed-earth walls. She'd been so focused on the river's energy that she'd barely noticed them, but now....

"Caleb," she said, "look at the walls."

He followed her gaze, taking in the intricate patterns carved into the earth around them. "What about them? Those are the same patterns August used to bind his minions to him. They're not going to help us."

"That's where you're wrong," she returned, and Caleb frowned, clearly not understanding what she was trying to get at. "They're *binding* patterns, right? So why can't we use them to bind the portal and close it forever? Just because August made the things doesn't mean we can't use them for our own purposes."

Understanding warmed Caleb's cola-brown eyes. "How are we supposed to get them to work for us?"

"They need to be powered by someone with the right kind of energy." She paused there before adding, "Someone with demonic blood."

August must have overheard their discussion

despite their best attempts to speak quietly, because his struggles against Ty became more frantic. "No!" he roared. "I will not be denied again!"

With a surge of desperate strength, he shoved Ty off him, throwing the half angel to the ground, and began chanting in harsh, guttural words that made the air itself writhe. Now Delia could see the shape of the portal beginning to grow solid on the far side of the chamber, even as the boundary between worlds grew thinner and thinner. Somehow, it felt hard to breathe, as if the emerging gate was starting to suck the oxygen out of the air itself.

"Do it," she told Caleb, her tone urgent. "I'll help you."

Mouth grim, Caleb pulled back a bandage on his palm, revealing a thin cut that looked as if it had only begun to heal. As crimson drops of blood hit the earthen floor, they began to glow with a strange inner light, oddly beautiful, as if he'd dripped a scatter of garnets on the ground.

Then they joined hands again, his blood smearing against her fingers. She couldn't pay attention to that, however. No, she had to focus on the shapes carved into the walls, sigils that seemed to twist in on themselves, almost like the ancient ouroboros symbol, but more complicated, darker... something that could trap energy within, just as it had trapped the minds of the men the demon August had seized for his own uses.

But if those shapes were traps, that meant they could also trap the magic being used to create the portal, could render it inert.

Caleb stared at her, dark eyes now intense with a combination of concentration and comprehension. The symbol placed at the north position of the compass began to blaze, red-hued light rippling along its mind-bending curves.

*I think it's working,* she said, and Caleb nodded.

*I think you're right. But don't stop.*

As best she could, Delia gulped in some air, forcing it past the tightness in her chest, and then moved her focus to the symbol at the east compass point. A few seconds later, flames moved along it as well.

Caleb's grin now reminded her of one that a warrior who'd just lopped off an enemy's head might wear.

*Have I told you that you're brilliant?*

*Not recently.*

A third symbol caught flame.

August snarled and raised his hands, dark energy forming around him like thunderheads on a hot summer afternoon. "You're going to regret this, you interfering bitch!"

But instead of attacking her directly or trying to break her contact with Caleb, the demon turned toward the weakening portal, now just a faint shimmer in the air. Mouth wide in an unholy grimace, he began tearing at the boundary itself with clawed fingers as he tried to widen the breach through sheer force.

Wind came out of nowhere, whistling in the still air inside the chamber.

Every scene Delia had ever seen in a sci-fi film where people got sucked out of the airlock suddenly began to replay in her head, and terror sent adrenaline surging along each nerve ending.

"He's going to try to pull me through!" she shouted at Caleb.

The suction was unlike anything she'd ever experienced before. Her feet lifted from the ground, and he hung on to her with grim fingers, his grin turning into a rictus of effort.

But the blood that smeared both their hands made his purchase tricky at best, and she slipped an inch or so.

Shit. *Shit.*

Delia stared into his frightened eyes and saw he'd just realized the same thing she had.

He wasn't going to be able to hang on much longer.

No way was he going to lose Delia. Not when he'd just found her.

Caleb tightened his grip. Deep down, though, he knew that brute force wasn't going to be enough to save her. He'd have to reach within and use powers he generally did his best to ignore.

Flames rippled along his arms and hands—not to destroy, but to clear away the blood that smeared his fingers and threatened to send Delia into the abyss. It touched her, too, and past the terror, he saw wonder in her eyes as those same flames licked her hands clean as well.

Every muscle screaming with effort, he pulled her closer, moving his grip farther and farther up her forearms until he was able to pull her close and hang on with both arms. His groin wanted to acknowledge the exquisite sensation of having her pressed against him like this, with only a bunch of sequins and a little fabric between her body and his, but he knew now was not the time for that.

Maybe it would never be.

Air roared past his ears, and he somehow understood that if they didn't get that goddamn portal closed soon, there wouldn't be anything left to breathe.

Delia shouted, "We have to close the circuit!"

Right. Three of the symbols still flickered with dark flames, but unless they were able to activate the fourth one, they wouldn't be able to trap the magic that kept the portal open.

White light flared behind them. Caleb risked a

quick look over his shoulder and saw that Ty had pushed himself back to his feet and had flung himself at August, who now had fully reverted to his demon form, all glaring red eyes and black scaly skin. Tall, misshapen horns protruded from his forehead, a sign that he indeed was a higher form of demon.

Not that Ty seemed to care. Caleb wasn't sure where the half angel had summoned the strength, because blood dripped down from a nasty gash in his forehead and his left eye already sported an impressive shiner, but the white glow surrounding him was brighter than it had ever been, as if the man understood he had to put everything he could into this final attack.

Which meant Caleb and Delia needed to do the same thing.

Their eyes met, and their wills combined. Flames rippled along the symbol on the west wall of the chamber, and in the next instant, all four of them blazed as brightly as if they'd just been doused with gasoline.

Under their feet, the ground shuddered.

The glowing hole in the world shivered, pieces of its energy breaking off like embers rising from a campfire. August let out a hideous shriek as he was pulled backward, away from Ty.

But too close to Caleb.

One bony hand shot out and grabbed him by

the wrist. "You should never have come back," the demon spat. "If I'm to be trapped in Hell for all eternity, so are you!"

And Caleb was torn from Delia's arms as the portal continued to collapse, sucking them into the thing as if it were some kind of supernatural black hole.

She gasped—but then she hastened forward and grabbed hold of him again, bare heels digging into the dirt in a futile attempt to keep him from being pulled in.

Then Ty was there as well, the white glow of his angelic energy surrounding her and Caleb as well.

For just a second, that glow turned almost acid green. August Sellers' demonic face distorted further, mouth widening as he bared his fangs in rage.

And then he was through the portal as it came crashing down, shivering into nothing, sparks flying everywhere.

The earth groaned again, and dirt began to fall from the ceiling again, faster this time, sending irritating flecks into his eyes.

Caleb wasn't sure what had just happened—had all their power combined to create the massive surge of energy required to collapse the gate once and for all?—but he knew one thing.

They needed to get the hell out of there before they were crushed to death.

"Hotel room!" he shouted at Ty, and the half angel nodded.

Caleb looked down at Delia. Her hair was starting to fall down and dirt smudged the tip of her nose, but she was still the most beautiful thing he'd ever seen.

"Hang on," he told her, and she wrapped her arms around his waist.

Then they were gone.

# Chapter Nineteen

— ⸨⸨ · ☾ · ⸩⸩ —

THE THREE OF THEM EMERGED IN A HOTEL suite Delia had never seen before. Sitting on the couch in the middle of the living room area were her friend Pru and, for some reason, Aaron Sanchez.

They both gaped at Delia and Caleb and Ty, with Pru's expression shifting at once to concern after she seemed to focus on the half angel.

"Holy crap—did you just do ten rounds with Riddick Bowe at Caesar's Palace or something?"

Ty reached up to touch the puffy skin around his eye, now turning spectacular shades of purple and dark blue. "No—maybe more like five with a demon under the Aquarius."

"Should I get you some ice?" she asked.

"Sure," he replied, then headed over to one of the unoccupied club chairs and basically fell into it.

Delia couldn't really blame him for wanting to collapse. Although she hadn't been physically knocked around like Ty Carter, she also felt as if she'd been pummeled, just in a different kind of way.

Aaron looked over at Caleb. "What happened?"

"We won," Caleb said briefly. "So I'm pretty sure you don't have to worry about selling the house now. The thing your grandmother was trying to warn us about isn't a problem anymore."

"Well, not exactly," Ty put in. Pru had just handed him a baggie full of ice, and he pressed it against his eye and winced slightly. The cut on his forehead had stopped bleeding, but he'd need to clean it up at some point. For now, though, it was probably better if he attended to his eye first.

Delia crossed her arms and sent him what she hoped was a steely look. "What do you mean? With Sellers gone—"

"He's gone," Ty broke in, "but the river is still without a guardian. Sooner or later, someone's going to try to exploit its power again."

This comment obviously didn't sit very well with Caleb, because he glared at the half angel. "You need to shut up about that. You're not roping Delia into being some kind of river guardian."

"Whoa, whoa." She held her hands up and

looked over at Ty. What the hell was he even talking about?

Clearly, she'd missed a lot during the time August Sellers was holding her captive.

But she remembered the terrible visions she'd seen while she was feeling her way around in the utter darkness of her prison—an older woman, possibly Alba, falling to the floor as unseen hands appeared to choke her to death. A car crushed by a semi on a dark highway under glittering, uncaring stars.

And the much younger woman, probably even younger than Delia, fleeing her apartment, a suitcase in each hand.

"August Sellers killed or scared off anyone in the Sanchez family who could have been the next guardian," she said, and everyone stared at her, frankly astonished.

"How do you know that?" Aaron demanded.

Considering it was his family they were talking about, Delia supposed it made sense that he'd be the one asking the questions.

"Because I saw it in a vision," she said. "Your grandmother didn't die of natural causes—I saw something choking her."

His wasn't the sort of complexion that could turn exactly pale, but he looked stunned nonetheless. "The doctors said it was a heart attack."

"Well, it wasn't," she told him. "I'm sorry."

He was silent for a moment. "Did you see anything else?"

She nodded. "There was a terrible accident—a car and a semi. It looked like it was out in the middle of the desert somewhere, but I didn't see any mile markers or anything that could tell me where it was."

But Aaron obviously knew what she was talking about, because his expression turned very grim. "My cousin Isaac. He was driving back to Laughlin from Needles, and a semi plowed right into him. He didn't have a chance."

"No, he wouldn't," Caleb remarked. "Not when a demon was gunning for him."

Yes, those were pretty terrible odds. Even though Delia knew she shouldn't expect demons to do anything but leave a trail of destruction in their wake, she still had a hard time accepting the notion that they would so wantonly kill off anyone in their way.

But....

"There was someone else," she said. "A woman who looked like she might have been around twenty-five. She was pretty and wore her hair in a French braid. I saw her hurrying out of an apartment and carrying a couple of suitcases."

Even as she spoke, she feared that maybe the final vision she'd seen hadn't been connected to any of this at all, that possibly the demons had allowed something random to slip into her mind's eye to throw her off the scent.

However, Aaron spoke up at once. "That must have been my cousin Eiza. She took off in the middle of the night right after our grandmother's funeral. Didn't say anything to anyone, just took her stuff and bailed out. I guess her apartment was month-to-month, so she didn't get in too much trouble over abandoning the lease, but...."

"She had to have known something," Pru said, apparently deciding to jump into the conversation once she thought there was a suitable opening. "Maybe she was just psychic enough to guess that something was horribly wrong about her grandmother's death."

Caleb ran his hand through his hair, pushing away the one stubborn lock that always wanted to fall over his forehead. "So she skipped town and hoped that would be enough to keep her from meeting the same fate. After all, if she wasn't in Laughlin, then she couldn't be a river guardian."

It seemed like kind of a cowardly thing to do, but then, Delia wasn't sure how she would have reacted if she'd been in Eiza's shoes. Facing down demons with Caleb at her side was one thing, but if she'd had to do it alone?

Maybe she would have skipped town as well... and hoped that would be enough to keep her alive.

"But," Caleb continued, now looking much

more cheerful, "with the demons gone, there's no reason for her to stay away. She can be the new river guardian, and Delia won't have to be dragged into any of this."

If she'd been braver, maybe she would have spoken up and said it was fine and that she knew how important it was to keep Laughlin safe.

Now, though...now she was just tired and wanted to go home to Las Vegas. The Sanchezes had been guarding the river for generations, and as far as she was concerned, they could continue to do that.

"Do you know where your cousin Eiza went?" Delia asked.

Aaron frowned. "I think I heard my mom say she was in San Diego. But I don't know for sure."

"That's all right," Pru said, her expression also much more chipper than it had been a few minutes earlier. "I just need her name and her last known address, and I can find her. Let me get my laptop."

Having a best friend who was a private investigator definitely came in handy.

"I think I have it on my phone," Aaron said as he dug his iPhone out of the pocket of his jeans.

Thank God the cell phone hadn't gotten lost during all the craziness of the past few days. Delia couldn't say the same for hers. She'd had her bag with her when she was snatched, but she assumed August Sellers must have gotten rid of it, along with her ID and her phone. That was going to be a real mess to sort out once she got back to Las Vegas.

"Yeah," he said a moment later, just as Pru returned with her computer and then set it down on the coffee table. "Eiza Mendoza, 4611 Desert Sage Drive, Number 15."

"Thanks," Prudence replied, typing away furiously. "And yep—there it is. She's now at 62 Seabreeze Way, Number 11."

"Is her phone number the same?" Aaron asked. "Because if she hasn't changed it, I can call her."

Delia couldn't help wondering why he hadn't reached out to his cousin before this if he had her information stored right in his phone. Then again, back when Eiza had fled town, probably no one had known why she'd felt the need to bolt, and she could see how Aaron might have thought her sudden departure hadn't been prompted by anything more than a bad breakup that had sent her in search of a change of scenery.

Besides, not all cousins were close. Hell, Delia didn't do much more than exchange holiday cards with her cousins in Seattle and Chicago, so it wasn't as if she could give Aaron Sanchez too much grief for not staying in touch with his cousin after she left Laughlin.

Pru looked back at her computer. "It's definitely a Nevada area code, so it doesn't look like her number was changed."

"Great," Caleb said. "Then Aaron can call his cousin and let her know the coast is clear, and she can come back and be the river guardian, and we can all get on with our lives."

That seemed like the simplest solution. On the other hand, there was a strong chance Eiza wouldn't want to return even after she learned that her reason for running off to San Diego was no longer a factor.

Delia hoped Eiza would understand why she needed to come back, though...if for no other reason than she was pretty sure Caleb would hop over to Southern California and do whatever he had to in order to convince her that she needed to come back to Laughlin. Delia definitely didn't want him strong-arming Aaron's cousin into compliance.

"Well, I'll start with seeing if she's okay," Aaron said. "Is it all right if I go into one of the bedrooms so I can have some privacy?"

"Sure," Caleb replied. "You can use the one I was sharing with Ty."

He pointed toward a closed door on the opposite wall, and Aaron got up from the couch, and went inside, although he didn't shut the door behind him.

Delia had halfway expected Ty to protest—he probably needed to lie down and rest—but he didn't say anything. In fact, the wound on his forehead already looked mostly healed, and when he pulled away the bag of ice, the puffiness and discoloration around his eye had diminished by at least half, maybe more.

His angelic blood speeding along the healing process?

It seemed as good an explanation as any.

He put the bag of ice down on the coffee table. Since it seemed to be made of some kind of plastic, the droplets of condensation that had formed on the bag weren't too big a deal.

"There's something that's been bothering me, though," he said, and Delia couldn't help smiling.

"Only one?"

"Well, it's the biggest one." He gave an experimental stretch of his shoulders, as if to gauge how his muscle soreness was healing, and then continued. "I want to know how August Sellers—whatever his real name was—knew about your powers, Delia, and how they could help him with his ritual. It's not the sort of thing that's common knowledge, after all."

No, it wasn't. Sure, people in the Las Vegas real estate community knew about her ghost-whispering talent, but absolutely no one other than the people sitting in this hotel suite had any idea that her gifts...powers, whatever you wanted to call them...had recently expanded far beyond talking to ghosts.

"I have no idea," she said. "I haven't told anyone anything."

Pru had been watching Ty as he spoke, her expression half perplexed. It seemed obvious enough that she'd also noticed his accelerated healing, although it didn't look as though she planned to comment on it.

"Don't demons just...know stuff?" she asked.

"Not necessarily," Caleb replied, even though Pru had directed the question at Ty. "It's not as if they're all linked psychically or anything close to it. In fact, most demons are all about chaos. They like causing trouble, but they're not masterminds."

"Except a few at the top," Ty put in. "They're capable of much higher-level thinking. So my best guess is that the demon calling himself August Sellers was in league with someone else even higher on the food chain, someone who must have been passing information along to him."

None of that sounded very good. The last thing Delia wanted to believe was that there was a network of executive demons—for lack of a better word—who'd decided she was a target simply because she'd gone up a few steps of the psychic ladder over the past couple of months.

For some reason, she thought of the dream she'd had not long after the battle at the Desert Paradise casino, of the man with the cold blue eyes. She'd mostly forgotten it since then...or, more to the point, done her best to put it out of her mind... but now she wondered if he had something to do with this.

No, that was ridiculous. It had been a dream and nothing else.

All the same, she couldn't quite stop herself from shivering, and at once Caleb sent her a concerned glance.

"Are you all right?"

"I'm fine," she said. "It's just the A/C is turned up really high in here, and I'm freezing in this dress."

"Well," Pru said as she set her laptop down on the coffee table, "I can help you with that. Good thing we're the same size. I've got some new clothes in my room—let's get you something a little more practical to wear."

That sounded like a great idea. She was taller than Pru, so any pants would be a little short on her, but high-water pants were a small price to pay in exchange for getting out of this damn dress.

Although...was that a flicker of regret in Caleb's eyes as she left the room to get changed?

Doubtful. It seemed more likely that he was annoyed they were wasting time on something as frivolous as a change of clothing when what they really needed to do was figure out how August Sellers had known she was a little more than your average Las Vegas real estate agent.

All the clothing Pru set out had tags from Kohl's still on them.

"We weren't expecting to stay overnight when we left Las Vegas," Prudence said as Delia adjourned to the bathroom to climb out of the sequined gown August Sellers had made her wear. "And we also didn't know how long we were going to be here, so I bought stuff for a couple of days."

Thank God for that—and also thank God for the new underwear. Delia supposed she could have stayed in the same panties if she had to, but it felt much better to pull on a new pair and a new bra, and then put the new clothes on top of everything. The pants were capri style, so the length didn't matter as much, and when she topped them with a sleeveless blouse that had some tonal embroidery on it, she felt almost human again.

True, everything was black, which Delia thought tended to wash her out, but she wasn't going to worry about the palette of her new outfit when the important thing was that she had one at all.

Her hair was a mess, but she removed all the pins and shook it out as best she could, and she thought it would pass. Luckily, it was naturally straight, so there was a limit to how destroyed it could actually get.

When they returned to the living room, she

saw that Aaron was already there, although he didn't look terribly happy.

"She doesn't think it's safe to come back," he said.

A perfectly natural response...but definitely not the one any of them had wanted to hear.

Ty's mouth opened, but before he could speak, Caleb said, "Let me talk to her."

Aaron's brows lifted slightly, although he seemed to realize it was better if he didn't try to refuse the request. "Okay. But I don't think you're going to get very far."

"Let me be the judge of that."

The other man shrugged, then handed over his iPhone. Caleb took it, the corners of his mouth lifting in a small smile.

"Hey, Eiza," he said, sounding completely relaxed and not as if he'd just faced a high-level demon and closed a portal to Hell. "My name's Caleb. I'm a friend of Aaron's."

"Friend" was probably a stretch, but since Aaron didn't protest, everyone else remained silent as well.

"I just wanted to personally assure you that Laughlin is safe now," Caleb went on. "A couple of friends and I just took care of your family's problem...the same one that made you leave town in the first place. We know your grandmother's death wasn't from natural causes, but the...person... responsible is gone and won't be coming back."

Another pause, longer this time. Delia wished she could hear what Aaron's cousins was saying, but Caleb had probably decided that putting her on speaker would have been kind of rude, considering the strain she was under.

"I understand that," Caleb said at length. "And I want to give you my personal promise that we'll come back and help out at the first sign of trouble. There won't be any, though."

Eiza spoke again, and this time, Caleb smiled.

"Yes, I'm sure of it. And I'll have Aaron give you our contact information so you know you can reach out at any time. Deal?"

He was silent, and then nodded.

"Perfect. Then I'll let your cousin know you'll be back in Laughlin tomorrow." He ended the call there and the handed the phone back to Aaron. "Okay, we're set. Eiza needs to pack up her things, but she said she should be here by tomorrow afternoon sometime."

That seemed almost too easy. But then Delia thought she saw the quirk at the corner of Caleb's mouth and guessed he might have sent a little demonic energy over the airwaves as he spoke to her, just enough to convince Eiza that everything was fine and that she needed to come home as soon as she could.

After all, the guy had always been there when Delia needed him...but his surprising dependability didn't erase the fact that he was still a quarter demon.

"And that means you're good to go, too," Caleb told Aaron. "Although I suppose you won't be able to sell the house now, since Eiza will need to live there."

To Delia's surprise, Aaron didn't look as dismayed by this prospect as she might have thought.

"It's okay," he said. "While I was talking to my cousin, I had to put her on hold for a minute to take another call. The real estate agency in Bullhead City wants a second interview, so things are looking up on that front, too. If I get the job, I'll be able to find something of my own either here in Laughlin or across the river, and I won't have to worry about getting the commission on my grandmother's house."

Thank God for that. As far as Delia was able to tell, they'd wrapped this whole thing up pretty neatly...well, except for the part where they had no idea how August Sellers had even known he needed to lure her down here so he could use her powers to open the portal...and now it seemed as if Aaron and his cousin might be able to get on with their lives.

"That's great," Caleb says. "It sounds like you

have a lot you need to handle, so you should prob-ably get started on that. We'll let you know if we need anything else."

"Um—" Aaron began, but Caleb had already put his hand on the guy's arm and was guiding him to the door and ushering him out into the hallway.

"Good luck with that second interview," he said, then closed the door behind him. He flashed Delia a smile and added, "Thought he'd never leave. But now we can get down to the next order of business."

# Chapter Twenty

—·‹‹·۰·››·—

ALL RIGHT, SO HE MIGHT HAVE USED A little demonic persuasion to get Aaron out of the suite at Harrah's, just as he'd beamed a bit of that otherworldly charm over to Eiza Mendoza so she'd agree that she absolutely needed to come back to Laughlin and pick up the mantle of river guardian. As far as Caleb was concerned, he hadn't been out of line. That was Eiza's job and responsibility, not Delia's, and Aaron had served his purpose and needed to be hustled along so the rest of them could get on to the more important stuff.

"Maybe there's some evidence in Sellers' office that might tell us how he knew about Delia," he said as he sat down on the sofa next to her. Although Caleb had thought she was stunning in that sequined gown, he had to admit she looked more herself in the clothes Pru had loaned her, even if she was wearing black from head to toe.

"And exactly how are we supposed to get in there?" Pru inquired. However, she looked vaguely amused, and he guessed she was just as glad that he'd gotten rid of Aaron Sanchez as he was.

"I doubt anyone knows Sellers is missing yet," Delia pointed out. "It feels like a century since we escaped that chamber under the Aquarius, but it's only been a half hour at the most. Also, it's past eight o'clock, and I doubt anyone expects to see him until tomorrow morning sometime."

"Unless he was supposed to be attending another river cruise," Ty said, although his tone was almost doubtful, as if he didn't quite believe what he was saying.

"No reason for that," Caleb replied. "The one he hosted did its job, even if we almost sank the boat. Besides, he was supposed to be opening a portal into Hell tonight. I'm pretty sure he kept his calendar clear."

Both Delia and Pru snickered a little at that comment, although Delia sobered soon enough. "I'm sure all that's true," she said. "But even if no one's going to be looking for him before tomorrow morning, I'm sure it's still going to be hard to get into his office."

"I could try swiping another key card," Pru

offered, although she also didn't seem too sure of herself.

"That won't work," Ty said. "Not that I don't believe you'd be able to get another one, but a key card someone's carrying on the casino floor wouldn't work to get us into an executive suite."

"Right," she said, and let out a breath that wasn't quite a sigh. "It's annoying, because I know right where his office is located. I looked it up on the blueprints for the Aquarius after I found out which suite was his."

Because of course she had. Although Pru occasionally got on his nerves, Caleb couldn't deny that she was very useful to have around.

"Well, that's something," Delia said, and was silent for a moment, mulling over the problem. "Couldn't one of you use your powers to get yourself inside?"

"We've never been in there before," Caleb pointed out. He hated this restriction on his teleportation talent, but it was what it was. "If I don't know where I'm going, I can't send myself there."

"But what if you knew what Sellers' office looked like?" Pru asked next. "Would that be enough to get you there?"

"Sure," Caleb replied, and Ty nodded, signaling he'd be able to manage the same thing. "But since we don't know what it looks like, I'm not sure how that's supposed to help us."

"Easy," she said as she reached for her laptop. "I'll just find an image online."

Even Delia looked skeptical, and she had a better idea of her friend's abilities than anyone else did. "How do you expect to manage that? I can't imagine Sellers would be too thrilled to have pictures of his office floating around on the internet."

"No, he probably wouldn't," Pru said, although she was smiling as she began typing away. "But it's hard to scrub that sort of stuff, especially if someone posted it in a locked-down Facebook account or whatever."

Ty straightened in his chair. Almost all the damage from his battle with Sellers had faded by now, with just some slight discoloration under his left eye to show that he'd been sporting a pretty serious shiner only a few minutes earlier.

"If it's locked down," he said, "how are you going to find it?"

Pru didn't look up. "O ye of little faith."

Another burst of typing, and another. Then she grinned in triumph as she spun her laptop around. "See?"

Sure enough, there was a Facebook post from someone named Ted Donnelly, one that showed a spacious office with an amazing view of the Colorado River below.

Underneath was a not-so-glowing caption.

*My asshole boss gets this huge office, and the bastard won't even dig into his pockets enough to throw us a holiday party this year. I don't know what happened to the guy—he's totally turned into Scrooge.*

"Well, then," Delia said with a grin. "Sounds like someone was a little disgruntled."

"Demons don't make very good supervisors," Ty remarked. "Also, even though he would have tried to hide it, once the demon inhabiting August Sellers fully took over, some of his true nature would have begun to assert itself."

That made sense. Demons were a lot better at making themselves look human than actually acting like real people.

Enough of the chitchat, though. Caleb leaned in to study the photo so he could impress all the details on his mind. In front of the floor-to-ceiling windows was a large desk of what looked like burled walnut...very expensive. A pair of fiddleleaf figs—real, not fake—stood sentinel behind the desk, bracketing the window. Part of the view was obscured by a trio of curved screens that sat on top of the desk, although a large leather-upholstered chair was just visible behind them.

"I've seen enough," Caleb said. He glanced over at Ty. "You good?"

"I think so."

Perfect. Time to get this show on the road.

"Then I'll take Delia with me, and you can take Pru."

For a second, Ty looked as if he wanted to protest that he and Caleb should go alone. But then the half angel appeared to realize that they'd have a much better chance of getting into August Sellers' computer if they brought Pru with them, and of course there was no chance Delia would consent to staying behind.

Especially since all manner of shit had gone down the last time they were separated.

"Okay," Ty said. "But we need to be in and out as quickly as possible."

Caleb was all for that. Although he didn't expect that Sellers would be able to claw his way back to this plane any time soon—or maybe ever—he also didn't want to deal with some over-zealous security guard coming along to investigate any movement in an office that should have been empty at that hour of the night.

"No worries."

Delia came over to him and calmly looped her arms around his waist. "Ready when you are," she said.

He couldn't allow himself to react to her, except for a nod to show he'd acknowledged her comment. A few feet away, Pru approached Ty almost timidly, although he seemed matter-of-fact enough as he put his arms around her and said, "This will be quick, but you still need to hang on."

A second later, the four of them materialized in front of the big walnut desk. Because the windows didn't appear to have any coverings, enough illumination from the lights of Laughlin streamed in to make the rest of the room visible enough. The photo Pru had found online hadn't shown the sitting area off to one side, with a leather couch and two matching chairs and a coffee table of what looked like hammered copper, but it was far enough away that it hadn't interfered with their arrival.

At once, Pru stepped away from Ty and hurried over to the desk. She had her head down, and Caleb wondered if she was blushing, or trying to conceal something about her reaction to the way the half angel had held her a moment earlier.

Hard to say. Although you could walk around in here without having to turn on the lights, some of the finer details were lost.

Caleb was glad of that, though, just because now there was probably a lower chance of anyone noticing they were even here.

He noticed Pru hadn't started working on the computer yet, but instead was opening the desk drawers and hunting around inside. Meanwhile, Delia and Ty stood behind her, looking awkward.

Well, they all knew that Prudence was the one who'd have to do the heavy lifting here.

"You think Sellers left a file in there with all the info about his demon friends?" he asked dryly.

Her mouth tightened in irritation. "No," she replied. "But, like I've tried to explain about a million times by now, I'm not a computer hacker. If I sit down and try to brute-force my way into the jerk's computer, I'll get locked out—and probably set off an alarm somewhere. This may not be the Pentagon or something, but I've learned that these casino types have plenty of safeguards built into their systems."

"Then what are you doing?"

"Trying to see if he taped his password somewhere," Pru said, her response somewhat muffled because she'd gotten down on her hands and knees and was feeling around under the desk. "You'd be surprised how many executive types do that. It's like they carry so many numbers around in their head that they can't be arsed to remember a password."

Maybe, but....

"You do remember that we're dealing with a demon here, and not some C-suite bozo with a degree from Wharton," Caleb pointed out.

"Doesn't matter. Sellers was a real person once, right? And the demon inside him took over at some point?"

That appeared to be the case. Sometimes demons managed to slither their way onto this plane without possessing anyone, but that didn't happen nearly as often as them simply taking up residence and then doing their best to hang on to their mortal shells, like some kind of diabolical hermit crab.

"I suppose so."

"She could be right," Ty put in. "Even demons can't completely override twenty years of bad human habits."

"And...got it!" Pru pushed her way out from under the desk, holding a yellow sticky note with tape on two sides, as if whoever had placed it down there had been worried that the original adhesive from the Post-It wouldn't be up to the task. "Jerk thought he was being cagey by taping it to the rear of the desk drawer instead of underneath, but it was there. Now let's see what's in this bad boy."

She settled herself in the oversized chair, looking very small and as if she had ended up sitting there because it was "bring your daughter to work" day.

Not that demons had daughters. At least, not that Caleb had ever heard of.

Delia and Ty moved closer, although they hung far enough back that they couldn't be accused of crowding Prudence too closely. She didn't look up, but instead typed a combination of letters and numbers and symbols on the login screen before her.

At once, the login disappeared and was replaced by pure black across all three screens.

"Cheerful," she commented. "Some people like something a little more colorful for their desktops, but I suppose demons don't go for that sort of thing."

There was still some kind of menu bar along the top, and Pru clicked on it and opened the file explorer. Caleb had always been a Mac guy, so he'd be the first to admit he didn't really know much about how Windows worked. Luckily, Prudence seemed to know what she was doing, because she opened a window that appeared to show all the files on the hard drive.

Leaning forward, she stared intently at the screen. Just a moment later, she said, "Gotcha."

"What did you find?"

"Oh, just a little folder labeled 'Styx.'"

"What?" Delia asked, moving forward. Her face was still pale, but she otherwise seemed recovered from her recent ordeal.

Caleb wished he could reach out to take her hand, but he wasn't sure how she would receive such a gesture. Instead, he retreated to his usual safe sarcasm and said, "You're really surprised there's a connection between our friends in California and August Sellers?"

"I guess I am," she said. "Especially since you just told us that demons aren't usually linked."

"Linked *psychically*," he reminded her. "I never said some of them couldn't be working together."

Ty ignored all this and asked, "What's in the folder?"

Pru clicked on it. Inside were a bunch of files with numbers for their names. However, their subjects were clear enough—photo after photo of Delia, one of them obviously the professional head-shot from the Dunne & Dunne website, but much more what appeared to be random snaps taken on the street, or in various places around town, whether they were of Delia emerging from Trader Joe's with a laden shopping cart or her picking up her dry cleaning...or pulling into the garage of her home.

"He was tailing me?" she demanded.

"I doubt he would've gotten his hands dirty like that," Pru responded. "I'm sure he just hired someone to follow you."

"Oh, that makes me feel so much better."

However, her tone was wry enough that Caleb could tell she was beginning to recover from the shock of seeing all those photos of herself.

The folder wasn't all about Delia, though. There were also images of Alba Sanchez's house and even a few of Aaron himself.

"Looks like Mr. Sellers had been planning this

for a while," Ty commented. "He was just waiting for all the pieces to line up."

Caleb didn't like the sound of that very much. "Even before that mess at the Desert Paradise?"

"Maybe," Pru said as she studied the files on the screen in front of her. "Some of these are dated back to the end of February, which would definitely have been before the poker tournament."

Delia had crossed her arms, almost as if she was hugging herself. The black top she'd borrowed from Prudence didn't have any sleeves, and the A/C in the office was turned up pretty high, but Caleb didn't think that was the real reason.

"So...was the ritual at the river sort of a backup plan?"

Of course. He didn't know why he hadn't seen it before, but then, it was kind of hard to detect a pattern when you only had one data point to work with.

"That's exactly it," he replied. "And it's what Hank Bowers and the rest of those possessed goons at the tournament were trying to accomplish. They wanted to open a gate to Hell with all the energies they were summoning, and when that fell apart, it was time for Sellers to step in and see if he could seal the deal."

"Those are some very determined demons," Ty said, and Caleb shrugged.

"If you'd ever been to Hell, you'd know why they want to get out of there so badly."

Delia glanced away from the computer screen at the lights of Laughlin, glittering across the surface of the river. It didn't seem as if the earth tremor they'd felt as the portal closed had traveled up through all those sublevels, because as far as he could tell, everything looked serene out there, thousands of mortals gambling and laughing and drinking and having absolutely no idea how close they'd come to utter destruction.

"But we beat them," she said, her voice firm.

"Yes," Caleb replied, "we beat them...this time."

# Chapter Twenty-One

—·《《·☾·》》·—

DELIA AND PRU DROVE BACK TO LAS VEGAS in Delia's Hyundai SUV, while Caleb followed behind in his big Range Rover. She wondered briefly why he hadn't taken his Mercedes, since it surely got better gas mileage, and then guessed he'd driven the bigger vehicle because he had passengers riding with him.

Ty, on the other hand, had said that it looked as if their work was done—for now, at least—and had promptly vanished. It was a handy way of getting around when you didn't have to worry about luggage.

But Caleb and Delia had needed to go back to Harrah's and pack up their things, among which were, miraculously, Delia's missing purse and sandals.

"Where on earth did you find these?" she

asked. She wanted to hug the purse, with all of its necessities of life, like her ID and cell phone and favorite MAC lipstick, but settled for slipping it over her shoulder.

"In the room where Sellers was holding you," Caleb told her.

She stared at him, shocked. "You found it?"

"We did," Pru put in. "But you were already gone. We figured we'd take your stuff so we could give it back when we caught up with you."

Back when that had happened, they'd probably been thinking more in terms of "if" rather than "when." But they had found her, against all odds, and now they were headed back to Las Vegas.

Headed home.

Pru was behind the wheel, though, because she told Delia that after everything she'd been through, she shouldn't have to drive another hundred miles. And while Delia had thought of protesting, she realized her friend was right.

Now she sat in the passenger seat and watched the dark desert flashing by outside the car windows. Part of her wished she could be with Caleb, but that was silly. This was her car, and that meant she needed to ride with Pru.

"Do you want me to stay with you tonight?" Prudence asked. They'd just passed a milepost that let them know Las Vegas was still fifty miles away, but Delia felt better with every minute that put Laughlin behind them.

She had a feeling it would be a long time before she went back.

Maybe never.

"I mean, you've been through a lot," Pru continued. "I think it might be better if you weren't alone tonight. I already have a toothbrush and a change of clothes with me, so it wouldn't be a big deal."

Although Delia was touched by the offer, she also knew she wanted to be alone.

Or rather, if she couldn't have Caleb there to keep her company, she'd rather be by herself...if merely to suss out why she thought his presence would be so much more comforting to her. An impartial observer would have probably commented that Caleb Lockwood wasn't the most soothing presence in the world.

However, Delia knew she was far from impartial when it came to Caleb.

"No, I'm fine," she said, and hoped she didn't sound—or look—as exhausted as she felt. "Honestly, I just want to go to bed and sleep for about a hundred years. I won't be very good company."

Pru redirected her attention from the road just long enough to give her friend a sharp look. "This isn't about hanging out and braiding each other's hair. I just think it's better if you're not alone tonight."

Once upon a time, Delia might have agreed with her. But the last few days had made a few uncomfortable thoughts bubble up in her mind, and she knew she needed time to sit down and sort them out. Having Pru hovering around and making sure everything was all right wouldn't help with that process at all.

"No, I'm really okay," she said firmly. "But I promise I'll call you if I start to feel hinky, and I'll text first thing in the morning to let you know I made it through the night just fine."

Pru's lips parted, and Delia worried that she was going to keep pushing the issue. To her relief, her friend shut her mouth again just a second later, as if she'd realized that it didn't matter what she said, that Delia had decided on a course of action and wouldn't budge.

"All right," she said at length, and her mouth twisted in a lopsided smile. "But don't bother with that early morning text. You know I won't see it."

Delia smiled in response. They wouldn't be getting into Las Vegas too late—a little before eleven, if her mental calculations were correct— and yet she had a feeling Pru would still find a reason to stay up for a few more hours after that and would want to get back into her usual routine of sleeping until at least ten in the morning, maybe later.

"Then I won't. Anyway, everything's going to be fine."

Or at least, fine for this short breathing space. She couldn't quite forget that remark of Caleb's, the one where he'd said they'd won for now. He hadn't added to the comment; he hadn't needed to.

They might have beaten August Sellers, but whoever was behind the Styx Group was still out there, watching and waiting.

And planning, no doubt.

Was the man she'd seen in her dream connected to them somehow?

*It was just a dream,* she reminded herself, even though she knew that reality wasn't what it had been a few months ago, that dreams and visions could be just as real as the actual, tangible things she could reach out and touch.

But Pru didn't know about the dream. She only knew that they'd defeated the current baddie and therefore had earned some time off.

So she didn't dispute Delia's statement and seemed content to be quiet as they drove the rest of the way into Las Vegas. And because Pru had told her during the drive that they'd covered for her as best they could, letting her mother know that urgent business in Laughlin might keep her occupied until Friday, Delia knew she could take tomorrow off to recover. She thought she'd prob-ably putter around the house, maybe go to TJ's and get her favorite comfort foods, like that awesome Greek pastry stuffed with cheese. It didn't land in her shopping cart too often because it was an unholy collision of carbs and fats, but she figured she'd earned it.

As Prudence pulled into the garage at Delia's house, though, she said, "Are you *absolutely* sure you don't want me to stay?"

"Absolutely," Delia replied. "But you'll still need to come inside to wait for your Uber."

Because Pru had told her she'd taken one over to Caleb's place, figuring it would probably be better not to leave her car parked on the street there for a period of unknown duration. None of them had known how long the rescue operation was going to take.

Hard to believe she'd driven down to Laughlin only yesterday afternoon. It felt as if she'd been away for a hundred years.

They got out of the Hyundai and headed inside. Delia had left on one of the can lights in the kitchen, figuring she didn't want the place to be pitch dark when she got home, although she flicked on some others as they headed into the living room.

Everything looked utterly the same, but the

house still didn't feel quite right, as if something fundamental about it had changed.

She knew that wasn't the problem, though. It wasn't the house that had suffered a shift at its very core.

No, that would be her.

Pru pulled out her phone and checked the app. "Only two minutes away."

She'd had Delia make the reservation as they were driving in so she wouldn't have to wait too long for the car to arrive. The timing seemed to be working out just perfectly.

"Thank you for, well"—Delia waved a hand in a direction she hoped was southward—"everything."

Pru's shoulders lifted a fraction. Not because she wasn't unmoved by Delia's gratitude, but more because she'd never been all that good at accepting thanks or praise.

"It's what friends do. I know you would have done the same for me."

Yes, she would have, without hesitation.

"Still—"

Pru's cell phone pinged right then, and she looked down at the screen. "Ride's here. I'll text you tomorrow after I get up, just to check in."

"Sounds good. I'm pretty sure the most exciting thing I'll do tomorrow is head out to TJ's at some point."

Pru grinned, surprised Delia a little by giving her a quick, fierce hug, and then picked up her satchel and her Kohl's bag of clothing and headed for the door. One final wave, and then she was gone.

The house felt strangely empty after she left, even though Delia was certainly used to being here by herself. She pulled in a breath, then went over and sprinkled some fish food into the tank. They all swam to the surface, mouths hungrily open, and a pang of guilt went through her.

No, it wasn't her fault that she hadn't been here to feed them, but the fish didn't know that.

Luckily, it didn't seem as if they'd suffered any irreparable harm by missing their feedings over the past day and a half, and once that was taken care of, she went into the kitchen to pour herself a glass of water. Thanks to the way Caleb and the gang had retrieved her purse from the room where she'd been imprisoned, she still had her phone and everything else, thank God.

At least she wouldn't have to go to the trouble of replacing the iPhone and her ID as she'd feared.

Her phone rang then, and she frowned. She doubted that Pru would be calling again so soon... and would have texted anyway unless it was a dire emergency...and as far as Delia knew, her mother had no idea that anything had gone wrong and wasn't expecting her in the office until Friday morning.

When she lifted the iPhone out of her purse, she saw it was Caleb calling.

"Just wanted to make sure you got home okay," he said.

Was it crazy to be so relieved to hear the sound of his voice? Of course, she'd had no reason to believe he wouldn't have also reached his house safely, but still, a wave of warmth went through her.

"Oh, sure," she replied, doing her best to sound utterly unconcerned. "Pru just left in her Uber. I was going to get some water and go to sleep. It's been kind of a day."

He chuckled. "That's for sure." A pause, and then he asked, "No sign of anything funky at your place?"

"None at all," Delia said. "I doubt anyone even noticed I was gone."

Except maybe nosy Mrs. Gallina, her next-door neighbor. But even if she'd butted in enough to reach out to Delia's mother to see what was going on with her daughter, she would have only learned that Delia was away on business in Laughlin, and that would have been the end of that.

Business. She supposed that was one way to look at reining in a crazed demon who wanted to open a portal to the underworld.

"Good," Caleb replied. "Same here." Another pause, and when he spoke again, something in his tone sounded subtly different, even if Delia couldn't have said exactly how. "You're not going to work tomorrow, right?"

"Yes," she said. "I figured it was probably better to take a mental health day, especially since my mother doesn't expect me to be in the office until Friday morning."

"Perfect. Would you be up for a little outing?"

She felt her eyebrows lifting. "I was just going to hang out and relax—"

"This would be relaxing," he cut in. "Someplace to go and decompress for the afternoon."

Come to think of it, a change of scenery might be a good idea. Yes, she'd been in Laughlin for a few days, but it wasn't as if she'd done any decompressing while she was there.

Pretty much the opposite, really.

"All right," she said. "As long as it's not rock climbing or whitewater rafting or something like that. I don't think I have it in me right now.

He made an amused sound. "No, I don't expect anything like that from you. But wear something comfortable, maybe some hiking shoes if you've got them."

She did...mostly because Bill Meyers, her ex-fiancé, had loved hiking. And although she'd appreciated the opportunity to get out of the city and breathe some fresh air—and often go someplace that sat at a higher elevation, where it was much cooler than it was in Las Vegas—on the weekends, she sometimes wanted to just hang out at home and relax.

Well, when she didn't have an open house to run.

"Where exactly are you taking me, Caleb?" she asked.

"It's a surprise. But we're not going too far, I promise. And it's nothing strenuous."

Okay, that sounded a little better.

And obviously, she'd much rather spend the day with him than sit around the house watching TV.

"All right," she said. "What time?"

"Eleven-thirty? I want to make sure you have plenty of time to get all the sleep you need."

Even though it was past eleven now, Delia knew she'd be up and about long before then. She could have a nice, leisurely morning, and then Caleb could come pick her up and take her...somewhere.

"That works. I guess I'll see you tomorrow at eleven-thirty."

"You sleep well, Delia."

"You too."

They ended the call there, and she returned the phone to her purse. A moment to pour herself the promised glass of water, and then she slung the purse over her shoulder and headed back to the main suite.

She was going to sleep like the dead tonight.

---

The idea had come to Caleb as he was driving home the night before. He didn't think he'd been imagining things when he'd intercepted some of the glances Delia had sent his way while they were doing their post-mortem in the suite at Harrah's. She might have just been through one hell of an ordeal, but at the same time, there had been something almost like hunger in her eyes.

Those were the sorts of looks a woman didn't send in your direction unless she was ready to be a little more than merely friends.

Unless he'd misinterpreted the whole thing and was just flattering himself.

Still, he needed to know where they stood. Maybe this was crazy and all he'd accomplish was blowing up the friendship they'd cultivated over the past four or so months, but still, he didn't want the situation to continue in this uncomfortable liminal state indefinitely. He wasn't used to feeling this way, had always been the one women pursued, rather than the other way around. All right, it had been a little different with Rosemary McGuire when he was in Southern California chasing down the *Project Demon Hunters* footage, but even then, her interest had been clear from almost the moment they'd met. Everything had been fine... until her angelic blood recognized the demon in him and she'd recoiled.

So now he was pulling into the driveway of Delia's house and hoping he wasn't making a huge mistake.

He got out of the Range Rover and went to the front door. Almost as soon as he rang the bell, she was there, smiling out at him.

"Just let me get my purse," she said.

She'd taken his advice about her attire to heart, since she was wearing a pair of army green cargo pants, an off-white scoop-neck T-shirt, and some pretty serious-looking brown hiking boots. Her long red hair was pulled back into a ponytail, and a baseball cap with a hummingbird embroidered on it completed the ensemble.

Caleb wasn't sure if a purse was the best accessory for where they were going, but he didn't say anything. She could always leave it in the car if necessary.

"Sure," he said, and waited while she disappeared somewhere in the house to fetch her bag.

When she came back, though, he saw she wasn't carrying her usual oversized purse, one that could fit her phone and her tablet and the little case she used for cleansing houses of any unwanted spiritual presences, but had a tiny thing slung bandolier-style across her chest, one made of canvas and looking as if it could fit her cell phone and some credit cards and not much else.

"Are you going to tell me where we're going?" she asked as she climbed into the passenger seat and then fastened her seatbelt.

"What would be the fun in that?"

She smiled...but she also shook her head, as if she supposed she shouldn't have been surprised by his reply.

And this morning she seemed all business, friendly but neutral, and he wondered if he'd been imagining those loaded glances the night before.

Well, if that turned out to be the case, this would be...interesting.

He backed out of the driveway and made his way through her neighborhood of large, tidy, Mediterranean-style houses until he reached the freeway. Delia didn't say much of anything, but when he turned off onto the 157 west toward Mount Charleston, a knowing smile touched her lips, one that seemed to indicate she knew exactly where they were heading.

"You've been here before?" he asked, a little surprised. Her footwear seemed to be a clue that she'd done some hiking in her life, but she still didn't strike him as much of an outdoor person.

"Yes," she replied, then paused for a second. "My ex-fiancé was into all the outdoorsy stuff, so we hiked pretty much all the places that were within an hour drive of Las Vegas."

She'd never talked about the man, so Caleb guessed he'd been in the past for a while. Still....

"The guy who left the UNLV sweats behind?" he asked, mentioning the clothes she'd given him to wear after he'd been attacked by demons at his old house.

Her expression now seemed a little startled, as if she was surprised he'd even cared about that one small detail. "Yeah, him. We got engaged about two years ago—he worked at one of the title companies we sometimes did business with. But after that, every time I tried to sit down with him and plan the wedding, he found some excuse for why it wasn't the right time. About a year after we announced our engagement, he broke it off."

Clearly, her ex-fiancé was an utter moron.

"I'm sorry," Caleb said, doing his best to sound neutral.

"Don't be," she replied, and her mouth lifted a little at the corners. "Better that he figured it out then and not after we got married. We would never have been compatible in the long run. Also, he hated Las Vegas. Last I heard, he'd moved to Reno."

Caleb wasn't sure if that was much of an

improvement, but if the guy wasn't a desert sort of person, then Vegas definitely wouldn't have been the right place for him.

"Anyway," she continued, "he loved to hike, and I went with him when I could. I'll admit it was nice to get out of the city and see some actual nature, even though I was never going to be the rock-climbing type."

"No rocks today," Caleb promised her. "Just...a picnic lunch."

He'd gone to a deli by his house and gotten a nice spread of meats and cheeses, and then picked up some fruit at Sprouts. And even though the day-use area at Kyle Canyon was supposed to be dry, he'd brought along a bottle of pinot noir, figuring what the park rangers didn't know couldn't hurt them.

"That sounds good."

They fell silent as he guided the Range Rover along the sometimes twisting highway. Already the landscape around them had changed dramatically, dry desert scrub giving way to junipers and ponderosa pines, the sky above somehow much bluer and clearer than it was back in Las Vegas.

Up ahead to the left was one of the familiar brown and tan Forest Service signs signaling the turn-off to the day-use area, so Caleb guided the SUV there. On this particular Thursday morning, a few cars were parked in the lot, but he guessed the people they belonged to had probably headed off to hike the Acastus trail, which began not too far from their destination, and wouldn't be anywhere near the picnic areas.

At least, he hoped he and Delia would have the place to themselves. This wasn't the sort of conversation where he wanted an audience.

He parked as close to the exit that led to the picnic areas as he could, then turned off the engine. "I have to get a couple of things out of the back," he told her as he unbuckled his seatbelt.

"Need any help?"

There wasn't that much, just a picnic basket and one of those hard-case totes that had storage space for a wine bottle and a couple of wine glasses. "No, I'm good," he said. "You can wait by the entrance."

She nodded, then undid her own seatbelt and got out of the Range Rover. He exited the vehicle as well, going around to the cargo compartment in the back so he could get out the basket and wine tote. Soon enough, he'd joined Delia, who was standing a few feet away from the front end of the SUV and looking around in appreciation.

"This is beautiful. You're right—it does feel good to get out and away."

The air here was probably twenty degrees cooler than it had been down in Las Vegas, and the breeze that rustled through the pines smelled amazing.

Maybe he should think about getting a cabin up here. He enjoyed Vegas, but, as Delia had just said, sometimes it felt damn good to have a change of scenery.

First things first, though.

"Glad to hear it," he said. "Let's go ahead and get all this set up."

They wound along the path, skipping past the picnic tables that were closer to the parking lot. Caleb had inspected the layout as best he could using Google Maps, and he knew there was one table set at the very end of the picnic area, one where the forest crowded close on almost all sides and would give them the privacy they needed.

However, he hoped Delia wouldn't suspect he had any ulterior motives for choosing that table over all the other ones, except maybe a desire to get as close to nature as possible.

To his relief, no one else had claimed that table. The forest wasn't silent, not with the breeze murmuring in the treetops and birds singing happily among the pines and junipers, but still, a quiet existed out here that they would never have been able to enjoy in the city.

He was also glad they'd come...even if this ended messily.

But he put those doubts aside as best he could,

and laid a cloth over the tabletop and set out all the goodies he'd bought at the deli and at Sprouts. Delia looked on with an appreciative eye, but when he set out the bottle of wine, one eyebrow lifted slightly.

"I thought you weren't supposed to drink in these picnic areas."

"You're not," he said blithely. "But I didn't see hide nor hair of a park ranger as we came in, and if we get busted, well, I'll deal with it then."

Her mouth twitched, although she didn't offer any other protests and merely said, "This all looks gorgeous."

He had to admit that it did. At first, he'd thought of simply getting them sandwiches, but he'd thought that didn't seem very romantic and that it would be better to set up some kind of mini charcuterie board.

"Well, I'm not a pro at this," he said, "but that deli has some great stuff."

"It definitely looks that way."

She sat down on the bench attached to the picnic table while he got out the wine and poured them a couple of glasses. Since she hadn't turned it down and told him she only wanted water—which he'd also brought along—he guessed she was fine with breaking that teeny little rule, too.

After all, they weren't going to hurt anything. They'd clean up the site when they were done, and no one would be the wiser. It wasn't as if they were a couple of high school kids who'd snuck up here to drink beer and leave a bunch of bottles behind.

He handed one of the glasses to her. "I think we need to have a toast."

Her blue-gray eyes glinted at him. Although she had a pair of sunglasses tucked into the neckline of her shirt, she wasn't wearing them now, probably because her baseball cap with that fun little hummingbird shielded her from the sun well enough.

"Sure," she said as she held her glass high. "What're we toasting?"

He wanted to say, *You,* but guessed that wouldn't go over too well, especially since he hadn't made any declarations of love yet.

"To beating the bad guys," he said.

"I'll definitely drink to that."

They clinked glasses and drank some of the pinot noir. It was fruity and medium-bodied, something he thought should go well with the bread and cheese and meat and the fruit as well.

For a minute or so, they were quiet as they put various morsels on their plates, then ate. He wanted to drink in every detail of Delia's appearance—her smooth ivory skin, the coppery shimmer of her hair as her ponytail hung down her back, her graceful fingers as she picked up pieces of bread and meat and cheese.

But he knew staring at her would only make her wonder what the hell was going on, so he did his best to act casual and as though this outing wasn't anything more than a friend taking another friend to a place where she could relax and truly breathe.

"You really think everything's going to work out in Laughlin?" she asked. She'd paused to wipe her fingers on a napkin and take off her baseball cap, probably because a few clouds had drifted in and were doing a decent job of blocking the sun. "Do you think Aaron's cousin will be able to handle the responsibility of being the river guardian?"

At least Caleb thought he could reassure Delia on those points. "Her family's been doing this for generations," he said. "Also, you had a vision of her being chased away by Sellers' minions. They wouldn't have bothered to get her out of the way if she weren't a threat to them. And, like I told her, I can come give her a hand if she needs one...even though I doubt it'll come to that. So I think she's going to do just fine."

A nod, and Delia reached for her glass of wine and sipped from it. "That's good. Because I really wasn't looking forward to having to drop everything and relocate to Laughlin just to hold back a bunch of demons."

Did he dare hope that part of the reason she

wanted to stay in Las Vegas was because he lived there as well?

That was probably presuming too much. Delia's whole life was in Vegas—she'd been born there and gone to school there, her friends and family were there.

Still....

"I don't think Sellers is going to be a problem anymore," Caleb said. "I'm starting to see a pattern here. When we banish one of these guys or defeat their plans, they don't seem to make a repeat appearance."

Delia tapped her fingers against the side of her stemless wine glass. It was actually plastic, since bringing fragile wine glasses out to a wilderness area like this wasn't a very good idea, but it worked well enough.

"But new ones keep cropping up," she said. Her mouth pursed for a second or two, and then he could almost see her force herself to relax. "I really should stop borrowing trouble."

"It's a lot, I know," Caleb replied. "The thing is, when we've kicked their asses, we usually get some breathing space afterward. So I think we need to focus on that for now."

"To breathing space," Delia said, and they touched glasses again.

For just a second, their gazes held. Her eyes widened ever so slightly, as if she thought she might have seen something in his face that she hadn't been expecting.

Rather than drink to finish the toast, she set her glass down.

Very quietly, she said, "Was there some other reason you asked me out here besides just getting some fresh air?"

There it was. She'd asked point-blank, and while he could try to obfuscate, he knew that wouldn't be very smart.

Delia Dunne was the sort of woman who expected the truth, no matter how uncomfortable it might be.

*Don't be a chickenshit,* he told himself.

"There was," he said. "I wanted—that is, I needed to know where things stood between us. Because I'm getting the sense that there's something more than friendship here. If I'm totally off base, then just tell me, and I'll leave the whole thing alone. But if I'm not...."

For a long moment, she only sat there, her entire body still, as though she thought that if she moved the slightest bit, if she opened her mouth, then everything would change.

But he knew it already had, simply because he'd told her he thought there was more than friendship between them.

Then, the words barely above a whisper, "You're not off-base."

Some women might have looked away. Delia, on the other hand, held her gaze steady, those blue-gray eyes so deep and clear, he thought he could get lost in them forever.

Somehow, he found his voice. This was exactly what he'd hoped to hear, but now that she'd all but told him she had feelings for him as well, he wasn't sure what to do next.

Be honest, he supposed. Ever since the moment he'd met Delia Dunne, he'd vowed to be truthful with her, and he wasn't going to change now.

Or rather, he'd already changed a whole hell of a lot from the man he used to be, and he wanted to stay the course. He might have been a quarter demon...but he also wanted to be the sort of person that Hell would vomit right back up because Satan knew he didn't belong there.

"I'm pretty sure I'm in love with you," he blurted, and she actually smiled at him.

"I suppose that's a good thing," she said. "Because I know I'm in love with you."

He wasn't sure which of them moved first. All he knew was that they were both standing now, a few feet away from the picnic table with its charcuterie spread and half-drunk bottle of wine.

His hands reached for hers, pulled her close. A tremor went through her, but she didn't resist, and instead took a step toward him so they were only standing a few inches apart.

Her face tilted up toward his, and he knew there was only one thing he could do.

He bent and kissed her, touched her full, beautiful mouth and tasted the sweetness of wine on her tongue. There were probably a million ways he'd imagined this moment, but he knew none of them had come anywhere close to this, to breathing her in and understanding that this amazing woman knew the worst about him and didn't care.

Or at least, she cared...but not that he was part demon.

The kiss lasted for uncounted seconds. Eventually, though, she pulled away.

Not very far, however. Her fingers were still laced in his, telling him that she hadn't ended the kiss because she was having second thoughts about being with someone who wasn't completely human.

"What now?" she asked softly, and he bent and touched another kiss to her mouth, a gentler one this time.

He smiled. "I suppose we'll figure that out together."

---

The Vegas Slayers series continues with *Devil May Care.*

# Also by Christine Pope
## (Series With Asterisks Are Complete)

LEGENDARY

(Urban Fantasy/Paranormal Romance)

Silver Linings

Lion's Share

Trial by Fire (February 2026)

Here Be Dragons (June 2026)

———

VEGAS SLAYERS

(Urban Fantasy/Paranormal Romance)

Speak of the Devil

Devil in the Details

The Devil Went Down to Laughlin

Devil May Care

Devil to Pay (May 2026)

The Devil's Due (September 2026)

———

THE WITCHES OF MINGUS MOUNTAIN

(Paranormal Romance)

Stolen Time

Borrowed Time

Killing Time

Wind Called

Demon Loved

Christmas Past

Season of Magic (April 2026)

Healer's Heart (July 2026)

---

PROJECT DEMON HUNTERS*

(Paranormal Romance)

Unquiet Souls

Unbound Spirits

Unholy Ground

Unseen Voices

Unmarked Graves

Unbroken Vows

Unholy Night

---

THE DJINN WARS*

(Paranormal Romance)

Chosen

Taken

Fallen

Broken

Forsaken

Forbidden

Awoken

Illuminated

Stolen

Forgotten

Driven

Unspoken

Hidden

Written

Given

Mistaken

---

FAMILIAR SPIRITS*

(Cozy Mystery/Paranormal Romance)

Spells and Spaniels

Cauldrons and Cats

Hexes and Hedgehogs

Charms and Chihuahuas

Runes and Ravens

———

LATTES AND LEVITATION*

(Cozy Mystery/Paranormal Romance)

Caffeine Before Curses

Muffins After Magic

Pastries and Prophecies

Eclairs and Ectoplasm

Sugar Skulls and Specters

Wedding Cakes and Wishes

———

HEDGEWITCH FOR HIRE*

(Cozy Mystery/Paranormal Romance)

Grave Mistake

Social Medium

Household Demons

Perpetual Potion

Jingle Spells

Wandering Monsters

Uninvited Ghosts

Prophet Motive

Ballroom Bits

Spell Check

Brew Confessions

Charm School

---

UNEXPECTED MAGIC*

(Urban Fantasy/Paranormal Romance)

Found Objects

Finders, Keepers

Lost and Found

Finding Destiny

---

THE WITCHES OF WHEELER PARK*

(Paranormal Romance)

Storm Born

Thunder Road

Winds of Change

Mind Games

A Wheeler Park Christmas

Blood Ties

Healing Hands

Wishful Thinking

Smoke and Mirrors

---

MISS PRIMM'S ACADEMY FOR WAYWARD
WITCHES*

(Fantasy/Academy Romance)

Misspelled

Dispelled

Expelled

---

THE DEVIL YOU KNOW*

(Paranormal Romance)

Sympathy for the Devil

Charmed, I'm Sure

A Wing and a Prayer

Wish Upon a Star

---

THE WITCHES OF CANYON ROAD*

(Paranormal Romance)

Hidden Gifts

Darker Paths

Mysterious Ways

A Canyon Road Christmas

Demon Born

An Ill Wind

Higher Ground

Haunted Hearts

---

THE WITCHES OF CLEOPATRA HILL*

(Paranormal Romance)

Darkangel

Darknight

Darkmoon

Sympathetic Magic

Protector

Spellbound

A Cleopatra Hill Christmas

Impractical Magic

Strange Magic

The Arrangement

Defender

Bad Blood

Deep Magic

Darktide

Star Bright

---

THE WATCHERS TRILOGY*

(Paranormal Romance)

Falling Dark

Dead of Night

Rising Dawn

---

THE SEDONA FILES*

(Paranormal/Science Fiction Romance)

Bad Vibrations

Desert Hearts

Angel Fire

Star Crossed

Falling Angels

Enemy Mine

---

TALES OF THE LATTER KINGDOMS*

(Fantasy Romance)

Dragon Rose

Ashes of Roses

One Thousand Nights

Threads of Gold

The Wolf of Harrow Hall

Moon Dance

The Song of the Thrush

---

THE GAIAN CONSORTIUM SERIES*

(Science Fiction Romance)

Beast (free prequel novella)

Blood Will Tell

Breath of Life

The Gaia Gambit

The Mandala Maneuver

The Titan Trap

The Zhore Deception

The Refugee Ruse

---

STANDALONE TITLES

Hearts on Fire (Paranormal Romance)

Taking Dictation (Contemporary Romance)

Golden Heart (Gaslamp Fantasy Romance)

Night Music: A Modern Reimagining of The Phantom
of the Opera (Contemporary Romance)

Ghost Dance: A Sequel to Gaston Leroux's The
Phantom of the Opera (Historical Mystery/Romance)

Flight Before Christmas (Fantasy Romance)

* Indicates a completed series

# About the Author

*USA Today* bestselling author Christine Pope has been writing stories ever since she commandeered her family's Smith-Corona typewriter back in grade school. Her work includes paranormal romance, paranormal cozy mystery, fantasy romance, and science fiction/space opera romance. She makes her home in Arizona.

*Christine Pope on the Web:*
www.christinepope.com

facebook.com/ChristinePopeAuthor
youtube.com/@ChristinePopeAuthor